Praise for
Devour

"Wow! This is one heck of a book! Reading it, I felt so many emotions, I didn't even know where to begin for my review. Mostly, though, I felt excited and exhilarated that this author had gotten this book so right. . . . Ms. Morel is a wonderful storyteller. *Devour* kept me on the edge of my seat from page one. Paranormal lovers everywhere will love this addition to their library."   —Romance Readers at Heart

"Interesting . . . intriguing."   —*Romantic Times*

"Ms. Morel's story should have a broad range of appeal, with elements of urban fantasy, horror, and romance all skillfully intertwined."   —Huntress Book Reviews

"Exciting. . . . Melina Morel provides a fast-paced story that werewolf fans will want to read."   —*Midwest Book Review*

Also by Melina Morel

Devour

PREY

Melina Morel

A SIGNET ECLIPSE BOOK

SIGNET ECLIPSE
Published by New American Library, a division of
Penguin Group (USA) Inc., 375 Hudson Street,
New York, New York 10014, USA
Penguin Group (Canada), 90 Eglinton Avenue East, Suite 700, Toronto,
Ontario M4P 2Y3, Canada (a division of Pearson Penguin Canada Inc.)
Penguin Books Ltd., 80 Strand, London WC2R 0RL, England
Penguin Ireland, 25 St. Stephen's Green, Dublin 2,
Ireland (a division of Penguin Books Ltd.)
Penguin Group (Australia), 250 Camberwell Road, Camberwell, Victoria 3124,
Australia (a division of Pearson Australia Group Pty. Ltd.)
Penguin Books India Pvt. Ltd., 11 Community Centre, Panchsheel Park,
New Delhi - 110 017, India
Penguin Group (NZ), 67 Apollo Drive, Rosedale, North Shore 0632,
New Zealand (a division of Pearson New Zealand Ltd.)
Penguin Books (South Africa) (Pty.) Ltd., 24 Sturdee Avenue,
Rosebank, Johannesburg 2196, South Africa

Penguin Books Ltd., Registered Offices:
80 Strand, London WC2R 0RL, England

First published by Signet Eclipse, an imprint of New American Library,
a division of Penguin Group (USA) Inc.

First Printing, September 2008
10 9 8 7 6 5 4 3 2 1

To Laura Cifelli.
Thank you.

ACKNOWLEDGMENTS

A big thank-you to the staff at the Denise Marcil Literary Agency: Denise Marcil, Maura Kye-Casella, and Katie Kotchman. Thank you to Lindsay Nouis of NAL. And a special thank-you to the multitalented artist Mabelyn Arteaga, who created my beautiful Web site at www.melinamorel.com.

Chapter One

When Pavel Federov and his assistant arrived on the scene, they found the fearful parents huddled with the police, everybody looking cold and scared in the light of the police cruiser's headlights. A small child, abducted by a stranger, was out there in the woods, taken from her bedroom in the middle of the night. When her parents discovered her missing, they saw the open window, the overturned furniture, and they called the police. One of the policemen called in Metro Investigations as special consultants.

"Pavel, glad to see you. Ivan, how ya doin'?"

The policeman greeted his acquaintances and got down to business, explaining what had happened, introducing them to the parents, and telling them the facts of the case.

"When was the last time you saw Yvonne?" Pavel asked gently. The mother looked as if she were in shock.

"At seven," she said, struggling to hold back tears. "We read her a story and put her to bed." She raised her eyes and looked up at the tall man with the accent and said, "Please bring my baby back. She's only . . ." At that point the woman leaned against her husband's chest and burst into sobs, too distraught to continue, terrified at what might be happening to her child in the hands of a stranger.

Pavel nodded as the man tried to comfort his wife. "And when did you realize she was gone?" he asked the husband.

"Two hours ago. We saw the open window, the chair on the floor, the blanket missing from the bed, and no Yvonne. We checked the house, put on the lights outside, and then called the police."

Pavel turned to the cop. "Did your guys lift any prints from the window ledge or the furniture?"

"Yeah," he said. "Come over here. Give Mr. and Mrs. Croft some space."

Pavel and Ivan looked concerned. They knew the cop had nothing good to tell them.

Several feet from the parents, Sergeant Murray said, "The guy's prints were in the system. Sex offender. Two months out of jail. He just did time for an attack on a kid in Rochester. She survived but just barely. I want the son of a bitch. I want him tonight before he hurts this one."

"If he hasn't already," Pavel said grimly. "All right. What can you give us to work with?"

"We found footprints leading from the house to the street. It's been raining and the ground is kind of wet. The prints continued into the trees, and the woods are so overgrown, it's sort of hard to make out anything, especially in the dark."

"Did you call in the dogs?"

"We don't have any dogs. The town cut the budget. But we called to the police department in the next town over. They're bringing them in. But not until tomorrow."

"Too late," Pavel said in disgust. "All right, Ivan and I will go into the woods and see what we can find. If he's on foot, he might know his way around, but in the dark, he's liable to get lost anyway. Okay. Ivan, are you with me?"

"Right behind you, boss."

Pavel turned to the sobbing woman before he and his assistant headed into the trees. "If she's there, I'll find her," he said quietly. "I won't give up till I do."

"Thank you," she said tremulously. "We'll be right here

waiting. As long as it takes," she whispered through her tears.

Making their way into the woods that surrounded the rural upstate town, Pavel and Ivan quickly disappeared from view, even with the headlights flaring into the trees. They had done tracking assignments before, but never with the urgency of this one. Somewhere in this tangle of trees and undergrowth was a terrified child in the hands of a predator. That thought alone made the men focus like lasers.

Walking slowly enough to get their bearings in the dense darkness, Pavel and his assistant crept through a tangle of new growth and paused. "Do you hear it?" he asked.

"It's a child," Ivan said. "She's crying. Not close by, either."

"Can you pick up a scent? I'm getting the smell of tobacco. And sweat."

"He's sweating from fear."

"Then let's make sure the sick bastard has plenty to sweat about. Let's go!" said Pavel.

With that, both men disappeared, and in their places stood two dark cats the size of panthers, lifting their heads to take in the scents on the night air, a mixture of trees, animals and humans. Then they reared back on their haunches and sprang into action, hurtling through the tangle of trees in the darkness, paws pounding on the forest floor, scattering bits of earth beneath them as they ran, homing in on the man's scent.

Half a mile ahead of them in the dark, a skinny, middle-aged man dropped the sobbing child he had stolen and sat down, exhausted. Out of shape and fearful of being spotted with his victim, he had run from the house as fast as he could, but now, wheezing and lost, he had to rest. The child stood watching him for a moment; then she turned and started running as fast as she could.

"Oh, shit!" In a second her captor was after her, shouting for her to come back while she moved silently in the trees, hiding behind a large pine tree as he staggered toward her, panting and gasping.

In the telepathic language of werecats, Pavel ordered Ivan to see to the child as they closed in on the pair, their paws thundering in the night as they raced toward the kidnapper. "I'll take care of him. You make sure the baby's safe," he said.

Hurtling toward his target, Pavel reached him before Ivan could seize the child. With a mighty leap, the panther-cat hurled him to the ground and bit him as they thrashed on the forest floor. The man shrieked with pain, helpless in the grip of the big cat.

Pavel had to force himself not to kill. He tamped down the killer in him while he flung the human against a tree, where he collapsed into a heap and lay facedown on the ground, whimpering with fright.

Satisfied that the kidnapper wasn't going anyplace, Pavel shape-shifted out of sight of his prey and returned to human form in the black pants and commando sweater of his company. As a werecat of the northern regions, he had been granted the gift of returning fully clothed by a god. Tonight, he was glad he had it.

"Ivan? Did you find the child?"

"Right here, boss. Pavel, meet Yvonne. And now we're going to take her home."

When Pavel and his assistant had the kidnapper handcuffed and on his feet, they called in the capture to Sergeant Murray, who relayed the news to the parents, who wept with relief. They had been preparing themselves for tragedy; now they were beside themselves with joy. In that dark forest, where death and danger lurked, those strangers had just given them back their child.

"What do we owe you, mister?" the father asked. "We want to thank you properly. You've just saved our family."

He shook his head. "The police will get a bill. All you have to do is take the little one home and keep her safe."

After he said goodbye to them, Pavel turned to Sergeant Murray and said, "The criminal is a lunatic as well as a pervert. While we were bringing him in, he kept screaming about being attacked by cats. Can you believe it?"

"Lots of strange things out in those woods, Pavel. You never know," the sergeant said with a wink. As a fellow werecat, he knew the score.

The long drive back to Manhattan seemed almost carefree compared to the gloom of the ride upstate. New York's only all-werecat security force had had a success tonight, and both men were glad things turned out well.

Later, when Pavel returned to his apartment and checked his voice mail, he found a message sent from half a world away by a shaman of his clan. From several time zones to the east came the raspy voice speaking slowly and deliberately, with the formality of another era.

"Beware the false ones who swear to uphold our traditions yet seek comfort with our enemies. They will cause turmoil. Even now chaos brews in the city of the Horseman, and the leader stumbles. All will be left in disarray."

If he hadn't known the reputation of the shaman who had left that message, Pavel Federov would have rejected it as nonsense, but the old man had foreseen too many things that turned out to be true. The only problem was, his predictions were often so hazy that until they materialized, nobody knew what he meant.

Pavel was a Russian Blue werecat, a member of an ancient group that had originated in the icy regions of the North. His residence might be New York, but geography meant nothing. His heart beat for his clan. And this intimation of disaster unsettled him.

Pondering the consequences of this strange message, Pavel took out his cell phone again and punched in the number of his cousin Vladimir, who kept odd hours. It was well past four in the morning.

"It's Pavel," he said when Vladimir answered. "I've just

received a call from the shaman. Sounds like something is going on in St. Petersburg. He used a phrase: 'The leader stumbles.' Do you have any idea what that could mean?"

"It could mean someone's in trouble. Someone important. Maybe even a human."

"Do you think it's political?"

"Hard to tell. People rise and fall from power. Maybe that's what he means. There are some who might say that the Hierarch of our clan stumbled when he married that flashy wife of his."

"Good point," Pavel said drily. "He had no business marrying outside the clan. And he did it anyway. I still can't believe it."

"I can see how he fell for her. Bella is a beauty."

"He's a fool. Those damned Siberian Forest cats are poison. He'll come to regret it, but by then it will be too late."

"Such cynicism. No wonder you're not married."

Pavel gave the phone a cold glance. His cousin was being tactless, but not intentionally. Sometimes people just forgot.

As if Vladimir had quickly realized his gaffe, he said, "Sorry, Pavel. I didn't mean it like that."

"I know. Well, call me if you hear anything. I'll do the same."

The clan might be anxious over nothing, the Russian decided. Talk, gossip, rumors. Sometimes he felt that people needed some kind of threat to liven up their dull lives. Not in his case.

No. Pavel's surveillance company had enough jobs to keep his whole staff occupied. Industrial projects, cheating spouses, computer crime, and even VIP bodyguard details. Just this past week, he had sent a man to infiltrate a network of crooked Wall Streeters. This evening they had helped rescue a child. Two weeks earlier they had nailed an embezzler at a bank.

That was small potatoes. Recently Metro had followed the vice president of a multinational corporation who was selling the secret formula of its leading sports drink for cash. Pavel's man got the whole thing down on video, and the veep was last seen calling his lawyer from jail.

This vocation paid well, Metro Enterprises provided employment for a handful of fellow werecats whose unusual skills made them invaluable to Pavel, and it eased the problems of citizens in need of a helping hand with their personal or corporate dilemmas, but it left Pavel with an emptiness that even large amounts of money couldn't fill. Vladimir had it right. He was a hopeless cynic who had seen too much crime, treachery, and plain stupidity to have the slightest faith left in anyone's better nature.

But, he reflected sadly, if Natalya were still alive, he wouldn't give a damn. The whole world could go off the rails, and he'd still find something to smile about if she were there. It was his tragedy that she wasn't.

Chapter Two

"Marc? There's so much static in this connection, I can barely hear you. Where are you calling from?"

"I'm at the warehouse. We've got trouble. Somebody's been going through our stock."

"Are you serious?" Vivian Roussel rose from her seat, cell phone in hand. The first thing that came to mind was the expensive porcelain they had just purchased. "What did they take? Any of the really pricey pieces?"

"I'm still trying to find out if they managed to steal anything. It's like they were going through the place and just targeting the paintings. None of the smaller boxes were opened. They don't seem to have bothered with those rare porcelains."

"You're sure?"

"Yes. They moved the paintings around. I've got our invoices here, and I'm checking to see if anything's gone missing."

"What do you think?"

"So far, so good. But it's too early to tell what's been taken."

"I'll meet you there," Viv said. "Give me forty-five minutes."

In all the years that they had been in business, nobody had ever broken into their shop or their warehouse. As Viv put the closed sign in the window and grabbed her coat, bag and keys, she felt violated in a strange way. In her very special circle, she and Marc were admired and respected, aristocrats of their species. Nobody had ever dared to harm them or even threaten them, especially not another werecat of their clan. Princely descendants of one of the legendary females of their kind, their clan held them in high esteem. The perpetrators must have been human, Viv decided angrily. That sort was so brazen.

"What about our security system?" she asked when she arrived at the warehouse to find her brother examining their property.

"They disabled it, so they had to be pros," Marc said glumly. "And I'd love to know just what they expected to find."

"Maybe they have us confused with somebody else. Our Russian imports don't have a provenance from the Winter Palace. Our pieces are unique and expensive, but it's not as though we have a cache of emeralds and diamonds on the premises."

"We wish," he said with a wry smile. "Well, I'm going to call the Leader and tell him the news."

The Leader, John Sinclair, was the head of Marc and Viv's werecat clan, the Maine Coon cats, and he was not pleased by the phone call.

"When you call attention to yourselves, these things happen. Human greed. Envy. Don't call the police. Handle it in house."

"But the police—"

"You handle it yourselves," he repeated in a near growl. "Meanwhile, tighten up the security. I'll send you information about whom to contact. I know a firm that's very good and very discreet. No police."

He might as well have said it was their own fault.

"Well," Viv said, once her brother relayed his conversation with their Leader, "I'm sorry we didn't invest in better protection. Obviously our system has flaws." She looked annoyed. "He told you not to involve the NYPD?"

"You know how he is about outsiders. If it involves our clan, we take care of it, although I think this is just a normal break-in. Nothing related to us as werecats, I hope."

"All right. How do we do this?"

"We have to find a better security agency." Marc raised his shoulders and his hands in a gesture of defeat. "I'll be choosier next time."

"Well, we'd better get somebody down here fast. We can't leave it like this. Who knows what will disappear if anybody finds out the place is unguarded."

"I'm on it," he said. "We have to show Sinclair we can protect our business."

"Pavel here. How's the weather up north?"

"Fine. If you like snow," the voice on the other end replied. "September, and they're already sweeping the stuff off the sidewalks. But you didn't call me from New York to chat about the climate. What's going on?"

"Here? Not much. The usual. I'm more interested in what's happening in Petersburg."

"Well, let's see. . . . Prices are out of control. You can't even buy a small apartment without a ton of money. Traffic is a nightmare. Nationalist demonstrations are popping up all over the place. We're living the wild and wonderful world of post communism."

"That's not what I mean, Yuri," he said with a grin. "I'm interested in news of the clan." Pavel waited. Then he asked, "Nothing?"

"Nothing much. The Hierarch and his company are in negotiations with foreign investors to drill for oil in a remote area of Siberia. Things are moving very slowly. There's talk about the government banning foreigners from the oil fields in the name of national interests. It's all iffy at the moment."

"Anything else? Any talk of trouble within the clan?"

"No," Yuri replied. "Just lots of gossip about the Hierarch's gorgeous wife. Madame Bella Danilov appeared at an exclusive reception for members of St. Petersburg's business elite. Madame Danilov opened a new boutique on Nevsky Prospeckt. Very busy lady," he said drily.

"Yes, isn't she?"

"Well, the members don't like her, but she seems to make him happy. A few members wanted him to step down but he refused. He told them if he could overcome an ancient prejudice, so should they."

"Bella must practice witchcraft. No Russian Blue cat before him would ever have considered mating with a Siberian Forest cat."

"Well, new times, new rules. But this doesn't make the clan happy," Yuri said seriously.

"Anybody unhappy enough to cause real trouble over this?"

"No," he said firmly. "The Hierarch is a popular leader. We may grumble about his lousy choice of a mate, but he's been good for us. He takes care of his own, and bottom line, that's what counts."

"Glad to hear it," Pavel said. "If I get back home for a visit, we can get together."

"Great. Hope to see you in the New Year. Oh," Yuri said almost as an afterthought, "this isn't clan-related, but it's big news here—the government and the Church have recently announced that the famous icon of the Virgin of Saratov was stolen sometime in the last three months. All efforts are being made to track it down. The usual."

Pavel reacted in shock. This was a national treasure, the holy icon Russians credited with sparing the city of Saratov from extermination by Tsar Ivan the Terrible back in the sixteenth century. Believers prayed to the virgin for protection against enemies of the motherland and for protection in battle. Werecat or not, Pavel had prayed to the Virgin of Saratov when he was a Special Ops soldier in the Chechen war, and he felt a devotion to her that had outlasted his combat duty.

"This is disgraceful," he exclaimed. "Who the hell would do such a thing?"

"Nobody knows. They questioned all the monks who live at the shrine, and they claim the icon was hanging in the church one day and gone the next. Workmen had been doing some repairs around the time of the theft, but they just vanished like smoke when the icon went missing. Nobody can find them."

"Naturally," Pavel said with disgust. "Keep me posted on this."

"Of course," Yuri promised.

Pavel put the phone back in his pocket and felt revolted. If the only thing concerning the brethren back home was the Hierarch's new bride, perhaps the shaman's worries were groundless. When was it news that a man, even one who led the Russian Blue werecats, had fallen in love with the wrong woman?

Pavel remembered nights as a young boy, when his old babushka used to retell the legends of their clan, of celebrated battles involving the Russian Blue cats and their fierce enemies, the Siberian Forest cats, of how the Siberians kidnapped and killed other clans' kittens and sacrificed them to their evil god, Moroz the Dread.

At that point, Grandma would piously cross herself and glance at the icons, then put her arms around Pavel and hug him. "Never, never let yourself be seduced by the Siberians," she would say. "Even now, the evil creatures still worship Moroz."

After that scare, she would make a hot glass of tea and talk of other things, but Pavel could never quite get over the uneasiness he felt regarding Siberians. He wondered if perhaps the Hierarch's babushka had neglected this talk. If so, it was a damn shame.

With all the upheavals of recent years, had people become

so totally callous that they would dare to steal a miracle-working icon wrapped in centuries of their country's history?

The thieves had to be humans of the lowest level, he thought with disdain. Werecats had more respect for sacred things.

Chapter Three

"Marc, I'd like to order another enameled tea service in the *boyar* style," Viv said. She sat at her desk in the office of Old Muscovy, their antiques shop, and scrolled through her inventory on the laptop. Then she suddenly rose to her feet in surprise as her eyes focused on a tall gentleman at the door, waiting to be buzzed in.

"What's the matter?" Marc asked. Then he turned to see what had startled Viv. In an instant he hit the release button for the door and rushed over to greet the Leader himself. "He doesn't look happy," Marc muttered to his sister just before he opened the door.

He wasn't. Tall, trim, and already going gray at the temples, the Leader nodded to the Roussels and exchanged formalities, letting Marc take his coat and allowing Viv to serve him tea. Then he said, "You know how much I've always liked you two, but lately you've been pushing the envelope. You did an interview on TV, and that probably attracted the burglar." He gave them a significant glance and let that sink in. "This business is fine, but keep your distance from the humans. You let the humans into your affairs, and it always bites you in the ass. Once they start digging, it could affect the whole clan. I felt I had to let you know how seriously I take this incident, in case you were still thinking of calling in the police."

"I can't understand why we were broken into in the first place," Marc replied. "It's never happened before. What did they expect to find? We don't carry appliances or other things that crooks can turn into quick cash."

Viv looked at the Leader and said, "Do you think they could have gotten our warehouse confused with another one? Maybe someplace where they store other kinds of goods? I can't imagine most thieves wanting Russian paintings and art objects. Besides, after I checked all the articles against our inventory, they were all there. It's very odd."

"Maybe we're making too much of this. People get broken into every day. Stores get robbed. It happens. We do business in a big city. Eight million people and not all of them are honest." Marc looked hopefully at Sinclair as he spoke.

The Leader nodded. "Well, this time, it could just be a random breaking and entering, but whatever it is, it stays within the clan. You're lucky nothing was taken. Have it investigated, and if it appears to be directed against you specifically as werecats, I'll put my Special Squad on it. But we probably won't have to go that far."

Sinclair's blue eyes rested on Viv for a second, and he gave her the kind of smile few werecats ever received from him. Even John Sinclair had a soft spot for one of the clan's aristocrats, a direct descendant of a werecat demigoddess. Viv glanced at him with her large amber eyes, and for a nanosecond, Marc could swear that the Leader nearly purred.

"I've made inquiries," Sinclair said. "Mac Dugan has worked with a security firm on the approved list. He'll give you their contact information. I was in the neighborhood, so I thought I'd look in on you." He glanced directly at Viv. "You're coming to the monthly meeting, I hope."

Viv didn't miss the tone of voice or the way his eyes caressed her. She nodded. "Oh, yes. I'll be there."

"Good," he said. Then with that resolved, the Leader said he had an appointment and left.

"Now *that* was a dominance display," Viv murmured. "Me boss, you underlings. He doesn't usually come calling."

Marc gave her a smile. "But it looks as if you're one underling he really likes."

"I'm not the kind of woman who likes taking orders. Our Leader is the iron-fist-in-the-velvet-glove type. Things have to be his way."

"He's the boss," Marc said with a shrug. "Be happy he likes you. That never hurts."

"You're right," she said with a lingering glance at the door. "We just have to be thankful we didn't lose anything and get on with it."

Marc nodded. Then he said, "By the way, did you receive an e-mail from Bella Danilov? I got one this afternoon. She wanted to know if we were pleased with the condition of the goods upon arrival."

"No," Viv said. "She probably just sent it to you. She seemed to like you."

Marc looked unexpectedly startled. He shook his head. "No," he said. "She was just a friendly person. And she's married to a very rich man."

"She didn't seem all that friendly to me. And I swear she's one of the werefolk. Maybe another cat. Or even a fox. I picked up on her pheromones and found them a little off, but that could be from the strong perfume she uses. She struck me as favoring her human side over the were side. And she treated me like a nonentity."

"Well, she wasn't that bad. She took us out to lunch at a nice restaurant and picked up the tab. Great place for Russian cuisine."

"True. But she was such a phony all the same. Any woman who has a cell phone encrusted with diamonds is screaming for attention. 'Look at me. I'm filthy rich!'"

Marc chuckled. "She's a spoiled darling," he said. "But

she did sell us a nice assortment of paintings, and she did help us get them through customs with a minimum of hassle, so for that, I'm grateful."

"Yes. It could have been much worse. I've had some pretty awful experiences with customs in the East. Madame Danilov certainly helped us there."

"So you see," Marc said, "even Bella Danilov has her good points."

"One or two," Viv conceded drily.

"You know, Mac already sent me the info on the company he's used. He gave me their number. Says they're very dependable. Let's hope that break-in was a one-shot deal," said Marc.

"I hope you're right. We have a lot of inventory tied up in that warehouse."

Both Roussels looked pensive. They felt shaken at being targeted since their high status in the werecat community had always prevented that, and they didn't like the idea that perhaps humans had managed to circumvent their security. The whole episode was unsettling.

As if reading her mind, Marc said, "I'll bet the burglars were human."

Viv shrugged. "That could lead to other problems," she said with a sigh.

Pavel's cousin Vladimir was a former Russian military man who worked as a houseman for a very wealthy and reclusive gentleman named Ian Morgan, an investor and collector of beautiful artworks. The fact that Mr. Morgan was also a vampire did nothing to diminish the respect Vladimir felt for him. Mr. Morgan, in turn, had nothing but admiration for the loyalty of werecats. They got along quite well.

"The art world is talking about the theft of the Virgin of Saratov," Ian noted one evening as he glanced up from the newspaper. "It's one of Russia's most venerated icons. What sort of crook would steal something like that when he couldn't possibly fence it?"

"One without shame or brains," Vladimir said grimly.

"People have lost all sense of tradition. They break into churches, into museums and seize national treasures. Then they try to sell them on the black market to sleazy millionaires. Disgusting."

Vladimir nodded. Then boldly, he asked, "Sir, has anyone ever approached you with something like that?"

Ian glanced up. "Yes," he said. "About thirty years ago, with an offer of magnificent Greek vases taken from an excavation in Bulgaria." He smiled. "I got in touch with Interpol and had the satisfaction of seeing the thief sent to jail. The head of antiquities in one of the Bulgarian museums turned up dead on the streets of the capital shortly after."

"Very good, sir."

"If I hear anything about the icon, I'll contact the police," he promised.

"If Pavel can help you, please let him know, too. With him it's personal. He credits the Virgin of Saratov with keeping him alive during the fighting in Chechnya."

"Vladimir, I had no idea you werecats held those beliefs. I thought . . ."

"We're eclectic in our belief systems, sir. We embrace many concepts."

Well, Ian reflected, *live and learn.* For an icon so steeped in Russian history, even the Russian Blue werecats were prepared to come to her rescue. Impressive.

Chapter Four

Monthly meetings on the estate of their Leader were a tradition among the Maine Coon cats. Sometimes the Leader invited the local members of the clan; sometimes he requested the presence of those who lived out of state. Clan business headed the agenda, and werecats with sharp eyes could often tell who the rising stars were by noting the seating arrangements. Protocal was rigid, and the dress code required human form.

Viv had driven out to the estate in the Jersey suburbs, been buzzed though the gates by security, and, dressed in an elegant black dress and silver jewelry, entered the foyer and headed to the ballroom where the meeting was about to begin. She smiled a greeting at various acquaintances as she accepted a glass of chardonnay from a waiter and strolled around, making conversation with serious-looking werecats from New Jersey and Connecticut. Suddenly the lights flashed, signaling it was time for the presentation.

To her surprise, the Leader motioned to her to sit up front, making Viv wonder if she was going to be held up as a bad example. She wished she had been able to persuade Marc to attend this time. She actually felt a little uneasy.

With everyone's attention on him, the Leader went to the podium and responded graciously as the audience, in regulation human form, applauded. White teeth flashing, he welcomed them and said, "With the vast array of technology at the disposal of humans and werefolk alike, life under the radar is becoming harder and harder to maintain. I'm going to show you a clip from a documentary broadcast last month to illustrate that."

Lights went dim as he turned on a large flat-screen TV. Immediately several humans appeared, swearing they had seen large jungle cats prowling the farming communities of the Midwest, killing livestock at will and causing chaos in the neighborhood. Gasps arose from several members of the audience as the next footage showed what the humans called a large black panther sauntering across a woodland clearing. The feral beast that had terrorized miles of farmland was one of them. In the next clip, he was dead.

"There, ladies and gentlemen. You see for yourselves what happens when one of our brethren chooses to go feral, when he throws off all restraints and allows the humans to find him. He went on a killing spree over four counties. This led to his execution by the local police and to numerous articles in the tabloids. We must never attract this level of attention."

"Leader?" A stocky werecat with a clothing store in the Bronx raised his hand.

"Yes?"

"Does anyone know what made him go feral?"

"His wife claimed he was under stress at work and he chose this way to attack his problems."

Another hand went up. "Did the humans realize he was one of us?"

"According to our people in law enforcement, they believed he was simply a panther who had escaped from a circus or a private zoo. But the point is, any kind of behavior that makes the humans take notice is deadly for us. We exist on our own terms. We don't intermingle any more than necessary. This is our strength. Those who abandon this principle always come to grief." He looked grim. Viv had a horrible feeling he was looking right at her.

After the presentation, the Leader motioned to Viv and took her hand as he escorted her to his study, the inner sanctum where major decisions were made. She hoped she didn't seem as nervous as she felt.

"Viv," he said as he directed her to take a seat, "we have to talk."

This sounds bad. She wondered what he was going to tell her.

When they were seated on the same sofa, he looked at her with unusual interest and said, "It's werecats like you and Marc who are the hope of our clan." He paused as he saw the questioning look in her eye. "You have the DNA of the greatest werecat who ever was, the demigoddess Krasivaya. And yet you show no sign of wanting to pass on this gift. You're shirking your duty to your clan."

"Oh," said Viv, feeling flustered. "Well, I haven't yet found the male I want for the father of my children. Krasivaya's genes deserve someone special." *Mind your own business*, she thought angrily. *My genes, my mate. Not your problem.*

Before Viv could react, the Leader shape-shifted, prompting a matching reflex in her. Nose to nose on the carpet, the two large Maine Coon cats, one silvery with white boots, the other black and brown, faced each other down, looking like shaggy mountain lions ready to tangle.

"Did you forget that I can read your mind when I wish? I am your leader. Don't be flippant with me."

Viv fought down the growl in her throat. She backed off and took a submissive posture while the Leader let loose with a series of growls and hisses that made her fur stand on end. Then, satisfied with the effect, he shape-shifted once again and returned to the sofa, a well-dressed executive in an Armani suit.

Thanks to a favor granted by a minor woodland god thousands of years ago, the werecats of the North enjoyed the gift of returning to their clothed forms when shapeshifting. Otherwise their ancestors would have frozen to death on the tundra.

"You can't waste your gift," he said quietly. "Choose a mate."

Fixing her with a wicked gleam in his light blue eyes, the Leader made her heart do a little flip when he leaned over and kissed her, gently, tenderly, caressing her as he deepened the kiss. She hadn't ever thought of him like that, and frankly, it stunned her.

To her distress, he picked up on that and said, "Think about it now."

"This is too sudden for me to process. You've been married for so many years. . . ."

"And now I'm a widower. I have to think of the clan, Viv, and so do you. We could have wonderful children."

Viv fought to block him out of her thoughts—a gift she rarely had to use since so few werecats could do what he did. She simply nodded. Nothing seemed real right now as she struggled to clear her brain.

"I want a mate I can be proud of," he said as he kissed her again. "I think you do, too."

Viv felt as if her world had gone upside down. Her Leader wanted her for her famous DNA, as if she were some kind of fruit fly in a lab. Because he was a widower, there was no impediment to his marriage with her, and he was such a snob, of course he would want offspring from the most distinguished werecat line of them all.

She had no desire to be the first lady of the Maine Coon cats. She liked her life as it was. John Sinclair was handsome, rich, and powerful, but she wanted love. It was her bad luck that she hadn't yet found it, and she didn't believe an estate with armed guards and an unlimited allowance would be where she'd discover it. Besides, she had heard gossip from some of the other werecat women about his active love life while his wife was still alive. And, of course, there was the story about the mistress he kept in a Park Avenue condo. She wasn't going to be his trophy wife and put up with a harem.

I have to tell Marc, she decided. *He was right about the Leader's interest.*

Still shaken by Sinclair's actions, Viv got through the rest of the evening as best she could and headed to the parking area with a group of werecats she knew from the city. She had barely driven three blocks when a big SUV careened around the corner and stopped just short of crashing into her car.

Viv's seat belt was the only thing that prevented her from injury as she slammed on her brakes and lurched forward. It didn't activate the air bags, but the force of the jolt took her breath away. Stunned from the inpact, she watched as two big men threw open the door of the SUV and ran toward her.

Something about their demeanor alarmed Viv. The looks on their faces suggested they were not simply good citizens coming to the aid of someone in distress; they seemed ready to attack. Whatever their intent was, it wasn't inspired by kindness or concern for her safety. They rushed the car, making a grab for the door handle, which was still locked. They screamed threats at her, beating on the hood, ready to drag her out of the car.

Pulling herself out of her stupor, Viv reversed so quickly she stunned them, forcing them to leap out of her way. Then gunning the engine and blaring the horn, she headed straight toward them, making them scurry back to the SUV, throw open the doors, and jump inside, peeling away so fast they were out of sight before she could catch her breath. Her hands tightened on the steering wheel as she watched them go; then she hit the horn in sheer fury.

By the time three of her brother's friends reached her and jumped out of their vehicles to ask if she were all right, the would-be assailants were long gone.

Hank, Joey, and Pat—all buddies of Marc's who went to Yankees games with him—insisted on taking her back to the Leader's home to let him know what happened. With his mania for keeping clan problems in house, they figured he could deal with it since the would-be carjackers were operating in his own neighborhood.

"Viv, were you hurt? Did you recognize them? How many were there?" the Leader demanded.

"I'm okay. There were two. They pretended they were going to crash into my car to make me stop, and then they jumped out and ran toward me. They were going to pull my door open and grab me, so I backed up as quickly as I could and pretended I was going to run them down. That's when they took off."

"Quick thinking," he said with approval.

"I considered going werecat when I saw them rushing the car, but I decided to save that for my last resort."

"Good. You kept your head."

"Leader, I can drive Viv's car home, and Pat and Joey can take mine. We'll make sure she gets home safely."

"No," he said possessively. "I'll drive her myself. My driver can follow, and you three can follow us. That way, if anybody tries something, we'll be prepared to handle it."

"Really, you don't have to do this," Viv protested. "The men will get me home safely."

"Nonsense. We take care of our own," he insisted, with a meaningful glance at Viv.

Hank, Pat, and Joey looked impressed. This was out of character for Sinclair. They knew he thought Viv was special. Every werecat of the Maine Coon cat clan felt Krasivaya's descendants were bluebloods, but their leader had never paid anyone a compliment like this.

"All right," he said. "Let's get the cars."

Once home, Viv thanked her friends, and then she greeted the doorman in the brightly lit lobby of her building on the Palisades and told him to be on the lookout for anything strange. It would take the men so long to get home that she almost felt guilty about letting them escort her like this. One BMW, one Mercedes, and two big SUVs leading up the rear. Really, such a fuss.

It would be something to joke about later on when everything was safe and two large men weren't trying to jump her.

I don't think I'm going to tell Marc about this right now, Viv thought upon reflection as she put the key in her lock and entered her apartment. *He'll just get upset.*

She got the surprise of her life when she pushed the button on her answering machine.

Chapter Five

"Viv, it's Marc. Pick up if you're there. Stay home tonight if you haven't gone out yet. I tried to reach you on your cell. You didn't answer. I also tried Sinclair's estate. Two men tried to jump me when I went to get my car, but I'm okay. I'm home now."

"My God," she exclaimed. What was going on? Had somebody declared war on the Maine Coon cat sept—or just them?

What was wrong? She and Marc had been in business for more than a decade and had never before had this kind of trouble. Had they managed to offend somebody powerful, somebody who would hold a grudge, somebody who could pay thugs to harm them? It was surreal.

Reaching for the telephone, Viv dialed her brother's number and was relieved to hear his voice. He was safe.

"Hi," she said. "I just got your message. Something similar happened to me when I left the meeting tonight. Two males tried to carjack me. I nearly ran them down, and then Hank, Pat, Joey, and the Leader escorted me home."

"Shit."

"Yes, my thoughts exactly," she said grimly. "But I escaped them. How about you? Did they hurt you?"

"No. They tried to grab me from behind, but I saw something in the side-view mirror as I was approaching the car, and I reacted. They lost the element of surprise and I let them have it with a few good kicks. I think I scared them more than they scared me."

"You're sure you're okay?"

"I'm fine. What about you?"

"I'm all right. Not a scratch."

"Good."

"Did they try to grab you near the shop?" Viv asked, concerned.

"No. I knew I wasn't going to the meeting tonight, so I dropped by a restaurant to pick up something to eat. I was coming out of there when they made their move."

"Then they must have trailed you from the shop."

"That's what I think," he said. "They know where we work. They know where our warehouse is. . . ."

The silence that followed was not a happy sort. The Roussels both felt threatened and hunted.

"I caught their scent," said Viv. "They were some kind of werefolk, but in all the excitement, I couldn't really decide which kind. We need protection. We need somebody really good, and we need them fast. Let's call that firm Mac and the Leader like. Do you have their number?"

"I have it on my desk."

"Well, we can't do anything tonight, but please give them a call tomorrow, explain what's been happening, and ask them to pay us a visit as soon as they can. This can't be random. First the warehouse and now us. And none of it makes sense to me. We don't deal in Fabergé eggs, for heaven's sake. I can't believe somebody is trying this hard to harass us and steal from us." She paused and asked, "Did you activate your alarm system when you got home?"

"You bet I did," Marc replied. "I hope you did the same."

"Absolutely. I also spoke to the concierge before I came upstairs. I told him to watch for anything suspicious."

"Good."

"And I'm going to take out my gun."

"Be careful of that," her brother said. "You haven't prac-ticed in a while."

"I remember how to use it," she replied.

"Maybe we ought to transform tonight," he suggested. "If anybody manages to break in, all they'll see is a cat."

"If anyone breaks in, they'll think they've disturbed a tiger," Viv said forcefully.

"Well, good night. Be careful," he added.

"You, too," she said.

When Viv hung up her house phone, she kicked off her shoes and lay across her bed, wondering how this drama had begun. What had they done? Their shop, the Old Muscovy, had traded in Russian and Eastern European art and artifacts for a dozen years without ever having problems like these. The worst thing that had ever happened was the time a car jumped the sidewalk and crashed into their front door. Luck-ily nobody was hurt, the insurance covered the damages, and they were back in business right away. Nobody had ever bur-gled them or tried to abduct them before.

And, Viv thought, if one of the recent episodes could be attributed to the risks of life in the big city, two made that highly unlikely. No. They were under attack. But why? And who was behind it?

None of it made sense, any more than the decision by her Leader to see her as a possible mate. He was an authoritar-ian snob who wanted an alliance with Krasivaya's descen-dant so he could claim bragging rights about a trophy wife. She hadn't liked the way things were headed ever since he had assumed command last year after an election that some considered flawed. A few members were investigating that.

The previous Leader was an easygoing gentleman with a charming sense of humor and a fondness for caviar. This one had an obsession with secrecy, staying under the radar, stay-ing out of the news. Rumors said that he'd been CIA in his previous job, so that made sense. But it didn't sit well with

Viv. Fortunately clan rules stated clearly and without any ambiguity that a female could choose her mate. If he tried to overrule her on that essential point and force her into the kind of alliance he wanted, she'd remind him she cherished her freedom. She'd fight to uphold it if she had to. With that in mind, she carefully placed her Beretta on the night table and lay back against the pillows, absolutely worn-out.

Pavel's secretary was trained to take down information and pass it on to her boss so he could decide who could best cover each particular case. Pavel took over from there, interviewed the client, and assigned a man to the case. In certain situations, he did the fieldwork himself, depending on the importance of the job. A call from an unknown party like Marc Roussel would ordinarily have rated the services of his number-two man, but the fact that Mr. Roussel cited a friend of his as a reference and worked as an importer of Russian art and artifacts aroused Pavel's curiosity. Moreover, he had heard about the Old Muscovy from other émigrés, and found himself interested.

Pavel surprised Marc by calling back within the hour and setting up a meeting.

"Would you be able to come to the shop?" Marc asked. "My sister works here, too, and I don't want to leave her alone right now in case those guys come back."

"I can be there by two o'clock. Is that all right?"

"Great. Ah, we buzz people in for security concerns. What do you look like, Mr. Federov?"

"Tall, dark hair, green eyes. I'm wearing a black leather jacket and black pants today."

"Okay, we'll be waiting for you."

"See you later."

When Marc ended the call and clicked his cell phone shut, Viv looked hopefully at her brother. "What did he sound like?"

"Slavic."

"You mean he's not American?"

"With a name like Pavel Federov?"

"He could be second generation."

"This one isn't. His English is fluent, but accented. He sounds businesslike."

"Well, if the Leader and Mac both use him, he has to be a real pro."

"Mac used his company last year when he suspected one of his employees was tapping the till. Federov caught the thief in two days."

"Very efficient."

"Dugan said he was thorough. Military man in Russia before he emigrated. And the Leader must think he's good," he reminded her.

Viv nodded, picturing some short, squat fellow with a buzz cut and a grim expression. What she saw when Pavel Federov arrived at the shop was something else entirely.

Chapter Six

The buzzer sent a zap of electricity into Viv's consciousness as she sat in the back room, going over accounts. With a glance at the clock, she ventured into the showroom, where she saw Marc opening the door to a tall man in black, a six footer who looked as sleek as a panther and just as lethal. This former military man was a tribute to physical fitness, Viv thought. He probably trained every day.

"Hello, Mr. Roussel," the visitor said politely with a firm handshake. "Pavel Federov, from Metro Investigations."

"Glad to meet you. There's my sister, Vivian. She and I own Old Muscovy together. Viv, come say hello to Mr. Federov."

"How do you do?" Viv said with a smile that was warmer than intended. This man was very, very attractive. Those green eyes of his recalled pure mountain streams in scenic landscapes. Then she saw a jagged scar on the hand he extended to her, and she remembered that mountain streams sometimes existed in turbulent, war-torn areas, too.

"Mr. Roussel, Miss Roussel," Pavel said as they all sat down for a conference amid the memorabilia of old Russia, "I have to interview you to determine how Metro Investigations can best serve you, so I'm going to ask some questions. Please don't feel offended. Now, first of all, do you have any known enemies?"

"No," they answered in unison.

Pavel smiled. "Let me rephrase that. Has either of you been involved in any recent disputes with a business associate or a personal acquaintance?"

"We're highly regarded," said Viv. "We try to cultivate good relationships with customers."

"Has anyone accused you of any wrongdoing, perhaps not keeping a promise, maybe even complaining of cheating them? I have to ask this." Pavel looked at his clients calmly. They seemed affronted.

"We have a reputation for fair dealing, Mr. Federov," Marc said. "There's never been any serious complaint lodged against us."

"I don't mean to imply it. I'm just trying to find a motive for the attacks you mentioned when you called us. It's possible you've angered someone. I'd like to find out who it is. Think carefully. Have you had any unhappy customers lately?"

Pavel watched as the clients glanced at each other, and then shrugged.

"Last month a woman in Brooklyn called to complain that our deliveryman took longer than he should have to bring her the cabinet she ordered, but there was a car crash on the route, and he was held up in traffic," said Viv. "She was very unpleasant about it. But I think she was just venting."

"Anything else?"

Marc shook his head. "Nothing comes to mind. We're very customer-friendly."

Pavel tried another area. "What about personal relationships?"

Viv glanced at him. "What are you implying?"

"An angry boyfriend?"

"I'm not seeing anyone at the moment," Viv said.

Pavel found that amazing. This woman was young, attractive, blessed with a face and form that could turn heads.

Her lovely chestnut hair reminded him of Natalya's, a melancholy thought.

"What about former boyfriends? Any hard feelings upon breaking up?"

Viv shook her head. "The men I dated were usually so involved with their work that I think they barely noticed I was gone."

Pavel doubted that.

Viv gave him an amused glance and said, "It's true. People are very self-involved in this town."

"What about you, Mr. Roussel?" Pavel asked, turning his attention to the brother. "Have you been involved with anyone who might harbor a grudge over a breakup?"

There was a pause. Vivian Roussel glanced at her brother in a way that Pavel found interesting.

When Marc failed to respond, Pavel asked politely if he could think of any lady who might be angry at him.

"Tell him," Viv suggested with an expression that suggested a few possibilities.

Pavel raised an eyebrow.

"Oh, come on, Viv. They don't hate me," Marc protested. "Marion, Jill, or Lilly would never stoop to something like this."

"All three spent quite a lot of time reviling you when the relationships broke up. But they were all quite nice," she said. "Wonderful women, really."

"They were all a little overwrought at the time," he protested mildly. "Their anger got the better of them."

"Yes. I suppose so."

Pavel's expression remained professional.

Roussel looked distinctly embarrassed. "They're not angry with me anymore," he said. "They've recovered."

"Were they so bitter that they might consider hiring people to inflict punishment on you?"

"No," Marc said. "I can't see them doing that. It's one thing to hate me and another to spend money on hating me.

And they're not the kind of people who would even know where to find someone in that sort of business. Besides, they've all found new boyfriends and they're happy."

"You may underestimate the fury of a woman scorned," Pavel replied.

"It would be out of character for these women to hire people to break into our warehouse or threaten us," Viv said. "I think they've moved on. And I can't believe they pose a danger to us. I always got on well with them. They wouldn't want to harm *me*."

"You're certain of that?" Pavel inquired. "They might just hate you for being part of the Roussel family. In emotional moments, people sometimes fail to make distinctions."

"Believe me, Mr. Federov, I was friends with all of them," Viv said firmly.

"Yes," Marc said. "I know they've spoken to Viv on several occasions. They're not a danger to us."

Pavel nodded and chose not to comment.

"If you're sure that these women wouldn't have wished to harm you, try to think of a reason a business associate would have."

"We really can't," Viv replied. "We've been trying to figure it out ourselves, and we always run into a brick wall."

Pavel wasn't used to this. Generally the clients had a long list of possible suspects all made out and ready for him to investigate. These two must be angels, he thought wryly. And he knew that was a lie. Angels did not exist in business.

Somebody, somewhere wanted something from them. All he had to do was find the who, the what, and the why. How hard would that be?

"I think I'd better begin with the women," he said.

Chapter Seven

Before Pavel left the Old Muscovy, he had asked for and been given a tour of the premises, observed the large collection of Russian artifacts, from polished nineteenth-century silver to early-twentieth-century porcelain to charming paintings, and he concluded that there was nothing that ought to have put the Roussels at risk for kidnapping or worse. It was an upscale shop, but highly specialized, and they didn't have a large inventory of precious stones or any million-dollar items. No, Pavel decided, the motive for the break-in and the rest had to be personal. He would treat it as such. He would also have to see their homes.

His new clients left him with a mixed impression. Marc Roussel was a nice guy, friendly and cooperative, but apparently something of a ladies' man. Vivian was beautiful and alluring, but he wondered if she could be concealing something about her own past. A woman as beautiful as that without a husband or lover? Hard to believe. Then again, with that kind of beauty and a successful business to her credit, she might just scare off a lot of men. She knew her worth, he thought with a smile. She might not want to waste her time on a man who didn't.

Pavel looked over his notes from the meeting with the Roussels as he sat in his office. A sixth sense told him there was something missing, something essential to understanding these people. He drummed his fingers on the top of his desk. What small clue had they given him to make him think this?

Closing his eyes, Pavel thought back on his visit to the Old Muscovy. Russian memorabilia filled the place. Lacquered boxes, porcelain tea services and figurines, silver teaspoons, and elegant enamel work nestled beside the amber necklaces, earrings, and pendants displayed in glass cases. Paintings of the forests, peasants, and aristocracy of old Russia decorated the walls. All to be expected in a shop like that. What was the odd note?

With a start, he remembered. The cats. He saw representations of American cats at strange places in the shop, and not of random cats, but of the breed known as Maine Coon cats.

These had attracted his attention because he first thought the Roussels had acquired porcelain images of the detested Siberian Forest cats, but upon closer inspection he had realized the figurines were not Russian at all. They represented the famous American cats, who were known for their stately bearing and their bravery in confronting their enemies.

Vivian Roussel had a certain elegance, a sensual allure, and a magnificent head of hair. Her brother was a good-looking guy with striking hazel eyes. Both looked like the epitome of WASP America. Could it be that these two belonged to the sept of Maine Coon cats, one of the oldest and most distinguished native breeds in their country?

Warily, Pavel wondered if his clients had gotten themselves in trouble with other werecreatures. If so, he had to tread carefully, for the clans might retaliate if certain boundaries had been crossed. Perhaps he had wandered into an interclan war.

Pavel always preferred to work for humans. They seemed much less complicated than werecats, who always had some drama in the background. That his highly developed senses couldn't detect their true nature could mean that they were

powerful creatures with the ability to block their pheromones, just as he sometimes could.

The friend who had recommended his firm was a werecat. Even that didn't prove the Roussels were, but it pointed
in that direction. He was probably going to uncover something connected with a castoff lover. Werecats were notori-
ous for their affairs, and from Pavel's point of view, personal
animosity always provided a much more vicious motive
than mere business differences. Jilted werecats were dangerous beasts.

Damn, he thought, these two werecats probably hid more
than they revealed, for instance, the reality of their origin.
Naturally they wouldn't admit it to a stranger; nobody
would. But Pavel was willing to bet anything he was right
about them. Apart from the cat totems in their shop, which
would allow another werecat of their sept to connect with
them, there was the matter of their eyes. Vivian's large
amber eyes were not of a shade ever seen in humans. Marc's
hazel eyes were equally distinctive. Only cats possessed
eyes like those.

Chapter Eight

"Gentlemen, we have a couple of new clients," Pavel announced at his staff meeting the next day. "Marc and Vivian Roussel, owners of a shop called the Old Muscovy. Someone broke into their warehouse recently, and a few days later unknown assailants tried to attack them. I interviewed the Roussels yesterday and accepted the case. We will have to install surveillance equipment at their shop and apartments, plant GPS monitors on their vehicles, and assign them codes with which to contact us in an emergency."

"Do they have any ideas about who is doing this?" asked Ivan, his number-two man.

"They claim they don't."

"Do we believe them?"

"Yes, at this time. One more thing, I believe our new clients are brother werecats, of an American breed."

"They're always the worst," Ivan lamented.

"These two seem to be honest and genuinely frightened by their situation. We will do our best to help them."

Vivian couldn't get Pavel Federov out of her mind. Never mind the fact that the man was tall, dark, and handsome. It was something else, those gorgeous green eyes that hinted of depths that she had never encountered before in anyone, human or werecat. He was just the most attractive male she had ever met in person. And she had met lots of good-looking men, having been a model shortly after college.

Those were strange days, Viv thought. "Discovered" when she accompanied a friend to a cattle call for extras in a film, Viv took a chance and called the number on the business card of a woman who had claimed to be a scout for a modeling agency. It turned out to be true, and Viv made a good impression. The agency loved her exotic eyes and beautiful hair, and this chance encounter led to employment for a few years until Viv decided she liked eating more than she liked posing for clothing catalogues or shampoo ads. Werecats prized their independence, and it rankled that her handlers were so inflexible about what she could and could not do. One day when a photographer sniped at her for a two-pound weight gain, Viv put down her foot, said goodbye, and walked out of the studio, never to return.

However, true to her Maine heritage, Viv had prudently invested her significant earnings and decided to go into business with her brother, who had a degree in Russian studies and a great love of Russian art. So that was how Old Muscovy was born.

With the fall of communism and a great influx of Russians into New York, the shop became fashionable with both émigrés and interior decorators, and business prospered. Life was good. Until this.

At Viv's second meeting with Pavel Federov, she listened attentively as he outlined his plans for her protection and Marc's. Their warehouse, shop, and apartments were to be guarded by strategically placed audio and video cameras. These would be monitored by his team, 24/7. In addition to that, their vehicles would be monitored by GPS, and they themselves would be provided with a small device the size of a dime that could be used to call for help in an emergency if they found themselves in trouble away from their home, shop, or vehicle.

"This sounds very comprehensive," Viv said with approval. "You seem to have covered all the bases."

"We try to be thorough," Pavel replied. "But there is one more thing. In view of the attempted carjacking, I would suggest bodyguards. These people failed once, but they may try again. And until we know exactly who they are and what they want, we should make it as difficult as possible."

"Ah, I don't know if I want to go with bodyguards," Marc demurred. "I mean, how will it look to customers if they suddenly see Mr. Muscle hanging around the shop? It might look as if we're expecting trouble. Besides, several shop owners on the block pay for a security guard to make the rounds. He checks all our stores, and he's dependable."

"We try to cultivate a pleasant image," Viv added. "With older clients, we sometimes offer tea while we discuss business. We try to be as gracious as possible. The sudden appearance of bodyguards might make customers think it's dangerous to visit."

"Including large, vicious types who are trying to harm you," Pavel replied.

"Pavel, with all the safeguards you've mentioned, I think you have us covered."

"We will have you under surveillance on video," he pointed out. "We will be able to follow your cars. But if somebody grabs you and throws you into the back of a minivan, it will take time to rescue you. Even *if* you're able to activate the emergency panic button," he said quietly. "Bodyguards will be there on the front line, stopping any aggression."

Viv and Marc glanced at each other.

"My men can be very discreet," Pavel said. "They are trained in all the latest methods of defense, but they can also be as low-key as you wish."

"I don't know if I want someone tagging along with me all the time," Marc said, still looking doubtful.

"It's in your best interest."

Marc shook his head. "I'll agree to all the other measures, but I'll have to think about the idea of a bodyguard."

After Marc stood up, indicating the meeting was at an end, Pavel turned to the sister and said, "Vivian, even if your brother doesn't think a bodyguard is necessary, you, as a woman, are more vulnerable. You told me you were nearly carjacked at night. If they had been successful, we might not even be having this talk."

"Are you trying to frighten me, Pavel?" she asked with a smile.

"I'm trying to make you appreciate the danger you're in. There's a difference."

As Marc went to the front of the store to greet a client, Pavel stood talking with Viv, admiring her beautiful long chestnut hair and her glorious amber eyes rimmed by impossibly long, dark lashes. She was the loveliest woman he'd met in a long time, and there was nothing flirtatious about her. He found that delightful.

When Vivian smiled, she meant it. She didn't seem to need to play games. That, too, reminded him of Natalya, and he remembered bitterly how optimistic and how full of life his fiancée had been before her brutal and chaotic slaughter.

Pavel worried Vivian didn't take her predicament seriously enough, and there was nothing he could do to impose bodyguards on her if she chose not to accept them.

Damn stubborn woman. She had to be a werecat, he decided. Independent to a fault. And if she could hide her true nature so well, she had to be a very high level member of her clan. Only the most skillful werefolk had that power.

She was an attractive mystery Pavel couldn't wait to solve. And she exuded the most delicious scent, he thought, the kind of scent that befuddled a man's brain.

Chapter Nine

"He's coming out of the restaurant. Get ready. The wife is about five paces behind him, talking to an acquaintance." The young man spoke hurriedly into a cell phone headset, communicating with an accomplice across the street. His voice reflected his edginess as he zeroed in on the target.

"Where is his car?" asked his partner on the opposite side of Nevsky Prospeckt with his hand on a Beretta.

"It's about three meters down the street. The driver is stuck behind our guy."

"I'm going in. Tell the others to follow."

As Dimitri Danilov, Hierarch of the Russian Blue were-cats and business tycoon, sauntered through the ornate front door of the Novaya Avrora restaurant, accompanied by two bodyguards, three young thugs in identical black leather jackets, black slacks, and dark sunglasses burst out of nearby cars and raced toward him, opening fire before the Hierarch or the bodyguards could even react.

"Bella! I'm hit!" The Hierarch felt something whistle past his ears at first, then sensed a terrible pain, followed by a large patch of blood beginning to stain the front of his light cashmere coat. He staggered and then suddenly collapsed to his knees, dead before he hit the sidewalk.

As people screeched and stampeded back into the shelter of nearby buildings or simply ran as far from the gunshots as they could manage, a striking blond woman sobbed and fought with a man who was holding her back from running out onto the sidewalk to the mortally wounded Hierarch.

"Goddamn you! I pay your salary! Let me go to my husband," she screamed.

As Bella Danilov watched from behind the door, the three gangsters fired several more shots at the bodies on the ground and then jumped into a getaway car that peeled away with tires screeching and horns blaring. Other drivers moved out of the way in fright and saw the gangsters make a dangerous U-turn and head off for parts unknown.

"Oh, Dimitri! *Dorogai!* My life is over, too!"

Bursting out onto the bloodied sidewalk, Bella Danilov threw off her bodyguard and sank, sobbing, to the sidewalk, where her murdered husband lay.

Cradling him in her arms, Bella rocked back and forth, keening a heartbreaking lament as she did, staring with unseeing eyes at the two other corpses beside him, his slain bodyguards.

While her anxious surviving minder used his cell phone to call the police, Bella knelt there wailing and vowing vengeance as several citizens slithered out from the shops where they had taken refuge and discreetly snapped photos with their cell phones, which they hoped to sell to the news services.

"Pavel! Are you there? Pick up the phone!" Vladimir's hand trembled as he punched in his cousin's number and kept glancing up at the TV screen. Horrific images, taken by a German tourist on Nevsky Prospeckt with a video camera, flashed across the screen, while a veteran CNN reporter warned viewers in a hushed voice-over that these pictures were not suitable for children.

"Vlad, it's six a.m.," Pavel said at last. "What's so important?"

"Turn on CNN. Quickly! It's the Hierarch. He's been assassinated."

For a moment, Pavel felt stunned. Then he leaped out of bed and grabbed the remote. "What channel?"

"CNN. Hurry."

The thirty-two-inch flat-panel TV came to life with a revolting shot of the sidewalk in front of the Novaya Avrora restaurant and the three bodies lying there, with a sobbing woman cradling one of them in her arms and wailing.

"Shit! They murdered him. That's what the shaman's message foretold. The leader stumbles."

"Who do you think is behind it?"

"Any number of people, starting with jealous clansmen and leading all the way up to the higher echelons of business and politics," Pavel replied. "Anyone that rich and that successful attracts powerful enemies."

"What a disaster for the clan," Vladimir lamented. "Dimitri Danilov was the best Hierarch in a long time. A man of talent and vision."

Pavel nodded. "Yes. I wonder if his brother will take over now. He'd be the direct successor."

"There might be some opposition to Boris as Hierarch. He's not as gifted as his brother. Or as popular."

"But he's the same blood, and in the midst of a disaster like this, I think the brethren will be swayed by the desire for continuity."

Vladimir sighed. "We can't even attend the funeral. The twelve-hour rule won't give us enough time to get over there and get to the cemetery. He was killed several hours ago. It will take time to get plane tickets, fly to St. Petersburg—hoping we don't encounter delays—get to a hotel, and reach the cemetery in time."

"I know. But of course, they can't postpone the burial."

Both werecats understood the custom and the necessity

for it. If a werecat was not interred within twelve hours of death, the body would change from human to cat form, thereby shocking any viewers who expected to pay their respects to a man or woman they knew as a fellow human. For the good of the brethren, werecats' bodies went to special morticians familiar with the requirements. Memorial services followed the next day with a closed coffin, and the burial took place quickly. Secrecy was paramount in these matters.

"Bella had better luck than her husband," Pavel commented thoughtfully. "Three men gunned down on the main boulevard of St. Petersburg, and she escapes death."

"The news said she paused to speak to a friend when the Hierarch and the guards exited the restaurant. Then her bodyguard grabbed her at the first sounds of gunfire and prevented her from rushing to her husband."

"Saved by a stroke of fate," Pavel replied. "She's a very fortunate woman."

"Well, I think that puts an end to Bella Danilov's interference in the affairs of the Russian Blue werecats. Ambitious as she is, no member of a foreign clan could ever take over the leadership."

"True," Pavel agreed. "But I still don't think it's the last we've heard of the lady."

"I hope you're wrong," said Vlad. "She's a Siberian. What role could she possibly play in our clan now?"

Pavel didn't know. But that didn't mean he felt she was out of the picture either.

"You're right," he agreed. "I'm too cynical for my own good."

Chapter Ten

After a few weeks of calm had passed, Viv relaxed a little and began to think that perhaps she and Marc had been a victim of a bizarre set of circumstances. It was a bit much altogether, but maybe there was no real plot against her and her brother. She really wanted to believe that. And Pavel Federov made her feel secure with all the high-tech surveillance equipment.

Everything connected with the recent string of events had been so bizarre. Viv was also glad she hadn't heard from the Leader. Perhaps he was too busy with his mistress to get back to her. Or maybe he was scouting some other werecat female with good genes. She hoped so. John Sinclair was just too controlling for her.

Marc sat talking in the back of the shop with a customer who wanted to order a porcelain tea service, while Viv stood at the window looking out onto the street. All was peaceful.

The usual Upper East Side passersby sauntered along the sidewalk: young mothers with stylish baby carriages and nice coats, young men with jeans and peacoats and long mufflers. October brought out the wool coats and gloves. Down the street a vendor already had his pretzel stand hot and ready, while a radio announcer had just warned of temperatures dropping to the midthirties tonight.

Viv wore a soft cashmere sweater dress with a low-slung

belt and a trendy pair of high-heeled Italian boots. The rust-colored dress brought out the chestnut tones in her long hair and flattered the amber in her eyes.

"Ah," she exclaimed. Coming down the street was Hank, Marc's buddy from the association, the one who'd driven her home the night she was threatened.

She buzzed him in as he stopped at their front door and greeted her with a wide smile.

"Viv," he exclaimed with pleasure as he opened the door and stepped inside. "You look beautiful. You know, I was worried about you, so I just had to come down here to see if you were okay."

"That's so thoughtful," she said with a smile. "But it's really not necessary. Nothing has happened since that night."

"Well, good," he said. "How's Marc? Everything okay with him, too?"

"Couldn't be better. He's in the back, talking with a client. Would you like to see him when he's done?"

Hank looked into her eyes and smiled. "He's not the reason I stopped by."

Viv appeared taken by surprise. The ink on Hank's divorce papers was barely dry, and he was giving her the look he used on every pretty woman. The kind of look a kid had when he saw a display of candy. Red males were all like that, she recalled. Marc was a prime example, she thought in amusement.

"Would you like to see the new musical that just opened at the Winter Garden?" he asked.

"Yes. But how would you get tickets? One of my friends tried, and they told her the first available seats were for March."

"Not if you have the right connections," Hank said with a gleam in his eye. "Two orchestra seats for Saturday night," he declared proudly. "With dinner to follow."

Viv hesitated. She really did want to see this musical,

which was the hottest thing on Broadway, but she wasn't certain that going there with Hank would be a good idea. He appeared so eager to get out and play the field after his acrimonious divorce from Brenda that she wondered if it might be a bit too soon.

From sad experience, Viv knew that male werecats had hormonal issues at times like these, and she didn't want to get entangled in a minefield of bruised male ego. On the other hand, maybe Hank would turn out to be different from what she expected. He had come to her rescue, and he seemed genuinely concerned for her safety. Marc always spoke highly of him. And if they clicked, she might find a mate who would be more congenial than her snobbish Leader.

With a few misgivings, Viv said, "Thank you. That sounds lovely."

"You know, if you take the bus into Manhattan, I'll pick you up here and take you to the theater. Then after dinner, I'll drive you home. We won't need two cars."

"Or I could drive in, leave my car at the parking garage, meet you at the theater, have dinner, and you could take me back to the garage so I could drive home."

That way, she would have control over the situation and not leave Hank too many loopholes. That worked.

"Really, Viv, with what's been happening, I'd feel more comfortable driving you back to Jersey. I'd worry about you going home by yourself late at night."

"I have a security specialist who fitted the car with a GPS device. In it, I'm under their watchful eye. It's actually safer."

"But you'd still be alone. You're better off with a male in the car."

Well, maybe Hank had a point, Viv thought. He wasn't leering. He seemed concerned. She didn't want to drive home after midnight by herself if she didn't have to, especially not right now.

"All right," she agreed. "Pick me up here at five o'clock when we close. We could have dinner before the show."

"Fine," he said. "That works, too."

"It was nice of you to think of me," she said.

"Viv, if you only knew how often I think of you," he said with a smile.

Oh, she thought. This would be interesting.

Chapter Eleven

"Vivian, it's Pavel. Just checking to see if all is well."

"Everything's fine," she said. "No trouble anywhere. In fact it's a lovely day."

"Glad to hear it."

This was not like Pavel to call clients in the middle of the day to chitchat, but Vivian brought out something in him that even he didn't understand. Normally he viewed customers as people who merited the very best service he could provide, but he believed in keeping a professional distance. Since he had met Vivian Roussel, he found himself thinking of her in ways that were not work-related, and this troubled him; but it didn't prevent him from making the phone call. He was fascinated by the idea that she might be one of his own kind.

"My monitors indicate no suspicious activity near your homes or your shop," he said. "Your brother is in the warehouse right now. He's inspecting the stock."

"Oh, yes. He said he wanted to check on things."

"He doesn't have to be anxious now. The video monitor is giving us a good picture, so you don't have to worry," Pavel assured her.

"I'm glad to hear it. We actually feel quite safe since we signed up with you."

"Good. But don't relax your guard," he said. "We still

haven't discovered who's behind your recent problems, but we will."

There was a slight pause on the other end. Then Viv said, "If you'd like to stop by and keep us updated, that would be fine. We're here every day but Sunday."

Pavel smiled. "You know, I think that would be a good idea." He was tempted to ask, "Are you doing anything after work today?" but it was a Saturday and he knew women took it badly if men asked them out on such short notice. Even though Vivian had told him she wasn't dating anyone, he didn't want to give the impression that he thought he could just call up and arrange a meeting like that. She would feel insulted.

Sometimes Pavel secretly read the American women's magazines to try to gain a better understanding of female psychology, and they all gave the same message: "Never lower yourself to accept a date for the same evening. Only a woman with severe self-esteem issues would do that." This beautiful woman didn't have any of those.

Instead, he said, "Could you pencil me into your appointment calendar for a Monday meeting? Perhaps we could discuss whatever we've learned over lunch."

That was the kind of thing a professional woman could accept: concern for the progress of a mutual endeavor. Nobody could fault him for that. It was modern and enlightened. *Dear God,* Pavel thought. It sounded like such a blatant ploy; she would see through him as if he were wrapped in cellophane.

He could swear Viv's voice had a smile in it when she said, "Mondays are usually slow. I'm sure I can get away for an hour, and you could tell me what's going on so far. Why don't you call me around ten o'clock Monday morning, and I can let you know the best time for lunch? How is that?"

"Yes," he agreed. "Sounds fine. I'll call you then."

"See you Monday," she said with a trace of genuine warmth in her voice. She sounded delighted.

Pavel was smiling. No, he wasn't smiling. He was grinning. He hadn't felt so happy in a long time, and it felt wonderful.

Why he should feel so damned pleased was a mystery, but he knew it was due to his desire to spend time with Vivian Roussel. That woman possessed something beyond the usual sort of feminine charms. It was something deeper than beauty, something that resonated in his soul.

He barely knew her and he found her incredibly enticing. What might it deepen into if he really connected with her? Pavel wasn't a creature who loved the superficial; he wanted to find his soul mate. If he was very lucky, this gorgeous woman might turn out to be the one.

Or, he thought gloomily, perhaps he was reacting mindlessly to the first woman who managed to push his buttons since he had lost Natalya.

Whatever inspired this frame of mind ought to be explored, he decided. He did not want to spend the rest of his life pursuing trivial affairs. He wanted a family, a home, and a real purpose in life once again. Maybe—if he was extremely fortunate—this chestnut-haired beauty with the lovely amber eyes might prove to be what he needed.

Pavel felt duty-bound to find out. The fact she probably belonged to a prestigious clan of American werecats was an impediment—but not one he wished to dwell on at the moment. His hormones were telling him things his brain didn't want to know.

When Marc returned to the shop, Viv nearly didn't hear him come in. She gave a start when she realized there was somebody in the back.

"Marc?"

"Yes."

"Oh! How did you get in without me seeing you?"

"The back door," he explained. "I glanced in the window, didn't see you, and wanted to know if everything was okay."

"You went round the back to sneak up on a possible intruder? Are you out of your mind?"

"I guess I just got carried away. Anyway, they have the place under surveillance, so I guess we're safe." Her brother gave her a grin. "I went to the warehouse to bring back another piece to go with the ormolu vases in case the client who asked about them wants the whole set. It might give him an idea."

"Good. Sometimes that works. Oh," she said as an afterthought, "I'm going to dinner and the theater tonight with Hank."

Marc reacted as if he didn't quite believe what he'd just heard. "Hank? The guy you once referred to as Mr. Studcat?"

"One and the same."

"Are you feeling well? I mean, I think he's great, but that's because we do guy things together. . . ."

"Like chase women, drink too much, and go to baseball games in a group with other studcats."

"That just about sums it up."

"Well, he asked me to a musical I'm dying to see, and since he was concerned enough to escort me home the night of the meeting, perhaps there's more to him than his 'cat on the prowl' persona."

Marc gave a laugh that was loaded with wicked undertones. "You and Hank. Damn, I never would have thought it."

Viv gave him an uncompromising stare. "Calm down. This is one evening. I'll go out with Hank to see if this is something I could pursue. Or not."

"Sure. And you said you never date divorced men."

"Oh, come on! He was concerned about me, and now he's asked me out. Don't start ordering the wedding invitations. It's just a first date."

"Whatever you say. You're a grown-up. You have a right to be happy." Marc was grinning with delight at the hope that she might actually end up with an old buddy of his. Viv knew he could picture them all hosting Super Bowl parties together, heading up to Vermont for skiing, buying season tickets for baseball games together. Just the kinds of things a good brother-in-law would want to do. Werecat males loved sporting events and were often good amateur athletes themselves. Marc had run track in college.

Of course, first she would have to marry Hank and develop a passion for sports. But, stranger things had happened.

"Did you drive in today?"

"No, I took the bus. Hank's going to pick me up later. He'll take me home."

"Well, good work, Viv. I always knew you two would click one day."

"Marc! You're really getting ahead of yourself. You've always told me Hank is a great guy, so now I'm going to find out. End of story."

"It's still a good move." He smiled. "I wonder what the Leader would think about it. Sounds like he has his eye on you, too."

Something like annoyance flickered over her face for a second. "He should remember the rule about females having free choice over mates," she said. "It's one I take very seriously, and I mean it. No male will ever force me into a marriage I don't want."

Marc nodded. Then he said, "I just want you to be happy, Viv. You pick whoever you want and I'll back you up. Just don't go out of your way to bust Sinclair's balls."

"I won't rub his nose in it," Viv said quietly. "But it will be my choice, and he'd better get used to it or he'll find out who he's dealing with."

Chapter Twelve

Viv knew things weren't going the way she planned when Hank told her over drinks that he'd been crazy about her since they were in high school. Not what she wanted to hear since Brenda, his former wife, had worn his ring since sophomore year.

"Oh, you had so many girls running after you, I doubt you noticed me."

"Sure, I did. I was dying to see you shape-shift. Man, I used to fantasize about that: what you'd look like au naturel. Would you be one of those cute calicos or maybe a brown-and-white tabby? Or even a blonde?"

"Silver tabby," she replied as she lifted a glass of wine to her lips.

"I know," he said with a wicked smile. "I saw you."

Viv nearly rose from her seat. "When?"

"When you were at summer camp with my cousin. I hid and watched you shape-shift. I thought that was the sexiest thing ever. Man, all that pretty silver fur. And those cute little white boots. My tongue was hanging out."

"You Peeping Tom!" she exclaimed. "That's disgusting."

"Teenage hormones, babe," he said with a grin. "Couldn't help myself."

Damn it, Vivian, you let your guard down for once in your life and you end up with this . . . studcat. No wonder Brenda dumped him. She took a deep sip of wine and glanced at her watch. It was going to be a long evening. Teenage werecat voyeur!

"Well, count yourself lucky," she said. "That was your first and last glimpse of the real me."

"Sure," he said with a wink. "Whatever you say."

Despite Hank's presence, the play was fantastic. She decided to take it as a reward for putting up with him. He strutted as they headed back to the parking garage, pleased that he'd scored a coup with the tickets. Now he had further plans.

"Let's go to a club I know down in SoHo. It's too early to call it a night."

"No, I'm really tired. I loved the play, but I'm falling asleep."

Viv could hear the clicking of her heels on the concrete floor of the garage as she hurried to Hank's car. She always hated entering these places at night, with or without an escort, especially now. Glancing nervously around as Hank strolled beside her, Viv felt the small pendant around her neck and liked the security it provided.

"You just want to go home?" he asked in disbelief.

"Yes. I'm exhausted."

Viv heard the click of the remote. Hank opened her door and watched her seat herself before he closed it and went around to his side. "Okay," he said. "Back to New Jersey. But I think you're making a mistake. We could have a good time here tonight."

At about the same time Hank's silver Lexus pulled out of its space, a black Mercedes did the same. It paused, then followed them down the lane, onto the exit ramp, and waited behind them as Hank handed in his ticket to the man at the booth. Viv glanced in her side-view mirror, saw the car, and thought nothing of it. Lots of cars were leaving New York at this time.

"I wonder how the bridge traffic is right now," Viv said.

"Put on the radio. They'll probably have an update."

As they drove in and out of traffic, heading for the Henry Hudson Parkway and the George Washington Bridge, Viv caught a glimpse of the Mercedes that had been behind them before.

Her heart skipped a beat. It was the same one. With the same two men in dark coats.

"I think we're being followed," she said.

"And what makes you think that?"

"Because the men who were in line behind us at the garage are behind us again."

"Probably a coincidence. How many people do you think are heading across the Hudson right now? Thousands. And sometimes they take the same path."

"This is true." She tried to sound convinced.

Hank drove silently now, but it was an uncomfortable silence. Viv could see him glancing furtively in the rearview mirror.

"Are they still there?" she asked.

"Yes."

"Try changing lanes," she advised.

"Okay."

He put on the directional and moved into the fast lane. So did the Mercedes.

"This is feeling a little strange," Hank said. "Have you and Marc gotten yourselves into anything that might draw the wrong kind of attention?"

"If you mean illegal, no," Viv replied. "We run an honest business."

"Then why are two guys tailing us?" Hank seemed worried now. His face lost its usual smile; he glanced back into the mirror from time to time, swearing as he observed the Mercedes behind him, staying doggedly with him.

"I'm going to alert our security service," Viv said as they

headed across the George Washington Bridge. "With any luck they can meet us when we arrive home."

"Call 'em now," Hank said with a shrug. "Our friends in the Mercedes are sticking to us like glue."

Viv pressed the button on her pendant and activated a light. "Hello, Miss Roussel," a voice said. "How can we help you?"

"I'm in a car heading for the GW, and there's another car behind me that's been with me since I left the parking garage in the city. It looks suspicious."

"We have you on our screen. What is your destination?"

"My apartment building in Fort Lee. There's a twenty-four-hour concierge in the lobby. I'll be safe once I arrive home."

"You're not driving your own car, are you?"

"No. I'm with a friend. I'm using my security pendant in his car."

"We have your address. We'll have a man sent to your apartment to meet your when you get there."

"I'm almost home," she said nervously.

"We're very quick," the voice replied.

"That's really high-tech," Hank said in admiration after Viv terminated her conversation. "Do you think they'll be waiting for us when we get there?"

"I hope so," she said. "Rather than those men in back of us. Whoever they are," she added.

This evening she had hoped to enjoy was beginning to look like a nightmare.

Chapter Thirteen

While Vivian was out with Hank, Marc Roussel drove his car back to the parking garage of his Upper East Side town house, gingerly removed a covered, medium-sized rectangular object from the trunk, buzzed himself through the security door, and took the elevator upstairs to his foyer. His heart thumped each step of the way, setting his nerves on edge, making him sweat even though it was the middle of October and the temperature had lingered at fifty-eight degrees all day.

When he told Viv earlier he was going to the warehouse, he was telling the truth, but he hadn't yet made his discovery. Once inside the storage depot, Marc had begun to go through each object in the place, searching for anything that could have triggered the persecution they were now experiencing. What the hell did they have? He was convinced it had to be spectacular, yet to the best of his knowledge, they had purchased nothing so extraordinary that men would hunt them for it. Maybe someone else knew something they didn't. It wasn't a feeling that gave him any comfort, so he drove to the warehouse, determined to inspect everything, even if it took days.

After three hours, Marc lifted a seventeenth-century mirror and gave a start. He didn't remember purchasing this. It was almost hidden behind a larger mirror, and when he examined it, he noticed something odd. On the reverse, almost as if it had been superimposed on the original backing, was a second backing. This was extremely strange. Why would it require two?

Marc was surprised and a little nervous. His first thoughts involved the smuggling of controlled substances. Had somebody placed a box behind the mirror and filled the interior with contraband drugs? Maybe he had a million dollars' worth of coke inside this thing. That would explain all the weird attacks. Somebody had stashed their haul in his warehouse somehow, and they wanted the goods back. Shit!

Gingerly, he examined the mirror and its gilded frame, looking carefully for any traces of white powder. Nothing. Then he felt all around the back of the mirror. Solid wood. Puzzled, Marc then turned his attention to the second backing, carefully feeling the edges with his fingers. What he found startled him.

"Can't be," he murmured. "Not possible."

Torn between growing fear and unbearable curiosity, the antiquarian sat down and popped out the top strip of the second backing until he got a better look at what lay inside. It looked like wood.

"This is like one of those matryoshka dolls," he muttered. Layer upon layer of hidden surprises. Then, frustrated by the task of getting out the piece of wood, Marc lifted the mirror upside down and began to shake it gently. Glints of gold shone in the dim light as the hidden panel within slowly revealed itself, hinting at sublime beauty. When he saw what he had in his hands, Marc trembled with awe and dread.

I'm dead, he thought. *It's all over. These guys—whoever they are—have got to be from the Russian mob. They'll kill us both.*

When he could stop shaking, Marc gingerly slid the painting back inside its hiding place. With his heart pounding, he took the "mirror" and a candelabrum, loaded them into his car and drove off.

As he headed home, plunged into gloom, he realized all his moves must have been recorded on the new video monitors. Marc just hoped his actions had been hidden by the large armoire next to the chair he sat in while he inspected the work. Why hadn't he thought of the damned cameras before? Oh, he was fucked. He had to get hold of Viv and tell her not to go home tonight, to go to a hotel until they could decide how to handle this. The whole thing was too much for them, probably too much for their new security team as well. Hell, maybe those guys were part of the plot? Who could tell? They were Russians, foreigners. Maybe even part of the mob. He hadn't located the source of the trouble until Metro Investigations had gone into the warehouse and wired it. But they only went in because of the earlier break-in and the attempted kidnappings.

Marc's mind was racing so fast, he felt almost irrational. Why did he have to get involved with Russian antiques? he wondered. He could have done something else, maybe gotten a job with the State Department, with some start-up company doing business with the new Russia, anything but this. And Viv was in danger, too. Things couldn't get any worse than this.

When he entered his town house, Marc turned off his alarm, then reset it, placed the mirror and its concealed treasure on a table, and took out his cell phone, punching in his sister's number. Nothing. Her phone was probably turned off since she and Hank were going to the theater.

Trying hard to sound as normal as possible, Marc left a voice mail message instructing her not to return to her apartment but to go to a hotel in Manhattan and call him when she checked in. Something had come up, and it was of the utmost importance *not* to go home.

He hoped she would listen to him.

Chapter Fourteen

"Do you really think your guys will be waiting when we get to your apartment?" Hank asked as he drove nervously while glancing into the rearview mirror. "Whoever's following us is not letting up. I've changed lanes. He keeps pace with me. Are you sure you're not mixed up in something weird?"

"This is the only weird thing *I* know about," Viv replied. "Marc and I are honest. We haven't cheated anybody, and we haven't played fast and loose with the law. I can't imagine why these people are trying to scare us."

"Do you think it's the mob?" he asked seriously.

"Why should the mob want anything from us? That's crazy."

"Well, who else? The feds?"

Viv shook her head as Hank left the bridge and turned into the local lanes, heading for her apartment. She prayed Pavel Federov's men would be there, although she didn't see how they could get there soon enough to be of help right now. Maybe if she and Hank drove straight into the parking garage beneath her apartment complex, they would be safe. Then again, the Mercedes might just do the same.

"Hank, I'm so sorry I got you involved in this. They want me, not you."

"Well, they aren't getting you," he said.

Viv could have kissed him. Despite all the studcat nonsense, Hank was a stand-up guy who wasn't going to fail to protect her. She was grateful for that, even if she did feel horribly guilty for putting him at risk just for being in her company.

When the Lexus entered the parking garage, the Mercedes did the same. Hank drove slowly down the rows of cars, ostensibly looking for a space. When his pursuers slowed behind him at a corner, he put the pedal to the floor and the Lexus shot forward straight out the exit and unfortunately into the side of another vehicle.

Air bags inflated, Viv screamed, and Hank was momentarily incapacitated. Suddenly doors flew open, men with guns appeared and screamed commands at them, and strong hands grabbed Viv and pulled her from the car.

Reeling from the shock of the crash, Viv staggered as she tried to stand up and fight off her attackers. On the other side, Hank jumped out of the car and attempted to tackle the kidnappers, but to Viv's horror, one of the thugs raised a handgun, fired three times, and sent Hank sprawling on the driveway, blood spattering his cashmere overcoat.

"Oh, my God! No!"

Viv shrieked in fear as she watched him try to crawl toward his assailant and grab him. The man turned back to his victim and fired again, putting an end to Hank's efforts.

"Cold-blooded cowards!" she screamed as a stocky character in a sweater and stocking cap took hold of her as she fought back, kicking and punching as best she could.

"Shit, lady! Behave yourself or I'll have to beat you down!"

By way of response, Viv doubled over and sank her teeth into his hand, eliciting a scream and a string of curse words from her abductor. He raised his hand and backhanded her viciously, sending her staggering across the driveway, straight into the arms of his partner.

"Come on! Let's get out of here. Somebody must have called the cops by now. Move it!"

Unseen helpers jumped into the vehicle that had blocked

their escape, taking off with a screech of tires, while two men dragged Viv toward the Mercedes, threw her into the trunk, and roared out of there like they were on fire. In the light of the driveway, a body lay inert, blood puddling around it—Hank, gunned down by Viv's kidnappers.

Frightened and desperate in the trunk of the car, Viv pressed the security device around her neck and spoke frantically into the receiver telling Metro their men never showed up and she was now being kidnapped in the trunk of a black Mercedes.

"We have you on the screen," the voice responded. "You're on Route Four."

"Get me out of this trunk," she whispered frantically, "before these two men kill me. I think they just murdered my friend. They shot him several times and he didn't get up. Help me!"

"Our men just missed you at your apartment. They are now in pursuit," the dispatcher told her with professional composure. "Try to remain calm."

Viv closed her eyes and had to work hard to remain focused. "Remain calm." Yes. Right now she didn't dare do anything else if she wanted to survive, but she felt raw fear tearing at her entrails as she curled into a fetal position and rocked back and forth with sheer frustration. Hank was probably dead because of her, and she shouldn't even have accepted the invitation that had cost him his life. And now she was at the mercy of men who might kill *her.* Why? This violence didn't make any sense. Had they confused her with someone else?

And, as her sharp senses became aware of the odors in the car, she noted with shock that she could detect the scent of a werecat, maybe more than one. The males who had abducted her must be werefolk.

The idea of being manhandled so disrespectfully by another werecat really stunned her. These bastards couldn't be from her own clan. And yet whom could she have angered enough to do this to her?

"We've never lost a client yet," the dispatcher said, and there was sympathy and compassion in his voice. "We're not going to start now."

"Please," she said through clenched teeth. "Just get me out of here before they park the car and kill me! I'm really frightened."

"Viv, if your phone is on, call me."

Marc listened, swore, and pressed END once more. Damn, she was out of contact, wherever she was. Hank wasn't responding to his phone either, and that was odd because the guy was always tuned in.

There had to be a good reason he couldn't reach them. They were probably still in the theater.

The more Marc thought about the possibilities, the more convinced he was of doom. The only thing to do was call Metro Investigations and see if they had Viv in their sights. They had all that high-tech equipment. They could find her.

When he got the call center, Marc was astonished to hear where they located her—in the trunk of a Mercedes heading down Route Four.

For a second he couldn't believe he had heard them correctly. Then he recovered and asked in a tight voice, "Is my sister all right? Do you even know if she's alive?"

"Mr. Roussel, I'm going to pass you over to Mr. Federov. Please stay on the line."

As Marc collapsed into a chair, his mind in chaos, he heard a click and then: "Mr. Roussel, Federov here. We have an ongoing abduction in progress. The gentleman who drove your sister home to her apartment has been shot and Vivian has been kidnapped. We're tracking the car right now."

Marc felt so disoriented he could barely think rationally. Hank had been shot. Was he going to survive? Who would want to harm *him*? Or Viv?

"How are you tracking them?" Marc asked when he regained his composure.

"GPS. Vivian has a pendant with a microchip. She's been in contact with us."

"That means she's still alive."

"Yes. She spoke with the call center. She's scared but otherwise unharmed."

"How long will that last? I mean when they get to wherever they're going . . ."

"We'll be right behind them," Pavel said quietly. "I've alerted our special-action team about the kidnapping, and they're on their way. Three SUVs are tracking her. Would you like the police brought into this?"

"No. Not as long as you can get Viv back yourself." Marc shook his head as he stared at the telephone. He couldn't believe this was happening. If Metro couldn't cut it, then fuck the Leader and call the cops. But he had to give them a chance first.

"I have to be there," he said. "Viv's my only sister."

"I would advise you to stay where you are, Mr. Roussel. We don't know if they have others waiting to abduct you, too."

"Then send one of your guys to come get me so I can join you in New Jersey. Your men have weapons permits, right?"

"Yes."

"Then I'll be fine. Just get me over there."

He thought he heard the sound of a sigh. Then Pavel said, "All right. My man Ivan will be at your town house in fifteen minutes. He'll give you the password "gulfstream" to identify himself. Be ready."

"Don't worry."

These things didn't happen to people like him and Viv. It was madness. But flustered as he was, Marc did one final thing before he got ready to leave home and rush across the Hudson to find his sister. He pulled down the folding attic stairs, went up to the attic with the treasure from the warehouse and stashed it behind some boxes. Then he nervously tossed a cloth cover over it and went to the foyer to wait for Ivan.

Chapter Fifteen

Inside the trunk of the Mercedes, Viv struggled to keep calm and tried to gauge her chances of survival. She was convinced the kidnappers were werecats since their pheromones gave them away. That meant she was dealing with another clan, obviously hostile to her own, or merely angry with her. She was certain she had no personal enemies who would want to harm her. The antiques crowd was more likely to use their tongues as weapons rather than hire thugs to settle scores; besides, the only other antiquarians she knew were humans.

Vivian tried hard to concentrate on something that might be useful. She knew most cars had a device that would allow you to pop the trunk from the inside, but because they were traveling at perhaps eighty miles an hour on one of the busiest highways in the area, she wasn't going to attempt using it right now. Too dangerous. Besides, everything was dark and she wasn't even sure if she could locate the mechanism.

There was only one option open to her, she felt, and that was the ultimate life-in-danger-pull-out-all-the-stops last resort. It might briefly confuse her abductors, but it would also pose problems for her rescuers, if there were any. And if Pavel Federov was as good as his reputation, he would have his whole staff working overtime on this one.

*   *   *

Pavel's worst nightmare was the classic hostage situation with crazed gunmen threatening vulnerable captives. If you couldn't neutralize the enemy, they might kill their victims, but in a rescue attempt, overzealous action might precipitate a disaster. This was what had happened in Moscow at the time of the theater takeover by terrorist gunmen, and Pavel had lost Natalya, the love of his life.

Now he himself was about to relive that grim night on a different continent, with a client he cared about far more than he ought to.

Pavel turned to his driver as they sped down the highway after the Mercedes. "I wish she had agreed to a bodyguard."

"So do I. It would have made things a lot easier."

Viv tried very hard to remember every lesson in survival she had ever learned. Her grandfather had told her things she tried to recall now as she lay on the floor of a car trunk, headed toward an unknown and frightening destination. The surreal quality of her situation almost disoriented her.

At that moment, Viv felt a change in the movement of the car. They were slowing down. She felt a gentle bump as the vehicle went onto another kind of driving surface and seemed to glide toward a nearby destination. They had arrived.

She concentrated very hard, erasing the sounds coming from the outside, thinking only of what she had to do. "Give me the power," she murmured. "Make me strong."

A few minutes later, the driver parked the car in the driveway of a house on a residential street, opened the door, and got out, followed by his accomplice. Both men were armed and ready to deal with any outburst as they approached the trunk.

"Go ahead," said the driver. "Let her out."

With a glance at his partner, the second man clicked the

remote and lifted the trunk door. In disbelief he stared first at the empty trunk, then at his partner.

"She's not there," he stammered. In the darkness, all he could see was a kind of fur rug. No woman.

As the two men wondered aloud what had happened to their passenger, arguing with each other about her disappearance, the pile of fur began to stir. Around the corner, the first signs of flashing lights approached.

Suddenly the driver screamed in terror as a large, shaggy cat the size of a puma leaped out of the trunk straight at him, knocked him to the ground, and tore his throat out. Dumbfounded, his partner lost control of his bladder, changed into a long-haired cat the size of a bobcat, and began running down the driveway, turning back to see the animal finish with his partner and pause before heading straight toward him.

Frightened out of his wits, the werecat ran as fast as he could, stumbling in the dark, colliding with a lawn ornament as he scurried away like a frantic crab, trying to outrun whatever was after him. The female was a fuckin' weretiger, maybe a werelion, he thought in the grip of hysteria. She was huge. And they hadn't even realized she was one of them. Why couldn't he get her scent? He lost his balance when he collided with a row of brick pavers and fell across the drive and under the shaggy paws of his pursuer.

Terrified feline screams ripped through the dark autumn night as the beast seized his throat and shook him like a rat, tearing a hole in his neck, biting the jugular, chomping down several times to make sure the prey was dead.

When the cat lay still, the larger furry cat with a magnificent plumed tail and white paws watched him for any sign of life. Satisfied that he was no longer a threat, the animal turned around and walked slowly up the driveway and around the back of the house. If any further attackers arrived, she had to be ready.

*   *   *

Sounds of three high-powered vehicles roared into the area, followed by Pavel in one car and Marc and Ivan trailing in another. The special-action team pulled up and quickly blocked the entrance to the driveway while the others took up positions and immediately noticed something lying across the far end of the long drive: a body dressed in a black coat with a dark stream of liquid emerging from beneath it.

"Get the lights over here," called the man in charge. "I think we have a fatality."

"Male or female?"

"Male."

"Holy shit! Look at the damage. Whoever got him tore him up good. His throat's been ripped out."

While two men examined the bleeding corpse at their feet, two others headed down the drive, where a smaller form lay on the grass.

"One more up here. He's dead. He hasn't got a throat anymore. And he's a big cat."

While the team fanned out around the back of the house, Marc arrived right behind Pavel, shocked at the sight in the driveway.

Werecats, he thought nervously as he looked at the two corpses. *The first one didn't have time to shape-shift.*

"There's nobody in the car. We found it with the trunk open. We searched it after we found these two with their throats ripped out."

Marc looked pasty in the blinding light of the car headlights. He glanced quickly at the corpses and then averted his eyes. "We have to find Viv," he said.

"Stay right here, Mr. Roussel," Pavel's driver directed. "We're going to look for your sister. You get back in the car. We have weapons in case the kidnappers had help."

"Then give me one," he said. "I'm a hunter. I know how to shoot, and I can help you if you need an extra hand."

Pavel turned to his driver. "If our client escaped from her

captors, she might be hiding in the backyard. It's dark. She could be trying to take shelter behind trees or behind some shrubs. Warn the men. After what she's been through, I wouldn't want her to get shot by our side."

Nodding, he called out, "Vivian Roussel, if you are in the area, make yourself known. My team is on the premises. The kidnappers are dead. We want you to show yourself if you are able. Just tell us if you cannot walk."

Pavel started to approach the entrance of the house. As he did, he heard a soft voice calling his name. Glancing down, he saw her. Viv was half concealed, kneeling behind a shrub, seemingly in shock. She stared at him, dazed. Her clothing looked ragged from the struggle.

"Are you all right?" he asked as he ran to her and helped her to her feet. "Marc," he called over his shoulder, "your sister is here. She's alive."

"Viv? Are you okay?" Marc pushed his way past the special-action squad. "Did they hurt you? Are you really all right?"

"I think Hank is dead," she said before she sank into Pavel's arms and passed out.

Chapter Sixteen

Marc remained at Viv's side as Pavel tried to question her about her kidnapping and the presence of other werecats in the area. Still dazed by the ordeal, she told him she and a friend had gone to the theater in New York, noticed a car following them all the way home, and then fallen prey to the kidnappers in a blocked driveway. She had no recollection of an animal of any kind. And she had no idea why there were two dead bodies in the driveway of this house, which she had never seen before.

"Mr. Federov, my sister is overwhelmed by her ordeal. I'm sure she would agree to questioning in a day or so, but right now I think she needs to see a doctor."

Everyone looked quite harsh in the bright light of the headlights. Pavel saw the futility of getting any useful information out of this traumatized woman, so he turned to Marc and said, "Fine. But she has to answer some questions in a day or so. I know she's the victim here, but we have to get to the bottom of it."

"Of course. And Metro will have to guard her so nobody else can get to her," Marc said. He looked at Pavel. "I'll take her home with me. We'll call her doctor and help her calm down so you can question her."

"Sure," Pavel said. "But she's pretty shaken up right now. It may take a few days."

When Viv was in the car with Marc and Pavel, she said, "Did Hank survive?"

"My men arrived just after the attack. They called the doctor whose name appeared on a medical bracelet he wore. He met them at a local hospital."

"But did he survive?"

"The last report by my man said he was still in surgery."

A sigh floated out as Viv sank back against the leather seat of Pavel's car. "Then he's alive."

"Just barely. They said he lost a lot of blood."

"I have to see him," Viv said.

Marc turned around from the passenger seat and stared at his sister. "I don't think you're in any condition to do that right now. You ought to have a doctor look at you."

"I was driven around in a trunk, but I wasn't shot. If Hank hadn't been with me tonight, he wouldn't be in the hospital right now. I have to see him. You know it's important. I can help him."

"There will be doctors and nurses there," Pavel said. "He'll be unconscious after the operation and he won't even know you're there."

"It doesn't matter," she said. "If he's alive, I can still help him."

Marc looked back at her. "I'll go see him. I think you should go home."

"Mr. Federov, take us to the hospital. It's important. You can guard me there as well as any other place."

"Then if you see your friend, will you go home?"

"Yes."

"Okay. We're on our way."

At the hospital, they found Brenda, Hank's ex-wife, who was sitting vigil beside his bed. She had been crying, and her eyes were red and blotchy when she spotted Viv and Marc at the door.

"How did you get in?" she asked in surprise. "They're only letting in family right now."

Marc walked up to Brenda and gave her a hug. Viv did the same. They glanced toward the door, where Pavel stood just inside. "A friend pulled some strings," Marc said.

Brenda pointed toward Hank, who looked near death, after his surgery. Tubes ran from his body to a rack near his bed. Monitors kept track of his pulse and his breathing. Then she looked at Viv and said, "Somebody told me he had given you a ride home when you were attacked."

"Yes. After they shot Hank, they threw me into the trunk of a car. I ended up someplace in Bergen County."

"What happened to the guys who did it?"

Viv shook her head as she looked sorrowfully at the man on the bed.

"What does that mean?" Brenda demanded.

"They're dead and I have no idea what happened. I must have blacked out, because the first thing I knew, I was hiding in the bushes of this house, and people were calling my name. It's just bizarre. I'm still trying to take it all in." Even though Brenda was a member of Viv's clan, she didn't want to give out details in such a public place.

"How come you and Hank were together in the first place?" Brenda asked with an edge to her voice.

Pavel listened carefully. He wondered, too. For a woman who claimed she wasn't dating anyone, this must have been considered a date by at least one of the parties.

"Hank asked me to go see a play I had wanted to see. It was just two friends getting together."

"I didn't think you were the kind of woman who would try to take over my husband like that," Brenda said, struggling with tears and anger. "I mean, we just recently split up. Did you ever go out with him *before* we divorced?" she demanded as her voice rose shrilly, overwhelmed by emotion.

Pavel moved into the room and positioned himself so that he could grab Viv if Brenda made a move to attack her. A catfight was the last thing he needed tonight. Both women were exhausted but keyed-up, and Pavel knew the ferocity of werecat women.

"Brenda, I know you're devastated by this, but believe me, there was nothing going on between Hank and me."

"Then why did you come straight here?"

"Because I feel horrified that he got shot, and I wanted to see how he was."

"Well, look at how well he's doing," Brenda sobbed. "Look at what happened to him. If he hadn't taken you out, he'd be fine." She covered her mouth with her hand and sobbed hysterically, shaking all over, and she glared at Vivian. "He has two children. And now they're going to grow up without their father. All because of you!"

"Brenda, would you like to come outside and maybe have a cup of coffee and tell me what the doctors said?" Marc tried to distract her from possibly hitting his sister. And as an old friend, he really did want to hear the prognosis. Two werecat doctors with hospital privileges here had worked on Hank, so he was in good hands. One of Pavel's guys had rushed him to the hospital and called the number on Hank's medical-alert bracelet.

"All right," she agreed, still sobbing. "Just for a minute. I don't want to leave him alone too long."

After the sound of footsteps faded into silence down the hall, Viv walked closer to the bed and gently took Hank's hand in hers.

Pavel gave her a questioning glance. She gestured to him to stay.

Then, as the Russian watched, Vivian Roussel began to chant softly in a language he didn't understand at first. In his mind, he recalled something similar from ages ago, something so old that it seemed to come from a place and a time nobody could even remember. From the ancestors.

Not caring that she had an audience, Viv continued her chanting and spread her arms out wide, encompassing

Hank's inert form as she invoked a force Pavel could only guess at. Indicating the four corners of the room, he knew she was calling on help from the four corners of the universe, asking the elements for help, begging the spirits to rally round this wounded creature.

Suddenly it clicked. Years ago, as a child, Pavel had witnessed a shaman performing a similar ceremony in the lands of the far North. This woman was one, too.

Silently he watched her conclude her prayers and then bow her head as she stood by the bedside and made another sweeping gesture before turning and sinking into the nearest chair.

"Are you all right?" he asked.

"Yes."

Pavel glanced at Hank. "Is *he* going to be all right?"

She looked up at him with a serious expression in those lovely amber eyes. "Yes. His recovery will go well."

Then as he watched, Vivian's head sank forward and she fell fast asleep.

Chapter Seventeen

"I think we all need to talk," Marc said quietly as he, Pavel, and Vivian left the hospital after keeping vigil with Brenda at Hank's bedside.

"Yes, and I don't think we should wait until tomorrow," Pavel replied.

"Then let's go to Marc's place. It's the closest one. Do you have your men watching it?" Viv glanced up at the Russian and silently hoped he would say they were.

"The entrance and exit are being monitored. So far, so good."

"All right," she said. "Then we can talk there."

When the three of them reached Marc's town house, Pavel drove into the garage, parked the car, and after making sure they were not followed, let Marc lead them through the security gate and into the elevator. Nobody said anything as the elevator lifted them to the foyer. Everybody felt drained. It was after four in the morning.

Once inside the town house, Marc turned to Pavel and said, "I think I know why these people are after us."

Vivian stared uneasily at her brother. "What's going on?" she asked.

"You and Pavel stay right there. I have to show you something."

As she and the Russian seated themselves on the sofa,

Viv glanced at him and realized he was studying her. Those light green eyes rested somberly on her face.

"I have to ask you some questions, too," he said.

"All right."

"How did a large man and a big cat end up dead in that driveway when you escaped unscathed—from whatever killed them?"

"I don't remember anything between being driven around in that trunk till the moment you found me on the porch. I don't know whose house it is or who my kidnappers were. It's a blank."

"Did they drug you?"

"No. There was no time. They grabbed me. I tried to fight them off, but I failed. They tossed me into the trunk of their car and hit the gas. I managed to activate that pendant and get in touch with your men. Nobody stuck me with a needle or held a cloth to my face."

"While you were in the car, did you hear sounds of an animal in the area? From what I saw of the wounds, those men had their throats ripped out by a beast."

Viv shook her head. "I'm sorry, "she said. "I must have blacked out. I just don't remember anything. It must be what they call post-traumatic stress."

Pavel's eyes narrowed. "You may be telling me the truth. But you're not telling me everything," he said.

"Pavel, I've been kidnapped. Our warehouse has been burgled. My brother and I both feel like we're running on borrowed time at the moment. Why shouldn't I tell you the truth?"

As Pavel was about to reply, Marc came back into the living room with a large antique mirror in his hands.

"Pavel, I want you to look at this."

The Russian rose from the sofa and watched as the antiquarian placed the large rectangular item on a chair. Then he saw him turn it upside down and slide something out, very slowly, very carefully. When it had emerged, Marc allowed Vivian and their guest a good look.

At first glance, Pavel went rigid, then snapped to attention and devoured the painting with his eyes as if he couldn't believe what he was seeing. Viv stared at his reaction, and then took a closer look at the very old icon before her. Magnificent. The detailing of the golden halos on the Madonna and child were gorgeous. Their painted robes glittered in the light. Expressive eyes looked out at the onlooker with tender compassion.

"This is the Virgin of Saratov," the Russian said at last. "She never left her place in that monastery—except for one brief time—until she was stolen three months ago. You'd better be able to give me a damn good explanation of how she ended up here." A warning glittered in his expressive eyes. His jaw clenched as he faced them.

"I found her in the warehouse this afternoon," Marc said. "I left on a lunch break to go back there and find out what we had that was so attractive to these guys. I started checking all the paintings against our invoices, and I found this disguised in the backing for a mirror. I had no record of it. We had bought one mirror, not two."

"Somebody must have planted it before we left Russia," Viv said with disgust. "That has to be why they broke into the warehouse. Whoever planted it wanted it back, and when they couldn't find it, they decided to kidnap us to see if *we* knew where it went."

She sat down again, plainly overwhelmed, her face drained of all color.

Pavel studied his two clients. He didn't know whether to believe them or not. The fact that they had one of Russia's holiest icons in their possession stunned him. The entire country was searching for it. The highest levels of the Russian government were involved in getting it back. And here it was in the apartment of an American antiques dealer who might or might not be a werecat. Hell, he *was* a werecat; so was Viv. But they didn't want to admit it.

"You have to tell me exactly how you think you acquired it," Pavel said in a stern tone.

"But we don't know."

"Then tell me what happened on your last buying trip. Or the previous one. It had to come from somewhere. When were you last in Russia?" he demanded.

"About two and a half months ago."

"The Virgin of Saratov was stolen about three months ago, according to a friend of mine. The government delayed announcing the theft because of its significance. Do you have any idea of how important she is to believers?"

Viv nodded. "She's supposed to have protected the city of Saratov from Ivan the Terrible. They had resisted him, and his usual policy was to slaughter everybody in town when that happened. Instead, the tsar allowed the people to keep their lives, but he took a huge ransom. When he went back to Moscow, the people celebrated their deliverance by building a special chapel to house the icon they credited with sparing their city."

"*Khorosho,*" Pavel said with a nod. "You've studied your history. Then you know that Orthodox believers venerate the Virgin of Saratov," he said. "They feel that if she could protect a rich town from the tsar, she could accomplish anything."

Viv glanced at him. "I saw the medallion you wear. You must be devoted to her, too."

"I am," he said simply. "And now we have to protect this lady until we can return her to her homeland."

Marc gave him a gloomy look. "I think we're dead if anybody finds out we have it."

"Not if we manage to act faster than your pursuers. And," Pavel added as he turned to Viv and looked her directly in the eye, "you'll have to start telling me the truth."

Chapter Eighteen

"Let's backtrack. It's late and we're all exhausted. Make me understand what happened the last time you went to Russia on a buying expedition. I have to know the truth about how the icon came into your possession."

"First I'm going to make coffee," Marc said. "I can barely keep my eyes open. Would you like some? Or anything else?"

While Marc went to the kitchen to prepare coffee for everybody, Pavel sat studying the icon, almost afraid to find any damage. This was a national treasure, the focus of prayers for millions of believers. He had a duty to get her home safely; and with the attacks on his clients, he knew he faced a daunting battle. Who had taken the Virgin? And for what purpose? Was a cartel behind this? Or was it the work of one lunatic?

"Vivian," he said at last, "when you and your brother were in Russia the last time, where did you go?"

"Moscow and St. Petersburg. We usually work with a variety of dealers."

"Are these the same each time?"

"We generally visit people we've dealt with before, but occasionally we go to a new man, based on references from our previous contacts. It depends."

Pavel opened his hands in an expansive gesture. "Depends on what?"

"On what we're looking for. Sometimes we search for things that we already have a market for. Samovars are very popular." She smiled. "I know it's sort of a cliché, but people like Russian samovars. You can't imagine how many upscale émigrés get emotional when they talk about sitting in Babushka's kitchen in her tiny apartment, with the samovar on the table. It's a sentimental favorite."

He nodded. "What else do people want?"

"Paintings. Still lifes are admired, especially nineteenth-century oils. We generally don't deal in icons. Eighteenth- and nineteenth-century portraits are popular, as well as silver and ormolu articles. Lately there's been an interest in twentieth-century art, but that's not really our area of expertise, although Marc collects early-twentieth-century posters. I prefer more romantic genres."

"Perhaps an elegant Vrubel in blues and violets."

She smiled. "I actually have one in my apartment. It's one of my favorites."

"He had a wonderful style, but he was quite mad," Pavel said.

Vivian glanced at him in surprise. "Did you study art in Russia?"

Pavel shook his head. "No. I once loved a woman who was an artist."

He didn't want to deal with the question he saw in Viv's eyes, so he asked, "Do your Russian dealers specialize in specific areas, for instance paintings, art objects, or silver, or do they offer a variety of things?"

"Well, Kornilov in Moscow is our source for the best silver. We also use a couple of others. For paintings, we have a whole range of people. Sometimes we buy privately from people selling family heirlooms. We try to give them a fair price." Viv added, "I think it's sad when that happens. We don't cheat anybody."

After going through their list of contacts in Moscow and St. Petersburg, Pavel found none who set off alarms. He would check them with his own sources later, but for the moment, everything seemed normal. And then Marc mentioned a name that surprised him.

"We also bought some things from Bella Danilov. She's a businesswoman who seems to dabble in lots of things. She's the one who owns the new boutique Boyarina."

Pavel glanced at Marc and Viv. "She was just in the news lately. Did you hear what happened?"

"Yes. It was on TV. Her husband was shot outside a restaurant in St. Petersburg, right in front of her, but the bodyguard managed to save her. We were shocked."

"Did you ever meet Mr. Danilov?" he asked.

"No. I heard about him from our contacts. He was quite a heavy hitter in financial circles. People said he was very smart—and crazy about his wife."

Pavel looked carefully at Vivian. "What was your impression of Mrs. Danilov?"

"Pretentious. Sorry," she apologized. "It's tragic that she lost her husband that way, but I found her a bit much. I have to be honest."

"I thought she was nice," Marc said. "She was quite a charmer."

"Yes. If she was dealing with a man," Viv said.

Pavel found that amusing. "Did you purchase anything from her?"

"Several paintings, mostly nineteenth-century genre scenes. And a few silver objects."

"And everything arrived in good shape?"

"Yes. No problems. We purchased from four dealers on that trip, and everything came home in one piece."

"If you don't mind, I'd like copies of the invoices from that trip. I'd also like to go through your warehouse. And," Pavel said with emphasis, "I'm going to try to find a safe hiding place for the icon while I make inquiries about returning it."

"This could be dangerous," Marc reflected. "The fact that we have it looks suspicious. We might be charged with stealing it." He hated to think of the Leader's reaction to the headlines that kind of thing would generate.

"What about the men who attacked me?" Viv asked. "I can't imagine that this is going to stop because those two are dead. We need to find out who is behind this, or we'll never be safe."

"One thing at a time," Pavel replied. "I'm going to assign a bodyguard now. You would agree this time, I think."

"Yes. I don't want to go through a second abduction."

"Good. Then I'm going to get in touch with an associate of mine and ask him to store the icon. Do I have your permission?"

"If he can assure its safety, that would be wonderful," Viv said. "We have no claim to it, and we'd like to see it go back home where it belongs."

"Fine." Pavel turned to glance out the window and grimaced. It was almost dawn. Damn.

Taking out his cell phone, he punched in Vladimir's number and glanced at his watch. He hoped there was still time.

Chapter Nineteen

"Morgan residence. Vladimir speaking."

"It's Pavel. Something's come up and I need to speak with Mr. Morgan."

"Trouble?" Vlad asked instinctively.

"Yes."

"The timing is not good," Vlad reminded him. "He's about to turn in."

"I know. I'm sorry it's inconvenient, but when he learns what I want, I think he'll be glad he took the call."

"Hold, please. I'll ask him."

When Ian Morgan heard Vladimir's cousin was on the phone with something important, his curiosity got the better of him, and he accepted the call.

"Very mysterious, sir," Vladimir whispered. "I have no idea what Pavel wants."

Ian was in his predaylight state, a time when he began to feel sleepy and craved repose. Vladimir observed the expression on his face change from mild interest to something else as he spoke with Pavel.

"Is it radioactive or toxic, by any chance?" Vladimir heard Ian inquire.

Pavel must have assured him it was not, because he nodded and said, "Fine. You may store it in the vault here. And we'll have a meeting later to discuss the reason for this."

As Vladimir watched intently, his boss said, "Yes. Bring it over as soon as possible. I will not be available at the moment, but your cousin can put it in the vault. We'll speak tomorrow night. Goodbye."

"Sir, shall I wait for Pavel?"

"Yes. He ought to be here within the hour. Let him in and put away this object he's so anxious to shelter."

"Very kind of you to help him, sir."

"Pavel has proved his value to me on several occasions," Ian said as he headed for the stairs leading to the basement and his daytime bedroom, a windowless room that had the look of a very luxurious bomb shelter. "I can return the favor."

Pavel left Viv at Marc's town house, after advising them to get some sleep, which was exactly what he was planning to do. Last night had rattled everyone, and before Pavel interviewed them again, he wanted to take care of more pressing business: the storage of the Saratov icon.

He called for Metro's armor-plated Hummer and asked two of his best men to accompany him on the trip across town. Getting out the Hummer was always a bad sign; it meant trouble. His subordinates noted that and proceeded accordingly.

The Russian wrapped the mirror with the false backing in an old comforter to cushion it on the journey, and when Pavel entered the vehicle with his cargo, his men appeared surprised.

"You taking home your laundry, boss?" one of them joked.

He smiled. "Not precisely. I have to drop off a package."

They didn't feel obliged to comment after that, and turned the radio to a techno-rock channel, which filled the vehicle with the kind of noise that made conversation unnecessary.

After arriving at Ian Morgan's town house, Pavel rang the

bell, was observed by Vladimir on the closed-circuit TV, and then buzzed into the garage. While his men waited in the garage, Pavel and Vladimir walked down the corridor to a flight of stairs leading to a subbasement, where a steel door guarded the outer entrance to the vault.

"No outsider is authorized to enter," Vladimir said. "Stay here."

"*You* may go inside?"

"Only into the foyer. Mr. Morgan is the only one with total access."

"Very astute on his part. I'd do the same."

Vlad nodded. "Me, too," he said. "Now please hand me this very important object and I'll take it into the first area. Tonight, he'll come and carry it into the vault."

"Vladimir," Pavel said, "what I'm holding is priceless beyond belief. Nothing must happen to it here."

"Please don't tell me it's nuclear."

"No. Nothing like that." He gave his cousin a sharp look. "It's nothing sinister."

"I'm sorry," Vladimir said. "You're being so mysterious."

"You have no idea how serious this is. You don't want to know. But you have my word that it won't explode."

"Mr. Morgan may feel he has the right to examine this package—since he's sheltering it."

Pavel nodded. "Yes. I will speak with him and tell him what I'm asking him to store. I'm relying on his sense of honor not to disclose the contents to anyone."

"Not even to me?"

"To nobody. Even looking at it could place you in danger. The less you know, the better."

Pavel glanced at his cousin to emphasize the point, and he noticed a look of bewilderment in Vlad's eyes. "Just don't try to find out what it is," he said in a kinder tone. "There are some secrets that are better left unknown."

Vlad took the wrapped package, expressed surprise at the

weight of it, and unlocked the steel door before him. "I'll be back up in a minute," he said. "Wait there."

While Pavel did, he heard a sound like a heavy bolt being slid into position, then the echo of footsteps as his cousin descended into the underground vault. Then very quickly, the footsteps came back up the stairs, the sound of a bolt grated again, and Vlad was standing before him and turning his key in the lock.

"Mr. Morgan will go there tonight and put it away. Right now, it's in a storage bin under video observation."

"Thank you."

"I hope people aren't going to try to kill you for whatever you've just entrusted to us."

Pavel clapped his cousin on the back and nodded grimly. "Me, too," he said.

Chapter Twenty

As attractive as he found Vivian Roussel, Pavel still suspected that her version of the events the previous evening wasn't quite accurate. While it was true that she had been kidnapped and thrown into the trunk of a car, the claim that she had blacked out at the time her abductors were themselves attacked and killed left Pavel with doubts. It was a werecat trait to be devious. They were complicated beings, unlikely to reveal themselves to strangers—even if those strangers were paid to protect them. He would have to take another approach.

When he called her cell phone, Viv answered on the second ring. She sounded better than he would have imagined after such an ordeal.

"How are you?" he asked. "And my asking isn't just a polite formality."

"I'm good. Marc and I are still trying to figure out who would have wanted to do this to us, but aside from that, we're recovering."

"May I come over there to speak with you?"

"Of course. When?"

"Within the hour."

He sensed a slight hesitation. Then she said, "All right."

"Oh, another thing . . ."

"Yes?"

"Any word about your friend?"

"As a matter of fact, Hank's condition is improving. His doctors can't believe how well he's coming along."

"Glad to hear it. You must have remarkable gifts," he said, then added, "Goodbye," and pressed the button to end the call.

An American werecat, a shaman, a beautiful woman. And that gorgeous auburn hair. Pavel tapped his fingers on his desk and thought about his client. Very attractive. Very feminine. Yet she must have been the one to kill the two werecats who had kidnapped her. And what a job she had done. Exactly as his old teacher would have instructed: aim for the throat. Take them out fast. Get out of there.

Since this was done while Viv exhibited feline form, no court would be able to charge her with anything. She was a hostage defending her life, in any case. The event never made its way to a police blotter, and those two bodies, both in cat form after twelve hours, went into a landfill. The fact that they turned out to be Siberian Forest cats bothered him. Why were Siberians involved in a kidnapping in New Jersey?

While Pavel reflected on Vivian's abilities, he felt an unexpected jealousy about this man Hank, who now lay in a hospital bed. Pavel saw how Hank's ex-wife had reacted when she spotted Vivian in the room.

It had nothing to do with the case, Pavel reminded himself. It could be nothing more than what she said: two old friends going to see a show because they wanted to. Then why had this Brenda react with such emotion? From what Pavel could tell, he and Marc both thought she might have slapped Viv if given a chance. And he knew there were plenty of high-status female werecats who were bold and passionate; stories of their love affairs were the stuff of legend. Was Viv one of these sirens?

You are a jackass, he thought. *You barely know Vivian Roussel, yet you spend time wondering about her love life.*

Get over it. You have a job to do. If she wants you to believe she has no man in her life, it's her business.

Pavel knew he could get a date any night of the week, and he often had, but so far it was just a distraction. Since Natalya's death he hadn't found a woman who moved him enough to wonder about her, speculate about whether she really liked him, and allow her to occupy his thoughts while he worked. Until Vivian.

We men are such idiots, he thought with wry amusement. *If women knew the hold they have over us, we'd be totally at their mercy.*

"I'm happy to be alive after last night," Vivian said after Pavel arrived at Marc's and sat down for tea. "I look upon this is as a kind of celebration. Marc is in his study with the computer, keeping up with overseas orders."

While Viv acted as the gracious hostess, Pavel questioned her again about the kidnapping and refused to accept her claim that she remembered nothing. He found her worryingly attractive, yet this stubborn denial grated on him. He knew she was concealing the truth.

"Think. You can recall everything that happened up until the time they opened the trunk to pull you out. Then it all went blank. I don't believe you."

She shot him a look of anger. "People sometimes go through trauma and find it so distressing that it disappears from their memory. It's a fact."

"Yes. But not in this case, I think. I've known people who fought in wars, killed the enemy in horrible ways, saw their friends killed, and remembered every revolting detail."

"And they sometimes suffer breakdowns."

"Yes. Unfortunately."

"And others blank it out to spare themselves the pain of remembering."

"True. But I think you're tough enough to have total recall. You're no weakling."

Viv merely looked at him and gave a small, feline smile. "I do have a strong will. But that rattled me."

"Of course it did. It would have shaken anyone. But you survived, and your armed kidnappers didn't. That leads me to believe you either killed them yourself or had someone—or something—available to do it for you."

Viv took a sip of tea and placed her Russian-style filigree-encrusted tea glass on the table. "I'm not certain you would understand."

"Try me. I've lived through things that might astonish you."

"Unless you and I have certain things in common," she said quietly, "you might find it difficult to credit."

Pavel looked serious. "We're dealing with an enemy who was brazen enough to steal one of his country's most cherished religious treasures. He respects nothing. He fears neither God nor man. This is the kind of person who attacked you. We need the truth in order to protect you," he said as he fixed her with a steady look from his beautiful green eyes. "It's the only thing that will help now."

Viv studied him carefully. She seemed to be weighing the pros and cons of her actions at this point.

Finally she said, "I thought there was something about you that makes you like me and Marc. It's only a guess, but I've rarely been wrong about these suspicions. It's the eyes that give it away. And the pheromones," she said as she looked straight at him.

He looked back at her and said, "If you agree to be truthful with me, I'll show you if your suspicions are correct."

"Fine," Viv replied. "You go first."

Chapter Twenty-one

"All right," Pavel said evenly. "I find it easier to deal with people if I know their true natures. I'm sure you feel the same."

"Agreed." Viv studied Pavel carefully and asked, "Would you like to go into another room if it would make you feel more comfortable . . . ?"

"That's not necessary. Unless you'd prefer it."

"I can handle it," Viv promised.

Pavel gave her a look that sent green flames straight into her soul. His mouth relaxed into a smile. Then he disappeared, and in his place stood a magnificent silver-tipped dark gray cat, about the size of a panther, his muscles rippling as he moved, his light green eyes staring straight at Viv.

Her mouth opened in a stunned O as she watched him. Though his human form was impressive, this splendid animal took her breath away. The silvery tips of his fur gave him an aura of such majesty as he advanced toward her that Viv was speechless with admiration for this creature of the dense and snowy forests. He looked like a prince of the jungle.

Pavel took advantage of her fascination and sat down beside her, allowing Viv to stroke his fur, a magnificent beast favoring her with his display of trust. Overwhelmed, she sank to her knees on the carpet to run her hands over his sleek fur and touch those hard muscles.

He pushed against her, willing her to recall what she was supposed to do. His paws clasped her leg as a hint of her obligation. He pressed against her and fixed his eyes on hers.

"All right, *koshka*," Viv said. "I'll carry out my part of the agreement."

She stood up and moved away, and then she turned around, and within seconds, a large Maine Coon cat the size of a puma emerged and strode majestically toward him, her silvery tabby markings creating a halo around her as she swished her long plumed tail at Pavel, her amber eyes large and beautiful as she saw the delighted gleam in his eye.

She was magnificent, all feline grace with splendid muscles that would allow her to hold her own with any of the big cats, a tribute to the gods who created her, a vision in silvery stripes.

Imperiously she walked with the sensuous movements of a lioness as she flaunted her form and her beauty before his hungry eyes. In the international language of cats, and using telepathy, he asked if she had always had the ability to shape-shift.

"Since I was very young. My mother taught me. She taught Marc, too."

"Did she also teach you about the ancient religion of the shamans?"

"No. That came from my grandfather, who learned it from *his* grandfather. My education is still unfinished, but I mastered enough to help those in need."

"Like Hank?"

"Yes."

The large Maine Coon cat strolled across the room, giving the Russian a good view of her well-muscled form. Beautiful. So much larger than the females of his own breed, so elegant, so glamorous, such color, such silky fur. What a gorgeous creature.

"You lunged at those men when they opened the trunk, didn't you? Then you killed them."

"Like rodents," Viv replied. "They would have tortured me to learn what they wanted. And I didn't know anything. Filthy werecat thugs. Siberians."

"You're sure?"

"I can generally sense other werefolk in my vicinity. And my kidnappers were werecats with a strong, harsh scent. Siberian Forest cats, the worst of the worst."

He processed that. "Did you know about me?" he asked as he moved closer to Viv and nuzzled her provocatively. She raised her head and rubbed it against him, responding to his caress.

"I wondered about you," she admitted. "Marc and I thought you might be one of the werefolk. Sometimes I could detect your scent, sometimes not. The eyes were the giveaway. Of course, my brother was afraid you might be something else."

"What?" he asked in surprise.

"We were actually concerned you might be a Siberian. You know, I have the ability to sense other werecats, but it's difficult to know the clan until they shift. You were hard to detect," she said. "You can disguise your pheromones most of the time."

Viv could see that Pavel was irritated by the remark about the Siberians. He must hate them. "Don't insult me like that," he said as he growled again, his green eyes flashing emerald fire. "I'm nothing like that breed."

"Then you Russian Blues hold yourselves apart from them?"

"Most of us do. It's bad to get involved with them. We stick to our own kind—with some sorry exceptions. Dimitri Danilov, our Hierarch, married one."

"No wonder I found her so repellent," Viv said. "Our clan has its rules, and they're very specific. No interbreeding. It's considered déclassé."

"What if *you* found yourself attracted to a cat from another clan?" he said, moving closer.

"Not likely," she said quickly. Too quickly, he observed. Those nimble paws moved back and forth as Viv tried to distance herself while he blocked her exit with his body.

"All clans have their own taboos," he conceded. "Sometimes I think it's absurd. But it makes us what we are." As he spoke, he looked into Viv's amber eyes with a longing that belied his words.

"I would never let Siberians close to me," said Viv. "The old legends don't lie."

"Yes," he said firmly. "Never let your guard down with them. And remember, some of them still practice blood sacrifice."

Viv flashed her eyes in disgust. "I'm not afraid of Siberians. My ancestor Krasivaya battled them aeons ago and always prevailed. We can defeat them again."

As Pavel moved closer to Viv to test the limits of her devotion to clan rules, Marc walked into the living room, saw the two huge felines, and stopped short.

"Oh, sorry," he said as he made a quick retreat. He wasn't about to ask what he had just walked in on.

Chapter Twenty-two

After they decided to be honest with one another, all three participants now felt they had established a greater degree of understanding, and if Pavel had admired Vivian in her human form, he was reduced to a state of sheer lust for her in feline shape. What a breathtaking animal. She made all Russian Blue females look feeble in comparison. He didn't know if it was the fantastic long, silvery tabby fur or her commanding presence, but once he saw Viv au naturel, he was captivated. Descended from a demigoddess, she looked like one herself.

With all this motivation to protect her, Pavel increased the video monitors, added bodyguards, and advised Viv to consider staying at Marc's until they could track down the thugs who were behind the attacks.

"How long do you think that will be?"

"Hard to tell. My men just called me to say they identified the thugs who threw you into that car."

"Who are they?"

"Small-time werecat punks who hire out as muscle. We're going to pay a visit to some of their friends and see if they can persuade them to answer a few questions."

"Do you think they will?"

"I think a few of them are likely to talk if they think it will help them avoid having the police look too closely at *them*."

"Our clan doesn't like to bring the police in to clan matters," Viv said pointedly.

"Don't worry. The cops won't come calling on you. We're only going to use that line to scare the Siberians. Of course, if they don't help us, there are always ways to make their lives miserable." He gave her a wicked smile.

"What about the two *dead* Siberians?"

"You know about the twelve hour rule. We waited, examined them for any clues they might give, and then two dead cats went into a landfill near Newark. No laws were broken."

"You're sure they were just low-level thugs?"

"The very bottom of the food chain."

She looked puzzled. "You don't think they tried to kidnap me because of the painting?"

"I think they tried kidnapping you as a quick way to raise some cash. You had a business. Your brother would pay to get you back. This type of hoodlum isn't a deep thinker. He's primitive. These two were not the sort who would know anything about art."

"Then you really don't think the kidnapping was connected with the painting."

Pavel shrugged. "I don't believe they're smart enough for that. But we're not letting down our guard, either." Then he glanced at his watch. "This evening I have an appointment with a gentleman who agreed to help us. With the, ah, hidden object. This afternoon I'm going to investigate some Russian angles."

Viv glanced at him.

"They have to be my countrymen," he said with a shrug. "The icon came from Russia, and unless some other ethnic gang of criminals was motivated to grab it, the thieves were Russians, too, especially given the significance of it to our people. If some gang from a raggedy-ass breakaway republic had stolen it, they'd be trying to blackmail the government into paying to get it back. That hasn't happened, so I don't think it's political."

"What could these people want?

"We don't know yet. That's what my crew is trying to find out." He hesitated, then said, "Viv, when you were inside Bella Danilov's shop, did you happen to notice if there were any mirrors like the one we just discovered?"

She tried to recall, but couldn't. "I remember lots of silver, some great paintings, but no mirrors. You know, I didn't like her, but I have to say she was a good businesswoman. She had all the paperwork in order and made sure everything arrived safe and sound. I'd suspect her the least."

"Well, glad to hear that," he said. "I'd hate to think the wife of our Hierarch was capable of such evil. Even if she is a Siberian Forest cat."

Viv raised her eyebrows. "I had no idea. Your Hierarch liked to live on the edge," she murmured. Then she shook her head. "From what I saw, Bella Danilov would be more likely to try to steal a shipment of Jimmy Choo shoes or designer dresses," said Viv. "I can't picture her going after something as dangerous as that object. It's just too risky."

Pavel noted that neither one of them wished to refer to the stolen icon by name. It was as if they were fearful of letting the secret out to some spy lurking in the woodwork.

"Good luck," Viv said as she let him slide his arm around her and give her a kiss before leaving. "Hope your friend can help us solve our problem." She gave him a glance that mingled irony and amazement as she said, "You know, Pavel, before I met you, I had never given the Russian Blues a thought. Frankly they seemed so . . . unimpressive compared with our own kind. And of course, there was the ancient taboo."

"And now, *dorogaya*?" he inquired with a raised eyebrow.

Viv fixed him with the full impact of her gorgeous amber eyes. *"Koshka,"* she murmured, "words don't do you justice."

When Pavel reached the vampire's town house that evening, Vladimir let him in and asked him to follow him upstairs to the salon.

"Any further trouble?" Vlad inquired as he led the way.

"Not yet," Pavel replied. Then with a smile, he added, "Mademoiselle Marais is here again, isn't she? I can smell her perfume. Spicy, like carnations."

"Yes. She's visiting. There's some talk of hunting in Canada, and she stopped by on her way up there."

Pavel knew Catherine Marais hunted werewolves for the feared but low-profile *Institut Scientifique* of Geneva; her reputation was such that any werecreature with a brain knew of her and treated her with respect. Mademoiselle Marais was one of the most deadly of modern werewolf trackers; she and her partner, Paul DuJardin, were the rock stars of their profession.

"I met her briefly once before," Pavel said with a smile, recalling a brunette beauty with a sexy voice.

"Thank God she doesn't feel compelled to pursue creatures other than those lupine scum," Vladimir replied. "Or I'd have to look for another job."

When the Russians reached the salon, Pavel shook his host's extended hand and Vladimir receded into the background, and then left the room. Ian Morgan introduced his beautiful mistress, who graciously recalled meeting Pavel on her last visit.

Without standing on ceremony Ian invited Pavel to have a drink and offered vodka. Ian abstained of course, but Catherine poured Pavel a glass and took one herself. An iced crystal bowl containing beluga caviar and lemon slices stood on a table, mother-of-pearl spoons beside the bowl. Small rounds of toast completed the setup.

"I've studied what you left," Ian announced. "It's magnificent. And authentic."

"Are you certain?"

"Absolutely. It has all the traits of the most refined masters of the art."

Catherine spooned some caviar onto a piece of toast and ate it, listening intently to the conversation.

"I brought it to you for two reasons, Mr. Morgan. The first, for your security system. The second, for your expertise in the art world. Now I'm going to ask for your help in returning it to its country."

Catherine Marais glanced at her lover and asked, "Should I leave you gentlemen to discuss business?"

"No," Ian said. "Please stay. I think you might be able to help us here."

Catherine smiled. "If I can."

Revealing information about the Virgin of Saratov made Pavel profoundly nervous. He didn't even want to tell Vladimir. He and the Roussels were so anxious to keep its presence a secret they were using euphemisms when referring to it among themselves. Now Morgan's mistress was about to find out. He wasn't certain this was a good idea, and he must have appeared uneasy because the vampire said, "Catherine is a woman of many secrets herself. She will understand the need for discretion. And she has valuable contacts who may assist us."

"What is this mysterious thing that's causing you such concern?" she asked lightly.

Pavel felt as if he were putting his head on the block as he replied, "The icon of the Virgin of Saratov."

"The one the Russians have been searching for since it was stolen from the monastery three months ago?"

"Precisely."

She turned to face Ian. "Darling, I've known you for a long time and have never had reason to doubt you, but I have to ask how it ended up in your home."

Pavel refilled his vodka cup and drank. "Mademoiselle, it's a long story."

"We have all night," she said with a steady look at them both. "Let me hear it."

Chapter Twenty-three

The vampire and his partner felt inclined to help Pavel since he wasn't trying to sell the treasure on the black market or make a profit. He and his clients merely wished to send it back home, where it belonged, and Ian wanted to do the same thing. Catherine's contacts might be able to facilitate the transfer.

"But first, I would like to see this legendary icon," she said.

Ian led them down to the vault, allowed them into the waiting area, disappeared down the inner stairs, and returned with the icon, its glints of gold smoldering in the haloes of the virgin and child and in the pattern of their garments. Catherine's eyes moistened as she beheld four centuries of devotion before her, and respectfully, she crossed herself.

"We have to get it back to them," she said simply. "I'll do whatever I can."

Now that he had secured powerful allies in his quest to return the icon, Pavel turned his attention to contacts back home, sending coded messages to a Moscow-based investigator he relied on for his skill in operating under the radar. He needed information on several people, he told him, all dealers in Russian antiques, and he named them. He needed to know if any of them had run afoul of the law, who their clients were, if they had any known gangster associates, and if they had ever had dealings with stolen church treasures. It was quite a list, but Pavel knew his man could find out the dirt, if there was any, and get back to him in a reasonable amount of time.

Time was truly of the essence here, because unless he knew who was involved in the theft, the Roussels were still at the mercy of unknown criminals, and Pavel preferred to know his enemy, the better to deal with them. Viv had to be protected at all costs.

To try to facilitate things, Pavel returned to his headquarters, where he switched on the video feed at Marc Roussel's place and glanced up at the screen occasionally as he delved into his computerized files. There he searched the database for Russian mobsters, with subgroups of Georgians, Chechens, Armenians, and others. He focused on criminal specialties—extortion, murder for hire, grand larceny, kidnapping—all the while trying to find something that would lead him to the criminal brazen enough to have stolen the Virgin of Saratov. The list was daunting and time-consuming.

The one group he discounted was the gang of incompetents who had kidnapped Viv. He learned that they called themselves the Rasputnikatz and were a minor league New York version of a midlevel Russian gang. Their rep was for quick and easy. Going after the Virgin of Saratov would have required a criminal mastermind, and Pavel didn't believe that all the Rasputnikatz combined could have come up with an IQ higher than ten. Only fools would have been unprepared for a fight when they opened that trunk. And since Viv and Marc were able to disguise their natures so well, those Siberians would never even have suspected they were dealing with a high-ranking werecat who would certainly outsmart them.

St. Petersburg

Danilov Enterprises had arranged a news conference, and a spokesman for the company, looking appropriately grim, faced a crowd of local and foreign reporters. Clearing his throat, he glanced around the room and announced the disappearance of Boris Danilov, the brother of the late Dimitri Danilov, and his successor as CEO of the family business.

"Do you suspect foul play?"

"Are any government agencies going to get involved in searching for him?"

"Please, gentlemen. One question at a time. You, sir," the spokesman said.

The reporter from St. Petersburg's largest daily newspaper repeated the question about foul play and asked if the firm's recent venture into Siberian oil could have attracted the animosity of a rival.

"There are lots of companies scrambling for drilling rights. They attempt to conquer their rivals with lawsuits, not murder."

"Sir, when was the last time Mr. Danilov was in contact with his business associates or his family?"

"Three days ago. When he failed to respond to cell phone calls on his private number despite repeated attempts to reach him, we decided to call in the authorities."

"After his brother's assassination, you have to be worried about his fate, of course," said a young woman in a fur-trimmed coat, "but isn't it the usual thing to receive a ransom demand in cases like these? Have you heard from anybody claiming to have kidnapped him?"

"No," the spokesman said tersely. "As of today, there have been no ransom notes. I've called this press conference to let the public know what we know, and to ask for your help in trying to locate our CEO. His family is devastated and in seclusion. We want your help in uncovering any useful information."

"Are you afraid this may affect shares of your stock?" a reporter from the financial newspaper asked.

The spokesman looked pained. He replied, "Our company is quite solid, as you know, and it will survive. We do not wish to be the object of rumors, which is why I've invited you here. We want the public to know that although Mr. Danilov has gone missing, there is no evidence that he has been harmed."

"At this point." That came from the back of the room.

"Yes. So, ladies and gentlemen, thank you for your time. I must get back to my office."

"Sir!"

"Yes?" He paused to take a final question from a young blonde in the front.

"I heard that Bella Danilov disappeared on the way to an appointment at a beauty salon yesterday. Any truth in that report?"

"Sadly, yes." And he quickly hurried off and took the elevator upstairs, leaving several of the reporters wondering what else he had forgotten to mention.

Chapter Twenty-four

"Bella, I don't know if this is a good idea. If our bargaining partners find out we're staging a hoax, our reputation will be ruined. Even my wife doesn't know where I am."

Boris Danilov stood at the window of a dacha on the outskirts of Moscow and toyed with a snifter of brandy as he glanced out over the snowy landscape. At his side stood Bella, his sister-in-law.

"Trust me, it's a good idea. If negotiations break down with the oil talks, Danilov Enterprises loses the chance to compete for the contract, but we get five million dollars under the table. We know we wouldn't have been able to undertake the project without a lot of upgrading, but they don't know it and they're desperate to buy us off. So we'll disappear for a week or so, lose the contract, and make money, anyway."

"Dimitri wouldn't have done this. He'd say it was a cheap stunt."

"He's dead," she snapped. "You have to be more aggressive. We're swimming with sharks here. You have to be the biggest and the best."

The new CEO took a sip of brandy and set the snifter down on a table near the window. He had a sneaking suspicion he might actually be out of his depth, and it unsettled him.

Dimitri's death had left him the de facto Hierarch of the Russian Blue werecats, but he never thought he'd ever as-

sume the leadership. A subordinate all his life, he was sometimes a resentful one as he saw his brother rise to the top,
knowing Dimitri was the one everybody admired and
fawned over. Truthfully, he felt incapable of supplanting his
clever older brother, the genius who had created an empire
in such a brief period of time.

The day Dimitri had been gunned down in broad daylight
on Nevsky Prospeckt had changed Boris's life forever. Now
he wondered why he ever listened to Bella and her grandiose
new plans for making millions. They already had plenty of
money. Had it helped Dimitri? Could he spend it in the
cemetery? Why not leave well enough alone?

Everything the old werecats said about these Siberian
Forest cats was turning out to be so true. They were con
artists, deceivers, scam artists; the list of unflattering quali-
ties could go on and on. And he had stupidly brought this
one into the heart of the family business. That was how
clever *he* was.

Boris took another sip of brandy and wished he were
back home with his wife and kids, instead of here with this
witch. His chance remark about the lack of security in the
old monastery church where the icon of the Virgin of Saratov reposed had given Bella the unholy idea that it could be
easily stolen. She had put out feelers to shady contacts in the
international art world and come up with a prospective
buyer. At this point, Boris was terrified at being implicated,
especially since Bella prodded him to use his ties to corrupt
customs officials to get the icon out of the country, no questions asked. When he had balked, she'd threatened to go to
the state prosecutor with details of dozens of his illicit business deals—like importing and selling drugs—if he backed
out. Boris was screwed. Werecat loyalty meant nothing to
her. Worse than that, he had racked up bills he couldn't pay,
so he had put his tail between his legs and said he'd do it. To
keep her claws in him, Bella had offered him a cut of the
deal. Twenty million divided by two. Now all they had to do

was retrieve the icon where underlings had stashed it and complete the transaction with the buyer.

"We'll go to New York and lie low until our time for negotiations expires," she said. "A private jet will take us there tomorrow. While we kill time, we'll take care of the *artistic matter*," she said with deliberate emphasis. "We'll pick up our money for the art transaction and then head home. We'll attribute our disappearance to threats by terrorists who will be implicated in Dimitri's death. That always works. My contacts in the State Security Services will swear we were in protective custody at an undisclosed location overseas, and upon returning, we will be full of gratitude to the FSB, our wonderful security services."

"You've already bribed them?"

"Of course. Two hundred thousand euros each, and they'll produce a file on our case backing up our story. They're dependable."

"We're so lucky to have such friends," he said with irony.

"This will make you rich. You're the new Hierarch. Start acting like one."

Bella turned away in annoyance and walked to the opposite side of the room, close to the eighteenth-century porcelain fireplace, which heated the salon. He could see the disdain in her manner, and he resented her for it.

"I have my own thoughts about this," he said.

"Good. Let's hope they're valuable. I always thought you must have learned something worthwhile during your time at the London School of Economics."

Boris didn't even bother to reply. He felt like saying, "At least I didn't get my education in a whorehouse," but why start a boring fight? He was just too tired.

"I'm going to bed. Wake me when we have to leave for the airport."

As he closed the door behind him, Boris felt as if he was walking into a black hole.

*　　*　　*

In the salon of the dacha, Bella paced up and down, occasionally shaking her beautiful, long blond hair as she did whenever she was agitated. Trying to work with Boris was like attempting to gather worms. He was always going in all directions at once, unable to make a decision and stick with it.

She had originally been taken with his tall, blond good looks—the man had the appearance of a male model. Dimitri had been shorter, although not by much, and a lot smarter; he had looked like a handsome and successful entrepreneur, which he was, right down to the Armani suits and Italian shoes. If Dimitri had lost half his brain, he still would have been sharper than his younger brother, but they had gotten on well, and Dimitri had never left Boris out of things.

Boris's only talent was as a gofer, and his usual job was to escort important out-of-town visitors to the nightclubs and the best restaurants in the city while they carried out deals with his brother. The only deals *Boris* made involved things like hash and cocaine.

Always on the alert for leggy blondes, he had discovered Bella in an overpriced nightclub in St. Petersburg, drinking with friends of his. With him as an escort, she had met and seduced Dimitri, shocked his clan by becoming engaged to him, and finally married him in a wedding that was outrageously costly even by the standards of Russia's billionaires.

And now poor Dimitri was dead, and all that remained of the inner circle of Danilov Enterprises was Boris and Bella. At last Boris had found his true calling: he was a puppet.

Exhausted from the stress of dealing with the new Hierarch, Bella shape-shifted and became a beautiful cat the size of a lynx as she searched out a warm place near the porcelain stove, then sank down and drifted into a deep and dreamless slumber, preparing for her trip to New York.

Chapter Twenty-five

Viv had gotten the visit she had been dreading. The Leader arrived at her home, looking concerned, and told her she ought to stay at a secure location while Metro carried out its work.

"You know I care for you, Viv," he said. "If you wish, I'll assign the Special Squad to work on this."

Viv felt worried, mostly over the matter of the mysterious icon—which she had no intention of discussing with John Sinclair or anyone else. Werecats took care of their own problems. The Special Squad generally dealt with security for the Leader. She didn't want to get involved with them and put herself in his debt.

"That's very flattering, but Metro will handle it."

"I've called you twice since the night you were kidnapped. You've avoided me."

"I didn't want to talk about it," she said.

He reached out and cupped her chin in his hand. Before he could kiss her, Viv moved away.

His eyes sent daggers at her. Coldly, the Leader grabbed her arm and pressed her against his chest before she could pull away. "Don't treat me as if I were nothing. I offered you the highest rank in our community. Think about it. And what were you doing out on the town with Hank? Do you think he could offer you something better?"

She pushed away and looked at him in amazement. "You're not offering me the highest position. *You* occupy it. And what I was doing with Hank is none of your business. Leader, I'm tired, and I have no ambition to be your wife. Please go home. Thank you for the honor, but I can't accept."

"You want to waste the inheritance from your ancestor on such an ordinary werecat? Think about your offspring."

"Believe me, I've thought about it," she said. "And I don't want a domineering father for them."

Angrily the Leader shape-shifted, with Viv following. Two large, shaggy cats the size of mountain lions stood almost nose to nose, eyeing each other, waiting for the other to make the first move. They began to circle each other, slowly, deliberately. Then the Leader lunged for Viv, grabbing her by the scruff of the neck, holding her down. Nimbly she flipped over and threw him off, sending him crashing into the sofa. With fury in his eyes, he leaped at her, holding her down once more.

"You're mine," he said telepathically as he crushed her beneath his weight, biting her neck to restrain her. He was going to mate now with her consent or without it.

"We choose our mates!" Viv replied. She felt a flow of adrenaline and let him have it as she bumped him off her back and slashed him with flying claws. Then she jumped on *him* and bit his ear, making him screech with pain and back off, wounded and stunned.

"Leader or no Leader, nobody takes me unless I say so," she flung at him. "It's my right. And you should remember who I am."

Glaring at the silvery beauty in front of him, the Leader was almost panting from the combat. He was older than she was, and not used to rejection. Werecat females made him more offers than he could handle. Nobody turned him down.

"I want you, Viv," he said. "Perhaps this isn't a good time. But we'll discuss this again when you're feeling . . .

more yourself. You've just been through a trauma. I understand."

What part of "not interested" don't you understand? The thought came to her mind before she could filter it out. He looked wounded.

"This is not a good idea," she said. "I know I have a gift I should pass on to my clan, but I must choose my mate, and in my own time, I will. Krasivaya's bloodline will not die out."

The Leader shape-shifted, looking regal and disappointed. Viv shifted and then checked to see if she had left lasting damage; she hadn't. But she had made her point.

"Don't reject something worthwhile for both of us," he said as he walked to the door and let himself out. "It would be a good alliance for our clan. It would take us to new heights."

After she shut the door, Viv did three things. She bolted all her locks, called downstairs to the guard from Metro to make sure the Leader's car had left with him in it, and then called Marc to tell him she was having her bodyguard bring her to his town house. She no longer felt safe. Worse than that, she had the distinct feeling she was dealing with a madman.

Pavel paid Viv and Marc an unexpected visit that evening to bring them dinner from a favorite restaurant and share the results of his initial findings, via his man in St. Petersburg.

Marc provided a good white wine to go with the chicken dish, and Pavel noticed a subtle change in his clients as they ate. Both appeared tense.

"I learned that two of your Russian suppliers have had some trouble with the police," he said.

"Stolen property?"

"No. Failing to secure the proper permits for some of their exports."

"Do you think it might be them?"

Pavel shook his head. "They're legitimate dealers. They claimed they didn't keep up-to-date with customs regulations. My investigator believed them. It happens all the time."

"That's two. What about the others?"

"Your samovar merchant seems to be a paragon of virtue by modern standards, except for his link to the wife of a well-known gangster. He's her favorite purveyor of nineteenth-century antiques. She and the husband are renovating an old palace in the Arbat district in Moscow, and this guy has the job of locating decorative objects to give it the proper ambience."

"Does she have him scouting sixteenth-century icons?"

"No. Too expensive."

"All right," she said. "What about the widow of your late Hierarch?"

"My man is still looking into her business dealings. With her it's difficult because she has a superior security system that makes things complicated."

"He's hacking into her computer?"

Pavel glanced at her with humor in his green eyes. "He's making every effort to investigate her," he said blandly.

Marc had been enjoying his food when he happened to hear something on the kitchen TV that caught his interest. Rising from the table, he walked quickly into the kitchen and turned up the volume. "Pavel," he called, "come in here. You might want to hear this."

The Russian went in, followed by Vivian. What they saw was startling. In the foyer of Danilov Enterprises was a man in a well-cut suit announcing the disappearance of the new CEO, Boris Danilov.

Pavel was caught by surprise. It had to be the first announcement, otherwise he or a New York member of the clan would have seen it. If Vladimir had spotted it, he would have called in the news. Then the American broadcaster added that the widow of the late CEO Dimitri Danilow was said to be missing as well. Some suspected foul play.

"Are the Danilovs under attack, too?" Viv asked.

Pavel threw up his hands in a gesture of bewilderment. He couldn't figure out who would profit by the removal of both brothers. The Hierarch had been involved in negotiations for oil rights in a contested area of Siberia. His assassination made room for his younger brother to replace him. The negotiations resumed, but the business empire Dimitri had created would undoubtedly flounder and then perish under the leadership of Boris, whom nobody respected.

Boris's assumption of the title of Hierarch had been given to him by default, since he was the Hierarch's kin, but clansmen in Russia and in America had doubts about his capabilities. Hushed rumors circulated about requests for him to step down if a worthy successor could be found.

Following the assassination, Boris's detested sister-in-law, Bella, let it be known that the new Hierarch was suffering from the trauma of his brother's murder and would energetically take charge once he had recovered from the aftershock. Within the clan, few believed Boris could do it.

That Siberian lost her meal ticket when the smart one was killed, and now she wants to take over the dumb one and keep him under her thumb. Pavel remembered that cynical remark and wondered if the speaker had been closer to the truth than he thought.

Echoing his thoughts, Viv looked at Pavel and asked, "Do you think Bella could inherit the Danilov empire if both brothers were out of the way?"

"There's a board of directors she'd have to deal with. I don't think they'd let her in."

Viv smiled. "If she's as devious and underhanded as I think she is, she probably got her husband to make out a will naming her his heir. He might have given her a huge interest in the business and sidestepped his brother."

"No. The Hierarch was enamored of her, but he wouldn't

have cut Boris out of his will. Family was everything to him."

"You never know," Marc said as he studied the photo of Bella now on the screen. "She's very attractive. And I'll bet her powers of persuasion would make you forget about anything but pleasing her."

"The Hierarch loved her, but he wasn't a fool," Pavel said defensively.

"But you say the brother is."

The Russian glanced at Viv. "And?"

"She might have been able to exert more control over *him*. If she's still alive," Viv added.

Chapter Twenty-six

"Viv, how are you? It's Hank. I'm out of bed and walking. Well, a little."

"Oh, I'm so relieved to hear you're recovering. Marc and I went to visit you in the hospital after they rescued me that night. I prayed for you."

"Well, it worked. My doctor says I'm healing nicely and ought to be back home before long."

"Did they transfer you to a place familiar with our people?" she asked. Werecats could experience recuperative powers that would astonish regular doctors. They preferred to be with their own kind.

"Yes. A private place in Brooklyn. It's very nice."

Viv smiled. "Is Brenda visiting you there?"

"Just about every day. She brings the kids. And the hospital's going to release me soon."

"Terrific. You know, I've wanted to thank you for trying to save me when they attacked us. You were very brave. I'll never forget it."

Hank paused. "I'm sorry I didn't protect you better, Viv," he said. "How are you? I heard they tossed you into the trunk of a car and drove you around New Jersey."

"They did," she said ruefully.

"What happened when you arrived at their destination? Did they try to hold you hostage?"

"Ah, they didn't get the chance. Something intervened and killed them."

Hank could picture the scene. Viv had gone werecat and those guys were killed right after they'd popped that trunk. Werecats knew what they were capable of when faced with death. A blueblood like Viv would defend herself ferociously, especially if she faced death at the hands of inferiors. Pride would make her ruthless.

"Well," she said cheerfully, "I hear you and Brenda are going to patch things up. I always hoped you would."

He laughed. "Yes," he said. "After getting shot and seeing how devoted she was at the hospital, I thought maybe we should try again. I love my kids and I want to be with them every day. Too bad it took a brush with death to show me what's really important."

"I'm so glad you've reconciled." Viv meant that from the bottom of her heart. She was glad Brenda was getting her husband back, and grateful she would be spared having to make up excuses why she couldn't go out with him.

"And, Viv," he said quietly, "I was semiconscious when you came in. I was pretty much out of it, but I knew what you were doing. I think those spirits all came to my rescue. Until that moment, I didn't realize you had the gift."

"I don't talk about it very often," she admitted.

"It's good to keep the ancient traditions alive," Hank said simply. "And I thank you for it."

"'Bye, Hank. Stay healthy," she said softly.

"Will do."

Years ago, her grandfather had started her education in the ancient wisdom of the werecats, teaching her some of his repertory of healing spells, showing her how to call upon the old gods to come to her aid in times of danger, and instilling in her the memory that she was a direct descendant of Krasivaya, the werecat Venus.

This beautiful creature had ruled a great Northern kingdom thousands of years ago when all the werecat clans fought for supremacy in the frozen lands of forest and tundra. Leading her clan with skill in battle and shrewdness at all times, Krasivaya could take on the size of a modern tiger as she battled rivals for land or influence. Some of her fiercest wars brought her tribe into conflict with the clan known as the Siberian Forest cats, a bloodthirsty collection of hunters and warriors who practiced infant sacrifice and killed their rivals' kittens on an altar to their god, Moroz the Dread.

In a legendary feat of daring, Krasivaya had once led an assault that destroyed Moroz's main sacrificial altar, overrunning the Siberians' stronghold and rescuing a terrified band of kittens, stolen from several clans, who were awaiting death at the hands of the Forest cats. That exploit cemented alliances with six other werecat clans and established her own people as protectors and liberators. Even today, in the memories of many werecats, the name Krasivaya evoked feelings of respect and awe. In her own lifetime, she was treated as a demigoddess and invoked as a guardian of the helpless.

As Viv sat by her grandfather, listening to the ancient legends of her people, Grandpa emphasized her heritage and her responsibility to help those in need, to recognize the world as a place where good and evil do constant battle, and to try to support what is right.

"As you go through life, you will find yourself forced to make choices," he had once said after spending the afternoon instructing Viv in the practices of the shaman. "Always let yourself be guided by your head *and* your heart, never letting one or the other dominate your thinking. Be rational, be kind, and be true to the essence of your being. You have the gift to shape-shift. Use it well, and use your abilities to improve your world, to protect those who depend on you. One day, you may be called upon to imitate Krasivaya," he had said very softly. "Don't fail us."

The memory of that conversation always evoked powerful feelings of respect and duty in Vivian. Lately Grandpa's words came to echo in her dreams as she pondered the cause of the recent disruptions in her life. Why, after years of completely normal business dealings with the Russians, had this problem surfaced? And why did the fact that Bella Danilov turned out to be a Siberian make her so uneasy?

Pavel's clan distrusted them, too. In the back of every cat's mind was the collective memory of the Forest cats' ugly past and the fear that, given half a chance, they might revert to it again. The death of the Russian Blues' Hierarch, the disappearance of his brother and heir, the weird possibility that Bella Danilov might have had something to do with planting the stolen icon in the Roussels' warehouse—all these things left Viv remembering Grandpa's advice.

Use your head and your heart. Logic and emotion. Don't get swayed by either, but take both into account.

Well, right now her head told her to be very suspicious of Bella, and her heart told her to embrace Pavel Federov.

She would trust her instincts on that.

Chapter Twenty-seven

"Yuri, we heard the news that both Bella and Boris have gone missing. What's happening up there?"

On his end, Yuri sighed. Pavel knew last names were unimportant here. Every werecat of the Russian Blue clan was intensely interested in the fate of only one Boris or Bella at the moment. It was the only topic of conversation right now.

"We think we may have lost our new Hierarch. Everybody is concerned," he said.

"Is there any possibility he isn't dead?"

"Sure. There's always that. But why the disappearing act? If they have to send out an official announcement to discuss the rumors, then they're expecting the worst. I think Danilov Enterprises knows exactly what happened and is hiding the truth."

"What's their motive?"

"Who knows? Maybe they don't want the stockholders to think the business is unstable."

"With a dead CEO and a missing replacement? That doesn't exactly inspire confidence. And it's odd that Bella vanished at the same time."

"The clan is in meltdown over this," Yuri said, and Pavel could hear the stress level in his voice. "We're under attack, and we don't know what's behind it. We would suspect

Bella, of course, since she's missing, too, but they say she and Boris have been fighting like hell lately, so I don't think they're in collusion. They really do hate each other. Now some of the clan want to call an election and choose a replacement Hierarch."

"If he returns and finds himself dumped, he'll never forgive us. We don't need that kind of turmoil—two angry Hierarchs claiming the title and the rest of the clan with divided loyalties. What a mess."

"Well, with all the uproar, I don't think any of our guys really wants to give his job away until we know more."

"I hope you're right." Pavel smiled. Yuri was an older werecat with old-school ideas. The younger members were more prone to action. He hoped the youthful faction didn't act hastily and remove the missing Hierarch from his position, since that might trigger clan warfare.

Before he said goodbye, Pavel asked one more question. "Has anybody heard anything about the missing icon? Any suspects in the theft?"

"Nothing, aside from a plea by the patriarch of Moscow and the president to return it to its place in the monastery. There aren't even any names being bandied around, aside from the usual ethnic minorities they blame for everything that's gone wrong."

"Very strange no ransom demands have been made, if that's the case." Pavel didn't really think there would be a ransom; more likely it was destined for a rich American collector. But he didn't wish to say so right now.

"Yes," Yuri agreed. "Maybe the thief just wanted it for himself."

That didn't make much sense either since whoever had sent it across the Atlantic to stash it in the Roussels' warehouse was trying to keep it safe until the right moment arose. That break-in had to have been an attempted repossession that somehow failed. Why? Had the thieves been too incompetent to find it there? Hadn't they had enough time, the right instructions, or the correct invoice?

"Well, thanks, Yuri. I'll keep in touch."

"Goodbye Pavel. Stay well," Yuri added with emphasis.

Damn, thought Pavel. Theft, he understood, but it was always caused by motive. Greed stood out as a headliner, second only to spite. But lately many treasured religious objects had been stolen around the world for the private collections of the superrich. If a man had everything money could buy, what was left to satisfy his lust for possession, except something so rare, so valuable that it would be unique in all the world? He knew this wasn't political. It was all about some greedy billionaire wanting one of Russia's greatest treasures for his own. That was why it had ended up hidden in the Roussels' warehouse, and although the Saratov Madonna was safe at the moment, that didn't necessarily mean she was free from danger. Until Pavel knew she was back in her homeland, he wouldn't feel he could rest. And he wouldn't feel Viv and Marc were secure, either, a thought that was just as troubling.

At least he didn't have to worry about the Madonna for the time being. Deep under the streets of Manhattan, carefully hidden away in one of the most secure private vaults in the city, she remained out of harm's way—thanks to an aristocratic vampire with a passion for art.

Chapter Twenty-eight

Viv was out of circulation while Pavel and his men tried to protect her, and inactivity was grating on her nerves. She was a woman used to freedom of movement, and this kind of confinement exasperated her. The only thing that served to distract her from her frustration with her own situation was news from a member of her own clan, the wife of one of the Leader's Special Squad.

Although Viv was under protective surveillance by Metro Investigations, she could receive calls on her cell phone. Pavel's experts had diverted the signal so that anyone tracking it would have been surprised to find it coming from Minsk. One afternoon, Sarah Jenkins reached her in tears, sobbing out her story over the phone.

"Viv, it was horrible. I think he's gone crazy. He—he attacked me!"

"Sarah. Who attacked you?" Viv asked in alarm. "Are you all right?"

"No," she sobbed. "I'm so upset. And I can't tell my husband. I don't know what to do."

Viv listened to the nearly hysterical sobbing, wondering what had happened and who had harmed her. When Sarah seemed a little calmer, she said, "Please, go back to the beginning. Tell me who attacked you."

There was a long pause, with the sound of stifled sobs, and then the woman said, "The Leader!"

"What?"

"It's true! He stopped by the house when my husband was out, and I thought he wanted to speak to him, so I let him in. All of a sudden he started acting strange and then he grabbed me, went werecat, and . . . he raped me. And two days after this happened to me, my friend Charla called me to tell me he did it to her. He's insane."

"You didn't tell your husband? What about Charla?"

"We were both too afraid. It's his word against ours, and he's the Leader."

Viv felt so outraged, she wanted to kill. She had managed to fight off Sinclair, but this young woman hadn't. It was an outrageous abuse of his power. She thought of Krasivaya, and she could imagine the punishment her ancestor would wish for this evil werecat.

"We have to take action. First, you must tell your husband."

"No!" she protested. "I'm too afraid."

"Sarah, we have to remove John Sinclair from his position. If not, he'll keep doing this. Your husband is on his Special Squad. He and his men can get close enough to him to take him into custody. We'll have a trial in front of the clan, and we'll remove him."

"No!" she wailed. "I can't. Charla is afraid, too. They'll think we encouraged him. And he'll lie and say we did."

"Then what do you want to do?"

"I don't know," she sobbed. "I'm frightened."

Viv struggled to find the right words. "All right. You've told me, and I believe you. I will have someone shadow Sinclair, keeping track of his movements, gathering evidence. If we can find enough to charge him with one more crime, will you come forward and testify against him?"

Sarah hesitated. Then she said, "Yes. But don't let him harm anyone else."

"If we track him, we can prevent that. But it would be better if you and Charla came forward right now." Viv heard what sounded like sobs again. She said gently, "Please think about it."

"Yes," Sarah replied. Then she clicked off, sounding too scared to say anything else.

Viv struggled with the desire to go werecat, race off to Sinclair's home, and tear him apart. After her own experiences with him, she had no doubt Sarah was speaking the truth. But according to the rules of her clan, such an accusation demanded a trial. Trials required witnesses. Those women were so frightened, they were in no shape to think about facing him in a werecat court. Yet. And Viv was hampered by her own problems right now.

This wretched excuse for a Leader had dared to use his position to prey on vulnerable females? He had dared to try to pressure *her* to accept him as her mate? Never in the history of her clan had such a Leader existed. Viv swore by the blood that ran in her veins that she would remove this evil beast as soon as she could. She wanted this other business to end so she could pursue that.

"Can't we go back to the Old Muscovy?" she asked Pavel when he came to visit her and Marc at her brother's town house. "Send the bodyguards over. They can stay with us all day."

"I have to get out of here," Marc said. "I need a break. We both do. We may end up at each other's throats."

Pavel gave them a bleak look. "You understand how dangerous your situation is. Vivian survived a kidnapping. You were both attacked on the street. You may attract more of the same."

"With surveillance cameras and bodyguards, your men can be there if anything happens. I'm willing—we're both willing—to give it a try."

Pavel didn't appear to be pleased with the idea, but he

agreed. "All right," he said. "We can guard you at the shop. But you still have to be in a safe place at night."

"A safe and separate place," Marc added.

The Russian hesitated. He glanced at Viv. "I have a good location where I can hide you," he said. "It's secure. There is a room with steel panels that slide into place at the first suggestion of a break-in."

"Sounds very high-tech."

"It is. It's my apartment, and I had it designed by an expert."

Viv looked at Pavel. After her recent conversation, she felt cautious.

"Strictly on the up-and-up," he said. "Because of the sensitivity of this case, it's the most secure facility I can think of. You can lock yourself in each night if you wish."

"I think I'll feel safe enough knowing you're there."

Marc looked thoughtful. "You'll have to guarantee her safety," he said.

Pavel nodded. "Of course."

"Where are we going?" Boris glanced out the windows of the Mercedes and failed to recognize the area as their driver sped along the highway leading from Kennedy Airport to New York City.

"An apartment I have in Manhattan," Bella replied. "I bought it—Dimitri and I bought it, actually—under the name of one of our companies. It has good security and nobody has ever bothered us there. Very anonymous."

"New York is a world financial capital. Don't you think they read the news? People might recognize us."

Bella flung him a look of sheer annoyance. "Boris," she said with an edge, "have you seen the contents of American newspapers? All they care about is blond starlets. We're unknown. The only danger here is from Russian expats, so we'll avoid them."

"How long do you think it will take?" he asked.

"If we fail to negotiate for five days, we'll lose the chance

to secure the Siberian oil contract. We will stay here for a week
and work on that other matter. By that time, I'm hoping to settle both things and walk away with a fortune in dollars."

Boris sneered. "I still think you should have negotiated for
British pounds sterling. Or euros."

Bella snapped at him. "I agreed to dollars because that was
what he offered. The end result would have been the same in
any currency you wanted."

"The euro or the pound would have been better in the long
run. Both currencies are climbing right now."

Bella found this lecture quite irritating, coming from a man
whose expertise revolved around knowing which nightclubs
were trendy. And he dared complain about *her* efforts? As
least she could generate money.

"Then, damn it, Boris, you can try your hand at negotiating
next time!"

This irritating creature's only function was to give legiti-
macy to her plans for the future of Danilov Enterprises, because while a Danilov remained in charge, the board of
directors wouldn't be able to remove her.

Boris, the new Hierarch of the Russian Blues and the new
CEO of Danilov Enterprises, was now her reluctant partner,
and he would remain one as long as necessary. With his constant need for money to maintain his lavish lifestyle and as-
suage his fear of jail, he would tell nobody about their deal
with the oil contract.

As for the other matter, he was so eaten up by anxiety that
she was afraid he might have a heart attack if things didn't start
to sort themselves out quickly. The sooner they made contact
with their buyer, the better they would both feel.

Bella could only marvel at Boris's lack of aptitude. She actually pitied his clan and was grateful that she had been born
to a werecat sept that had a strong sense of self. These Russian
Blues needed her to take charge of them because if they looked
to this new Hierarch for guidance, they would all go straight to
ruin.

Chapter Twenty-nine

The Danilovs had barely settled in at Bella's Manhattan condo when she picked up her cell phone and made a call that led to a shouting match with the person on the other end.

Insults flowed from Bella's mouth, followed by a rapid-fire series of threats, more shouting, and finally an ultimatum to "Get it or else you'll end up in the river."

"Trouble?" Boris asked.

"Yes. But only a minor inconvenience."

"In connection with?

"That other matter," she snapped at him.

"Ah, your minions botched the job."

Bella appeared to be considering if she ought to admit the truth. Then she shrugged and simply said, "Yes."

She thought Boris looked ready to reproach her, so to cut him off, she added, "We will recover it. It's only a matter of time. So far they haven't been able to find it."

"How far along are they with the plan?" he asked.

"They broke into the warehouse where the icon was hidden, but they couldn't locate it. Meanwhile the owners changed their security system and hired some competent help. Our idiots lost two men so far, and now they're whining about 'additional risks.' They're getting cold feet."

"What if the Roussels spotted the icon first and hid it?"

"No. It was camouflaged pretty well. They aren't smart enough to discover it. Nobody could have," she said flatly.

"So what do we do now?" he asked.

"We have a morale-raising meeting with our helpers and light a fire under them. We don't want to stay here any longer than we have to."

Boris agreed with that. He wanted to get home as quickly as he could. "I'm going to call Marina and tell her I'm safe. She shouldn't have to worry."

He almost thought Bella was going to forbid the phone call to his wife, but he could see she briefly considered the idea and then rejected it.

"Make it brief. Just tell her you're all right and you're involved in an important business deal. You don't want her holding news conferences and attracting more attention than this needs, all right?"

Boris nodded and took out his cell phone with the international connection. He should never have allowed this witch to blackmail him into going along with this scheme. If it hadn't been for the money, he wouldn't have agreed, but Marina was nagging him to buy a bigger house, and he needed a dramatic increase in funds in order to please his wife. When would he ever learn?

He felt disgusted with himself, ashamed he'd betrayed his brother and his clan, and he cringed at the idea of replacing Dimitri as Hierarch. He wasn't worthy. He was a fake, a puppet whose strings were pulled by an amoral bitch for whom nothing was out of bounds. Uneasily he felt he'd made a deal with the devil.

On Marc and Viv's first day back at the Old Muscovy, two large men planted themselves on the premises and surveyed the scene from front to back, the one watching a video monitor in the back room, the other keeping an eye on things in the showroom. Trying not to think too much about her recent troubles, Viv found it difficult to concentrate on her work.

Around one in the afternoon she heard the buzzer ring. Hoping to see Pavel, she glanced toward the door and was taken aback when Bella Danilov stood in the entrance, waving cheerfully. Bella gave her a thousand-watt smile, showing beautiful white teeth, and pointed toward the handle. Viv couldn't believe her eyes. Walking toward the door, she buzzed her visitor in and greeted her.

"Hello, Vivian. I'm so glad to have caught you at the shop. How are you?" That low-pitched voice with the Russian accent overflowed with charm and warmth.

Viv could scarcely believe her eyes. Or ears. "I'm fine. How are you, Mrs. Danilov? I'd like to extend my condolences," she added quickly. "Marc and I were both shocked when we heard about Mr. Danilov's death. There was some speculation you had been harmed, too. It was all over the news."

"Thank you. It was so difficult for me, for all of us who loved Dimitri." There was the trace of a soulful sigh. "But life goes on, doesn't it? Even in the midst of such a loss as his. And of course, nobody understands how very hard it is to deal with this."

Viv flashed her bodyguard a significant glance; he took one look at her and understood. Then he moved closer so he could eavesdrop on the conversation.

"Such a tragedy," Viv said, hoping she sounded sympathetic. "Will you be staying in New York for a while?"

"For the time being. I had to get away from the scene of so much misery. I needed some breathing room," Bella declared, exhaling another tiny sigh.

"Well, I certainly hope you find it here. You've been through so much."

Viv hoped she didn't sound too false. She felt sorry for any widow, but somehow Bella Danilov seemed as if she could recover quite well from whatever fate dealt her. And all the rumors in the werecat community about foul play were wrong. Leave it to her to land on her feet.

"You're probably wondering why I called," Bella said.

"Well, I am surprised to see you. Can Marc and I help you in any way?"

"I was just checking some of my deliveries to the States, and I wondered if there were any irregularities with your shipment. Did everything arrive properly?"

"Yes. In perfect order. Nothing damaged."

"That's wonderful. Did you check it all?"

"Of course. Everything is there."

"Mmmmnn," Bella murmured thoughtfully. "You know, I'm taking a great risk in letting anyone know I'm in the country, but I think I can trust you to be discreet. After what happened in St. Petersburg, I need to recover, and I thought I could do that here."

"Of course I won't broadcast it," Viv assured her. "Is there anything Marc and I can do?"

"Oh, no, but thank your for offering. I was just thinking that since I was in the city, it would be nice to visit your shop. I've heard such good things about it."

Now, of all the things that Bella Danilov could have wanted to do on a secret visit to New York, this was the least likely activity Viv could imagine. Back in St. Petersburg, Bella had treated her as if she were part of the furniture; it made no sense for her to drop in for an impromptu visit and act as if they were old friends.

"Well," Viv said graciously, "since you're here, let me give you the grand tour. And would you like a cup of tea?"

"That would be lovely," Bella answered, looking like a happy schoolgirl as she removed her coat and draped it over a chair. "Do you have Darjeeling, by any chance?"

Chapter Thirty

As soon as he saw Bella Danilov walk into the shop, Pavel's man in the back punched in his boss's cell phone number to alert him to her presence at the Old Muscovy. He was as startled as Viv.

"Watch her carefully. Don't let Miss Roussel leave with her—under any circumstances. I'll have somebody trail her when she goes." Pavel paused, then said, "She must be wearing a coat, right?"

His employee said, "Of course. It's cold out there."

"Then get to it and plant a tracking device on it if possible, and don't let Miss Roussel leave. I don't care what you have to do or what you have to tell her. Just keep her in the shop."

"Right."

Pavel found this impromptu visit very suspicious. He had kept his St. Petersburg and Moscow operatives busy checking out the businessmen Viv and Marc had purchased from recently, and so far nothing suspicious had turned up. Not one of them had been involved in anything dealing with medieval icons. One had sold Marc a mirror dating from 1829, and that was the only mirror on any of his invoices. They still didn't know who had planted the icon in the undocumented one.

While Pavel was sitting at a panel of monitors watching

Bella Danilov and Viv, he noticed something "off" about Bella's demeanor. She was smiling and cheerful in the phony manner he recalled from footage on the nightly news, but something in her expression gave her away. She was carefully observing everything in that shop, as if she were taking inventory.

Bella had gone missing from Russia at the same time as her brother-in-law, but the financial newspapers were concentrating on the disappearance of the CEO, and she was merely the wife of the former one. The tabloids felt free to dwell on Bella's escaping death that day on the Nevsky and vanishing around the same time as Boris. There were a few opinions in one newspaper that her disappearance seemed a little too suspicious right after her husband's murder, and misguided references were even made to a possible "close relationship" to Boris, but those vanished after protests by lawyers from Danilov Enterprises. That line of speculation ceased after a few days anyway when her story was replaced by a gory murder/suicide among the moneyed set. But suspicions had been planted.

Dimitri Danilov's death had shocked the Russian Blues deeply, and the clan closed ranks behind his brother, even if there were some who had reservations. But the combination of bad judgment, assassination, Bella's prominence, and the rise of a sadly inferior new Hierarch disturbed them. Perhaps their clan was suffering from some curse arising from a transgression far in the past, unknown to anyone in the present day, something that could ruin them, little by little. Werecat readers of the tabloids were starting to wonder about their first family.

When Bella returned to the condo, she was surprised to find that Boris had left without a note or a message on her cell phone. This displeased her. Left to his own devices, Boris was likely to go out drinking, and right now, that could lead to spilled secrets.

"Stupid ass," Bella muttered as she opened and shut doors, searching frantically for him. He had left. He was someplace in New York City, probably drunk and drawing too much attention to himself.

Bella knew Vivian Roussel had been amazed to see her, but from her manner, that was all. She didn't flinch or look especially nervous or give any indication of any emotion except the normal surprise of seeing an acquaintance from thousands of miles away suddenly pop up in her boutique. Normal reaction. Discovering her response was the only reason Bella had risked the scouting expedition.

Bella's nerves buzzed with tension, but she felt relieved that the Roussels were fortunately still in the dark.

But where had the mirror gone? Bella had hoped that she might find it displayed in the Old Muscovy. That was a long shot, of course, but stranger things had happened. Her helpers had searched the warehouse and missed it, so that had to mean that somebody else had taken it, and since only the Roussels had access to the place, they must have removed it, simply accepting it as an attractive decorative item. No doubt they had it in one of their homes by now—if they hadn't already sold it. Bella had checked out the contents of their boutique, and she knew it wasn't there.

Her incompetent American help had botched the job when they'd kidnapped Vivian. Now they would have to try again, but this time, she would turn to people whom she could trust. Through her network of clan members, she knew she could find allies whom she could count on to do whatever she required if the price was right.

Shit. It was as if she had to pay a special nuisance tax to get the job done, what with the bribes at the airport, the payments to the goons, and now the need to hire more muscle. All she did lately was pay, pay, pay.

Bella could hardly wait to collect her own little bonanza. She hated being paymaster to the world!

Chapter Thirty-one

As soon as Bella Danilov left the Old Muscovy, one of Pavel's men tracked her to a chic condo in Manhattan, a charming but out-of-the-way place in a building that served as a low-profile sanctuary for visiting movie stars or others who wanted an elegant but discreet shelter.

The concierge was as taciturn as he ought to be, but when he saw a handsome cat walk into the lobby, he accepted his visitor as an amusing distraction. The cat explored a while, eventually slipping into the elevator with a couple of tenants who found him adorable. Domestic cat form was the preferred mode for werecats undercover. They tended to super-size for harder work—or play.

Once the tenants had gotten off at their floor, Pavel's man shape-shifted into human form and followed the signal from the device planted in Bella's coat. Third floor, apartment 3D. At the sound of footsteps approaching, he sauntered back down the hall as a couple got out of the elevator and headed to an apartment at the far end. Casually pushing open the door to the emergency staircase, he descended to the first level and went out a rear exit that brought him out onto the sidewalk. He couldn't wait to get back to Metro to tell the boss he had just found Bella's hideaway.

* * *

That evening, Pavel sat nervously in his own kitchen, watching Vivian prepare a meal. She had turned down his offer to order out, and had insisted on cooking, in an effort to do something useful while she was accepting his hospitality. One of Manhattan's finest grocery stores had supplied the ingredients and Viv was carefully preparing a salad with a variety of greens. Tilapia à la provençale was to follow, accompanied by a good wine and a fruit course for dessert. Pavel tried to help, but his offers were waved aside.

"I do know how to cook," he said as he sipped a glass of mineral water. "I had to learn in the Special Forces."

"But did you have anything edible to practice on? I heard that in Special Ops, you learn how to survive on roast grasshoppers and things like that."

"Well, yes. You have to go on survival training. But where I was, it was too cold for grasshoppers. We shot and ate whatever was available."

Viv glanced at him in curiosity. "What was the most exotic thing you ate?"

Pavel reflected as he poured himself a glass of mineral water. He shrugged. "Well, *you* might consider it exotic. A sable."

"A sable? Seriously?"

"It was him or nothing. And he kept several of us from starving."

She shuddered as she tore up more greens. "I wish you hadn't told me that. I'll never be able to look at a sable coat the same way."

Pavel gave a thin smile. "Me, either," he said.

After dinner, which turned out well, Pavel made Russian-style tea and told Viv what his man had learned about Bella.

"She's keeping a low profile, staying at a very elegant apartment she may own, off the beaten tourist track."

"Is she alone?"

"My man trailed her to the apartment building via the signal from the GPS device we planted in her coat while she paid you a visit. We don't yet know if she has a companion, but we will. One of our female operatives will bug the place when she shows up as the cleaning lady."

"If she's staying with a man, then maybe they were both involved in getting rid of her husband or stealing the icon, or both."

"We don't have any proof of either crime."

"Yet."

"Right. And we have to keep that in mind."

"Have your men finished checking all the antiques dealers we worked with?"

"Yes. They didn't find any hint of impropriety in their dealings with clients."

"And Bella?"

Pavel grinned. "Well, that's quite a story. Arrived from somewhere in central Russia back in the midnineties, took several jobs that used her computer skills, made it her business to become indispensable to her male bosses, caused a divorce in one instance, and ended up working for the Hierarch after his brother met her in a club and introduced her."

"Bella knows how to make friends."

"Bella's friendships took her from hand-me-downs to sables. There are thousands of girls like her: all driven to escape their shabby backgrounds and make new lives with the richest men they can find. Postcommunist economics."

"Do you think her marriage to your Hierarch was all about the money and nothing else?"

Pavel shrugged. "He was crazy about her. She appeared affectionate with him. But who knows? One thing for certain: as his wife, she could have anything she wanted anytime she wanted it." He looked serious. "For that reason, I don't think she would have killed him—or had him killed."

"Then," Viv said, "what do you think was behind the assassination?"

Pavel took a sip of tea, and he shook his head. "My suspicion is a business rival. The Hierarch was engaged in a bid for oil rights. And he wasn't the only one."

"Maybe somebody got tired of negotiating and hired an assassin to improve his chances."

He nodded. "It's possible. These days, stories like that fill the newspapers. The business climate is dangerous. The whole damn country is dangerous."

"Would your Hierarch have had anything to do with stealing the icon?"

"No!" Pavel exclaimed. "He was a person who respected tradition and the faith of Orthodox believers. He loved our history. In fact, he paid quite a bit of money recently to have one of Petersburg's old palaces restored. The man would never have stolen such a treasure. He was probably the biggest werecat philanthropist in the country."

Viv glanced at Pavel and said, "All right, he was an honorable person. What about the younger brother?"

"Oh," he said dismissively, "Boris is a lightweight. He might be lured into all kinds of trouble. But he wouldn't have the cunning or the ability to get involved in such a dangerous scheme."

"You never know. He did manage to become your Hierarch, didn't he?"

Viv knew she had rattled Pavel, as if she had forced him to confront the impossible. She said, "Why don't you make a few calls to Russia and see if he's turned up there—or anyplace else?"

"I will," he promised. "In fact I'll do it right now."

Chapter Thirty-two

"Yuri, Pavel here. Any new information about the Danilovs?"

Pavel heard something that sounded like a curse, and then his contact said, "According to a source whose cousin works as a maid in Boris Danilov's home, Marina Danilov was hysterical when her husband disappeared, going around the house moaning that they'd probably killed him just like they'd killed his brother, scaring the kids, and smashing things. Very dramatic."

"Marina used to be a bad actress in trashy movies. Are you surprised she'd carry on like that?"

"No. But this is the interesting part. After receiving a phone call yesterday, she pulled herself together and went out shopping and dining with her best friends. She went from several days of full-blown hysteria to 'Let's do lunch.'"

"She knows he's safe," Pavel said. "The gravy train rolls on."

"Sure. Our source couldn't believe the change in her."

"Okay. Thanks, Yuri. Again, sorry I ruined your sleep."

"I'll return the favor sometime soon. Good night."

When he hit the END button and folded the cell phone, Pavel looked at Vivian. "After getting a phone call, the new Hierarch's wife went from weepy to happy. Boris is safe."

"Good. But where is he?"

"Maybe in New York with his sister-in-law."

Viv considered that. "How are we going to find him?"

"If he's with her, Bella is going to want to keep him on a short leash. He's a drinker. He's indiscreet. She wouldn't trust him on his own."

"Same apartment?"

"I'd bet on it. Once the new cleaning lady places those bugs, we'll know for sure."

"In the meantime, let's go exploring."

Pavel shook his head. "*I'll* check on it. You stay here. Remember, you're in my apartment because it's the safest place in the city right now."

Viv gave him a disdainful glance. "I'm a werecat, descended from Krasivaya. Your Hierarch doesn't scare me. I've dealt with worse," she reminded him. Pavel and Viv were standing nose to nose. He irritated her by smiling. "I'm serious!"

Pavel nodded. "So am I."

"You're an accomplished security expert, so I'll be perfectly safe with you," Viv pointed out.

"Sorry. You're not pushing my buttons. I don't think it would be a good idea for you to roam around the city right now."

"Let's do it in small-cat form. Who'd be suspicious of a couple of cats? If things get rough, we can always supersize."

Pavel's green eyes narrowed with amusement. "What I would like to do with you as a cat is something quite different," he said with a seductive growl.

Viv's glare turned to a smile. She'd had the same thought. "I think we ought to keep our minds on the objective here and not get sidetracked." She felt a strong urge to shapeshift, which she tried to ignore. Her desire to mate was unbearable.

Pavel smiled back, all kinds of sensual thoughts tumbling through his mind, by the expression in his eyes. Viv found him so attractive, she had a hard time behaving. Nobody had appealed to her in years the way Pavel did, even though he was from a foreign clan. The taboo was fierce—which made him all the more enticing. Thoughts of the Leader's reaction made sweat start beading on her forehead. That might be even more dangerous than facing the icon thieves right now.

"*Dorogaya*," he said softly, "I don't want to see you harmed. That's what you're paying me for. I'll take the chances."

"But if Boris is the heavy drinker you say he is, we could probably track him to a bar and grab him."

Pavel looked dubious. "I doubt Bella would allow him that much freedom."

"She left her little hideout to come see me. He could find his way to the nearest bar if he wanted."

"There's no guarantee he'd be that predictable."

"Does he know the city?"

"I don't think so."

"Then he might do what any stranger would do if he wanted a drink: ask the concierge where the closest bar is."

"Possibly."

"If he gets restless, he's going to want a drink," Viv pointed out. "And if he's staying with the widow Danilov, he's going to require lots of alcohol. Believe me."

"All right," Pavel said. "Then we'll start staking out the bars. I'll put someone on it."

"And what will we do?" she asked.

For a moment, Pavel simply gave her the sexiest smile that had ever registered on her radar. He put his arm around her waist and drew her close. "Let's do this," he said and softly kissed her mouth.

Viv's best intentions of honoring the ancient taboos collapsed in the time it took to put her arms around his neck and kiss him back. She leaned into him as he hugged her tighter, and she startled him by the warmth of her response. She wanted him, and she wanted him right now.

Viv's hands caressed his chest as she sought out buttons to undo, and then realized he was wearing a T-shirt. Undaunted, she slipped her hand under it and felt him react to her touch and pull her closer to him.

Pavel kissed her as he slowly undid the pearl buttons of her silk blouse, and then continued to kiss her as he pulled it out of her skirt and up and over her head as he flung it into the air.

"I hope you don't do this with all your clients," she murmured as she came up for breath.

"First time," he replied, cutting off the conversation with more kisses.

"This breaks all the rules," she whispered as Pavel released her briefly. She stood staring at him, torn between her desire and her fear of the Leader's retribution—if he ever found out. She wrapped her arms around Pavel as he picked her up and carried her into his bedroom.

"Vivian, I won't force you to do anything you feel is wrong," he said as they both landed on his bed. He leaned over her as they stretched out, and he nuzzled her neck, pushing away her long hair and trailing kisses down her throat and into the lovely valley between her breasts.

Viv smiled into his eyes and caressed his hair. Then she said seriously, "I have to warn you, our Leader thinks I should be his mate."

The Russian gave her an amused smile. "I can understand that."

"No, it's not humorous," she said. "I've told him very forcefully I don't wish it. If he knew about this, he would attack you, Pavel," she said seriously. "I've just learned there's a bad situation in my clan. I haven't even told Marc yet. Our Leader is out of control. He's raped two of our females. My clan will have bring him to trial. I've already promised to have him put under surveillance to build a case."

Pavel looked serious. This surprised him, but he would offer help if she wanted it.

"I claim the right of all Maine Coon cats to choose their mates," Viv said without hesitation. "And if possible, I'd like Metro to help me keep watch on our Leader so we can prevent him from harming anyone else."

"Agreed. Now I think we shouldn't talk so much," he murmured. "Our kind is always so much more natural when they just act on their instincts—don't you agreee?"

Pavel sat up briefly and took off his clothing, then removed the rest of Vivian's and slid under the covers with her.

"I'd say that's a good idea," she whispered as she covered his mouth with kisses.

Chapter Thirty-three

The next day Viv and Marc were back at work under the watchful eye of Metro's men, Viv took her brother aside and told him what she'd heard about the Leader. He was shaken. And then he revealed he'd heard some unsettling things a few weeks earlier about Sinclair's newest ideas about security. He was evidently preparing for some kind of dictatorship. Hank was worried, too.

"We have to stop him," Viv said. "I'm having Pavel assign men to track him so we can gather evidence. You could network with some of the members you trust and set up a special meeting for an impeachment. One of the females will testify if someone else will. She's frightened to do it alone. I'll testify that he tried to rape me."

"We have to make sure we have enough support. This has never happened before in the clan. Members might hesitate."

"Our clan has never before had a criminal for a Leader," she replied. "And we can't keep this one. We have to depose him."

Marc nodded gloomily. The proud Maine Coon cat clan was being undermined by a vicious megalomaniac, and right now he and Viv had to contend with their own problems with the Siberians. They felt caught in a vise.

In his town house that night, Marc felt secure enough to suggest to his bodyguard that he wanted to get out. He was used to a social life, and he felt like a prisoner under house arrest. Nobody had tried to kidnap him since the large guys with the muscles had taken up their position at the shop. He was willing to bet the enemy had given up.

"Mr. Federov wants you in our sight," his new bodyguard told him.

"I'd like to attend a gallery opening. You can come, too. They sent two tickets."

"I think it would be smarter to stay home."

"I have to get out. This is driving me crazy. It won't be hard to guard me. We'll be in the same room."

The bodyguard gave him a disapproving look.

"It won't be a problem. It's casual."

"I'll have to check with headquarters," the bodyguard replied.

After some discussion, the bodyguard André closed his cell phone and told Marc they could go. Another guard would meet them near the location.

The gallery opening was a pretty lively affair, with a group of A-list types and their hangers-on, followed by the definite B-list groupies and a mix of others of indeterminate status, most of them dressed in black and all of them interested in the refreshments.

One of the city's chichi caterers provided stylish fare that mingled low-calorie count with creative uses of color. Marc sampled the sushi appreciatively. He recognized a few business acquaintances and greeted several pretty blondes who were networking among the art. He noticed that André refrained from eating or drinking and kept a discreet lookout.

While the guests were circulating, admiring the art or eyeing one another, Marc felt there was something odd about a few of them. Nothing he could put his finger on, but he could feel that he wasn't the only werecat in the room.

"André," he said, "there are other members of the brotherhood here."

André knew what he meant. It was werecat slang for their own kind.

"Which clan?"

"Don't know. But I don't think they're our people."

"I think we ought to make it an early evening, Mr. Roussel. Say your goodbyes to the hosts and let's leave. Be very natural. No rush. But we have to go."

Marc ate another piece of sushi and sauntered over to the artist who had invited him to the party. He praised his work, expressed his regrets, and explained he had an early-morning meeting with clients.

"Nice and easy," André instructed him. "Get your coat and move out the door like there's no rush. When we get onto the sidewalk, we make a quick right turn and hop into the car, which will be waiting for us."

As Marc and his guard exited the party, they were aware of two men who noted their departure and headed across the room to leave right after them.

"You know, I don't want to sound paranoid, but I think we're being followed."

André pulled a walkie-talkie out of his pocket and said, "Bring the car around. We've got company."

As Marc and his guard picked up their pace and headed in the direction of the SUV that drove toward them, André gave Marc a push and shouted, "Run!" as their pursuers broke into a trot and tried to overtake them.

Three loud bangs filled the air as somebody fired at them. André let out a howl of pain as one of the bullets found a target, but he drew his own weapon and ordered Marc to run faster as the waiting SUV approached, headlights blinding them.

When the vehicle pulled over and screeched to a stop, André, even in his weakened state, could see there was something wrong. His partner was gone and a stranger was at the wheel.

"Siberians," he said as he gritted his teeth with pain and

grabbed Marc. "Don't go in. Come on, we have to make a run for it. Now!"

As the driver of the SUV shouted to his associates, Marc and André ran into a dark parking garage and hid. With the two pursuers nearby, Marc made a decision, shape-shifted, raced out in big-cat form the size of a puma, and lunged at them from behind. He inflicted enough damage to buy time, and then took off through the lot with André, even though the guard was clearly in trouble. He lurched painfully on a wounded leg.

Marc shape-shifted again as they ran for their lives, not stopping for breath until they reached a dimly lit bar located on a sidestreet, somewhere in SoHo. A few patrons glanced at the newcomers, then went back to their drinks as the two visitors slid into a booth.

"I chewed those two up pretty well," Marc said with satisfaction. Then he glanced at his companion and saw even in the murky light that he was grimacing in pain.

"I need a doctor," said André. "Fast. I'm calling for backup."

Chapter Thirty-four

When Pavel recovered from their lovemaking a few hours later, he and Viv were curled up in big-cat form in his bed, with him nestled against her magnificent silvery fur and savoring the moment. He nuzzled her affectionately and then hopped off the bed and shape-shifted, disappearing into the hall.

Viv stretched out to full length, languid and very pleased with their first mating. She relived their passionate lovemaking in both human and feline form. Then she stood up, shook herself, and leaped down from the bed and onto the thick carpet where she shape-shifted and picked up her scattered clothing.

As a werecat, Viv felt the same urges an ordinary cat would feel. The desire to mate was strong. As a woman, she felt she had been a little too carried away by passion, and now she wondered how things would develop from here. She wanted this man, even if he was a stranger and from a different clan. He made love in a way that thrilled her.

"You make me very happy," he said as he met Viv in the hall and gave her a look that sent a spiral of lust straight to her core.

"I could say the same."

"Then," he said as he gently lifted her chin and kissed her, "we should take it as a sign that this is a special relationship that ought to be nurtured."

She didn't know if it was anything more than sheer lust that attracted her so strongly to this gorgeous Russian, but she was more than willing to find out. No male, werecat or human, had ever moved her the way he had. It was as if he was the other half she had been missing for so many years.

The mood was shattered when a phone call came in from Metro's call center. Viv heard him ask, "Where are they now?"

There was an explosion of Russian that sounded very angry, and then she heard, "Get back out on the street and search for the attackers. Send two others to case the area. I'm coming, too. I'll go to the bar and get them."

When he hit the END button and flipped the cell phone closed, Viv glanced at him. "Trouble?" she inquired.

"Your brother and his bodyguard went to a gallery opening in SoHo earlier tonight, and they were spotted by the enemy. André was shot and wounded. Marc tangled with them."

Viv rose from the chair and looked stunned. "Where are they now? Is Marc all right?"

Pavel gave a nod. "They're holed up in a small bar in SoHo for the moment. My man was supposed to pick them up, but while he was waiting, he was carjacked and knocked unconscious. Marc and his guard ran for it. Metro's call center just got a call from them asking for help. Marc's okay."

"I don't want those filthy animals to get their paws on my brother."

"We won't let them. I'm ordering my men to cover the area and look for werecats while I go to the bar to get André and your brother. Marc's tracking device will take us to him in case he and Andre have to leave before I reach them."

"Well, I'm not staying here while Marc is in trouble. I'll go with you."

Pavel looked at her very seriously. "That's a bad idea. I don't want to have to worry about you while I'm hunting. It's safer for you here."

"Marc is my brother. I'm not going to sit here without doing something to help him."

"*Dorogaya,*" he said patiently, "if Marc had listened to his bodyguard, they wouldn't be in this mess. I don't want the same thing to happen to you."

Viv shook her head. "I can spot him before you can. It's better if I go with you."

"We're dealing with scum. I wouldn't want any woman I know to fall into their hands, least of all, one I care for."

"Well, I survived an encounter with them before and I came out on top," she said stubbornly. "They ended up in a landfill and I'm still here."

"This is not a good idea."

"Do you have a better one?" she replied.

En route to SoHo, Pavel contacted a doctor who worked for Metro, another werecat, and told him to get ready because he was bringing in a wounded employee. He also called two of his men who were patrolling the area and ordered them to meet him at the bar.

Both cars converged on the dark sidestreet within minutes of each other. Viv and Pavel and two tall men in black entered, drew a few bored glances, and looked around the room. It was small, with very bad lighting, a good hiding place.

"There they are," said Viv as she finally spotted her brother.

Pavel and one of his men lifted André to his feet and helped him out while Marc threw forty dollars on the table to cover the drinks they had to order to stay. They were out of there before anybody had a chance to look twice.

"Pavel!" Viv took his arm.

Standing in front of the two cars were three tough-looking young guys grinning at them, waiting to start something.

"Hey, babe," said one punk, indicating Viv, "you want to add me to your to-do list?"

Pavel tilted his chin in the direction of the cars, and the others helped load André in. "Get him to the doctor," he ordered. "I'll handle this." As the SUV pulled away, carrying André to the clinic, he walked over to the three jerks and said, "Excuse me. I don't think I heard what you said to the lady. Maybe you'd like to say it to me." His eyes gleamed with evil intent. He was itching to go werecat. Viv could smell it in his scent.

"Hey, man, I don't swing that way," one of the punks said with a laugh. They all looked at Viv, who had stayed behind, not wanting to leave Pavel. They couldn't believe she hadn't gotten out of there.

"I think these guys need manners one-oh-one," she said with a glance at Pavel. "Agreed?"

"Right."

As the three street punks started toward them, intending damage, they saw their prey disappear behind the SUV. Bewildered, they looked at one another stupidly and saw something strange walk from around the back of the vehicle and stand facing them, teeth bared, just waiting to lunge. Two big cats, about the size of panthers, one dark silvery gray, the other shaggy.

"Oh, shit! Oh, shit!"

The three young guys practically trampled one another in their rush to get out of there.

"Man, it's that bad weed you bought," one of them screamed as he ran down the street, the sound of big sneakers pounding on the pavement. "Now I'm seeing tigers. I hope they get your ass!"

Viv glanced after them and gave Pavel a swat with her paw. "I thought they were the Siberians who tried to grab Marc. Did you know they were just stupid humans?"

"Thought they might be the bad guys," he said. "Looked dumb enough to be rogue werecats."

"Males," Viv said. "Let's shift and go get Marc."

Chapter Thirty-five

"Marc, I know you're used to an active social life, but until we get the piece back to its owners, I think it's the safer for you to avoid going out at night."

Pavel looked serious. His operative André looked abashed. Two days after his injury, he was back at work, due to the doctor's care and the amazing recuperative powers of werefolk. If the wound wasn't life-threatening, a few days would generally heal it.

"Well, when is that going to happen?" Marc demanded. "We've handed it over to your contact for safekeeping. When are the Russians going to come take it home?"

"As soon as the transfer can be arranged. I think you can appreciate the need for secrecy. The highest levels of diplomacy are involved in this."

"They'd better kick it into high gear," he said. "Otherwise neither one of us is going to survive."

"You and Vivian will be all right during the day with my men on the premises. At night, just stay put for maybe the next thirty-six hours. This will be over before you know it."

Marc nodded. "That's what I'm afraid of." And he gave Viv a look that was full of foreboding.

Since his trip to New York, Boris had found distraction by dining anonymously at various restaurants, as long as they had a good bar. Bella tended to want to shop, but she was strong-willed enough to forgo that ultimate pleasure in order to keep a low profile.

She felt flustered and furious by the fact that all her elaborate plans for stealing the treasure had imploded before she got to New York. As a woman who had reached the top by resolute scheming, Bella could barely cope with the wreckage of her most audacious plot yet. She had taken huge risks, used Boris's contacts to arrange for the theft and transport of Russia's most cherished icon, lined up a buyer, and now because of some stupid, anonymous underling, it was—momentarily—out of her grasp.

"Damn!"

The sound of the telephone jolted her out of her gloomy reflections. Bella walked to the table and picked up the phone, wondering who might be calling her. So few people had this number.

"Mrs. Danilov?"

"Yes. Who is this?"

"A friend."

"Then why don't you tell me your name?" she replied, about to hang up.

"Stay on the phone," he said. "You don't really know me, but I know quite a bit about you."

"So does anyone who reads the newspapers."

"I have someone here who is very close to you."

Bella felt a momentary frisson. She stiffened.

"Don't you want to know who?"

"There is nobody in New York who is close to me," she said. And she hung up.

Bella had scarcely had time to cross the room to get her cigarettes when the phone rang again. She forced herself to ignore it. It continued to ring. She lit a cigarette. The ringing began to drive her wild.

"Who the hell is this?" she demanded as she grabbed the phone and shouted into the receiver.

"You may call me Bill," he said. "I have somebody here who wants to talk to you. Here he is."

"Bella, be polite to these people," Boris said. "They're serious players. They snatched me off the street, and they want what they think we have."

"Why did you have to go roaming around the bars? This is what happens."

"I think they're your people," he said nervously.

"Why?"

"They know about the, uh, transport of that object we're all concerned about."

"And?"

"It looks as if they want a cut of the action."

Bella hung her head, shook it, and then started to swear so fiercely, she feared she was becoming hysterical with rage.

"Let me talk to the one who calls himself Bill," she said abruptly.

"Yes?" he replied.

"Who are you?" she demanded.

"A member of your own clan. We think what you did was very daring, but apt to create trouble for the entire clan if you get caught."

Bella took a drag of her cigarette. What else could go wrong with this plan? Perhaps those Roussels had broken the mirror containing the icon, and *she* was about to inherit seven years of bad luck.

"So you want me to call it off?"

"No, actually we want you to go ahead. We simply would like a chance to participate."

"Not on your life. I took all the risks. I should take the profits."

"Yes," said Bill, "but we're holding somebody who also has an interest in the success of the plan. Since the death of his brother, he's become an important man. How would it look if he were to die and leave a note behind—which would end up on the front page of the tabloids—blaming you for the assassination of your husband and the theft of a national treasure? Very bad for business, right?"

"Boris is not going to kill himself," she said impatiently. "And I didn't kill Dimitri."

"Whatever you say," Bill replied cheerfully. "But we will stage the suicide, write the note, and send it to all the papers. Then you can sit back and watch the fallout."

Bella clenched her teeth in sheer frustration. "How did you grab him? In a bar?"

"Yes. We had a very pretty young woman start up a conversation with him, and when he was about to follow her outside, we pushed him into a car and brought him along with us. He's become quite talkative."

"He's a fool," Bella sneered.

"Yes, but he's also a Hierarch. You'd do well to keep that in mind. He's not exactly fond of you."

At that, Bella kept quiet. Boris might be a dupe who could be manipulated by his constant need for cash, but deep down, his dislike of her might make him willing to do or say things that would come back to haunt her. She still needed his cooperation, and now she had to figure out a way to deal with this new disaster. They said they were members of her clan, so they must have had some tie to the New York Siberians who were supposed to retrieve the icon from the warehouse and return it to her. Were they working together?

"All right," she said wearily. "What do you want from us?"

Chapter Thirty-six

"Pavel," Viv said, "how long do you think it's going to take to get the object shipped back to its country?"

"Catherine Marais is holding talks with key people. They're making plans."

"Good. By the way," she said quietly, "have you managed to find out what John Sinclair is up to?"

"One of my men is shadowing him, hacking into his computer, making inquiries about his friends. So far we've uncovered lots of offshore banking, debts at casinos in Las Vegas and Atlantic City, fights with his mistress, and expensive presents for her. Busy fellow."

"What about our women?"

"Right now he seems to be concerned about the relationship in New York. He's not molesting any females from your clan. And by the way," he said with a smile, "the girlfriend is a Turkish Angora."

Viv's eyes flashed. "That hypocrite! On top of everything else."

"We also learned that he left the CIA under something of a cloud. He engineered a disaster in Bosnia and never regained the confidence of his bosses. They kicked him to the curb after that." Pavel glanced at Viv. "How did he manage to take control of your clan?"

"Clever packaging. Good spin doctors. We were foolish."

Viv and Pavel sat in his state-of-the-art kitchen, drinking a glass of wine after they had finished dinner. He had cooked, and Viv couldn't believe how good the meal was. The man had many talents. And he was so sexy he ought to come wrapped in asbestos. Every time she looked into those beautiful green eyes, she wanted to shape-shift and mate like wildcats.

"How is your employee?" she asked. "The one who was injured when they stole his SUV the night Marc nearly got kidnapped."

"He's recovering."

"Any idea who was behind it?"

Pavel looked at her with those dark-fringed green eyes, and Viv felt her muscles contract. She struggled against the desire to shapeshift.

"It has to be Bella. André recognized his attackers as Siberians he interviewed right after you were kidnapped. At the time, we thought they were just bottom-feeders. Now it looks like she hired them. Of all the antiques dealers you visited, she's the only one who dropped in to case your shop after the icon went missing. You said she treated you like a poor relation in St. Petersburg, and now she wants to be your new best friend. I watched the video of her in your shop. She poked around every corner, looking for something. She has to suspect you have what she stole."

Viv nodded. "That had to be the reason for the visit."

"And when we tapped her phone, we discovered her missing brother-in-law's in New York, too. Very interesting situation."

Viv smiled. "Then you still have a Hierarch."

"Unfortunately he's now in the hands of some members of Bella's clan who want a share of the action. We heard this on the audiotape. They're threatening his life as well as her reputation if she fails to cooperate, so I think Bella's going to make the right decision and cut them in."

"But that doesn't mean a thing since we have the icon and she doesn't."

"Yes," Pavel said, "but maybe these guys don't realize that."

Viv nodded. "But if Bella's hustling them, they'll probably kill her. And your new Hierarch."

"Good riddance to her."

"But what about your Hierarch?"

"Since he's the only we have at the moment, as stupid as he is, we'll have to protect him."

"Even if he helped steal the Virgin of Saratov?"

Pavel shook his head. "If he did such a thing, it would make him subject to the full penalties of our law. He would forfeit all claims to our loyalty. Do you understand what she means to our country? This is a powerful protector of the people. Werecat as I am, I believe she saved me from death several times during my combat service. No Russian Blue in the world would serve a Hierarch who disgraced us like that."

Viv stared down into her wineglass. "How dangerous was it in Chechnya?"

"I don't like to talk about it. It was bad for us and bad for them. Insanity on both sides. I came close to having my head blown off by bombs on several occasions. A wall collapsed right over me and left me standing in the outline of a blown-out window. A member of my unit shot a sniper who had me in his sights because one of their bombs lit up the area and took away his cover. Not good memories."

"And you lost the love of your life."

"Yes. That happened in a theater in Moscow, but it was the war that caused her death." Pavel suddenly looked much older and exhausted. "I nearly went mad with grief. I resigned my commission and retired to a monastery just to be alone. Then, after six months, I got in touch with Vladimir and asked him if he thought I might find work in America."

"And you did."

"Yes. I began by working as a security specialist for an agency, and then I moved up and finally opened my own. We don't do bounty hunting or anything like that. We stick pretty much to high-tech surveillance. Or low-tech if that's what the situation calls for. We do bodyguard assignments from time to time. I've done special assignments for Mr. Morgan, so I've come to know him. Very fine man."

"And the werewolf hunter?"

"Mademoiselle Catherine Marais is very professional, very competent. She and her partner are feared by were-wolves all over the world." Pavel smiled. "Did you know that she and her partner took down the last Montfort were-wolf?"

"Impressive. She must be an expert."

"The best."

"Ah," said Viv with a wicked smile, "it sounds as though you're quite an admirer of this French huntress. Perhaps there's more to this than you'd like to tell me."

To Viv's amusement, Pavel looked genuinely discon-certed. "No," he exclaimed, "I have no relationship with this lady. She's a business acquaintance," he said as he gave Viv a seductive smile and leaned over the counter to kiss her softly on the lips. The kiss lingered, causing Viv's tempera-ture to rise as she responded. She returned the kiss.

They straightened up, and Pavel walked around to Vivian and took her in his arms. "You're the only woman I'm inter-ested in," he said as he lowered his mouth to hers and kissed her fiercely. "I think you're more than enough to keep me busy." He kissed her again, then again.

"Oh, *koshka,*" Viv murmured, as she ran her hands over his chest, "we could be busy forever."

"All right," he said as he pulled her closer to him and led her into the bedroom. Pavel felt her warm, yielding body against his, and he whispered, "Why don't we begin right now?" And his kiss lingered on her lips. "I love you. You're such a seductive creature. And your human form is enchanting," he murmured as he sank down onto the bed and took her in his arms.

Viv caressed him tenderly as they kissed. Then she became more aggressive and ended up on top of him, with her long chestnut hair undone and falling over him as they embraced and thrashed around in their excitement.

Pavel managed to undress her and himself as they kept kissing, and neither one of them knew how they didn't fall off the bed and onto the floor with all the rolling around.

He felt Viv's legs open and wrap themselves around him as she clung to him. He could feel the rapid beating of her heart as he positioned himself on top of her and kissed her neck, her breasts, her mouth.

When he entered her, Viv uttered a cry of passion that made him want to please her, possess her, fill her with such satisfaction that she would never even want another male in her life.

"Oh, *koshka*," she whispered as they rocked with the force of their lovemaking. "Don't stop! Don't even think about stopping. Oh, Pavel!" She breathed as she flung her arms around him. Her words died in a gasp of pleasure so intense she thought she'd die.

When they were exhausted and lying entangled on the expensive sheets, Viv snuggled up to her lover and kissed him lightly on the cheek. "I think they were wrong when the old lawgivers forbade us to mate with other clans," she murmured. "I wouldn't have known what I was missing."

"So I've helped you see another side of the law," he said sleepily as he rested his head on her breasts and lounged happily beside her. "Very good."

"Perhaps we ought to rethink some of the old notions," she said lazily. "Times change. People change."

But somewhere deep in her soul, she feared she would pay a heavy price for this forbidden pleasure. She couldn't even bear to think of Sinclair's reaction.

Chapter Thirty-seven

Bella Danilov experienced such hatred that she had trouble maintaining her human form. This stupidity affected her at such a primal level that she longed to go werecat and chew him up. Damn Boris! She should have known he'd screw up and leave her open to this kind of blackmail. These New York Siberians could murder him for all she cared. Oh, shit! His death would be bad for her, so she had to keep him alive. With all the likely rumors circulating about Dimitri's death, the last thing she needed was to have a second dead Hierarch in her vicinity.

Damn, she thought. *Of all the things I could have done, why did I have to get involved with this?* That was naturally a rhetorical question; she knew why she had chosen to steal the Saratov icon and ship it to the United States. She wanted to make millions.

Someone help me, she thought as she reached for her cigarettes and selected another one from the pack. *All this bad luck started with Dimitri's death. And now I have to make sure this fool stays alive. What a curse.*

As one of the American presidents once said, "Life is not fair." Didn't she know it.

Catherine Marais had been in touch with the Russians and she arranged for a top-level diplomat to view the icon so he could verify its authenticity. He agreed to the conditions: blindfold until he arrived at the location, then no attempt to determine where he was. Catherine would vouch for his safety. Determined to bring the icon home and restore it to its rightful place, he would have agreed to almost anything to get a look at it. Pressure from the public and from the Kremlin combined to make a powerful incentive for risk.

That night as Vladimir drove across town with Catherine, two of Pavel's men trailed them, keeping watch for any unwanted company. They were in touch with Catherine by cell phone, using earpieces for greater mobility. When the gentleman, a Mr. Lubov, met the car at the appointed place, he got in and Catherine handed him a blindfold and a pair of dark glasses to go over it.

"I'm sorry for the inconvenience," she said apologetically, "but the person who has been entrusted with the icon had nothing to do with its disappearance and doesn't want visitors because of it."

"I understand, mademoiselle. Believe me, as soon as we have the painting, that's the last he'll have to worry about it. But are you certain it is the Saratov madonna?"

"Oh, yes. How it came to be in the United States is a mystery, but it is definitely the stolen icon."

"You have no idea how precious she is to my country. Since the days of Ivan the Terrible, she's been regarded as a protector of the nation. Now I hope I can bring her home."

"You will, Mr. Lubov, as soon as you can guarantee the arrangements."

When Vladimir, who had finally been brought into the secret the day before, drove his passengers into the underground garage of Ian's town house, he and Catherine led their blindfolded guest into the area of the vaults, where Ian was waiting for them.

"You may remove the blindfold," he said quietly. "I hope your trip wasn't too uncomfortable, sir."

The diplomat shook his head as he pulled off the dark

glasses and the black cloth. He blinked as his eyes became accustomed to the light again. "I'm fine. Now I believe you have something you'd like me to see."

"Wait here and I'll bring it to you."

The Russian nodded and glanced around the bare room, at his two companions, and at the steel doors that closed behind the man's back. Catherine and Vladimir stood next to him, all three of them anxious for the next step.

When Ian emerged with a rectangular object covered with a dark cloth, the Russian stood immobile as his eyes went right to it. He stood a little straighter and he drew in a sharp breath as he watched his host remove the cloth. "My God!"

Dumbfounded, Lubov stared at the icon. He gingerly stretched out his hand and touched it, unable to disguise his emotion at the sight of the resplendent Madonna. "This is the Virgin of Saratov," the diplomat said in awe. "My God, I can't believe it. I was so afraid it would be a hoax."

"Are you certain?"

Lubov nodded. "Yes. When I was a child, my grandmother's brother was a monk at the monastery there. Stalin was so desperate during the war that he actually permitted a few old men to keep it open so they could pray for the war effort. He knew the importance of the Virgin of Saratov."

"So you saw the icon there?"

"Oh, yes. My old uncle was devoted to the Madonna, and he used to hold me up so I could get a good look."

He turned to Catherine and said, "This is no forgery. Back in the days of Peter the Great, a Swedish army fought the tsar, and he ordered the monks of that time to bring him the icon so he could take it with him in battle. It received a bullet wound, and if you look carefully, you will see the spot in the wood where the Swedish bullet grazed it. Not many people know this. The monks did, and they told me the story."

All eyes went to the icon, and with Lubov pointing the bullet damage out, they discovered it.

"Then," said Ian, "let us make arrangements for her return."

In a shabby apartment in Queens, Boris Danilov sat nervously between a couple of members of Bella's clan who appeared to be waiting for somebody or something. He glanced around the room and wondered if they lived here or simply used it as a place of business, since the apartment seemed like a sad time capsule of the seventies, all orange accents and shag carpets. Poverty and bad taste had left it adrift in the era of love-ins and disco boots while the rest of the world had moved on.

"Are we waiting for someone?" Boris asked. "Will it take long? I'd like to be on my way, if I can."

"You go when we say so," one of his abductors said.

"Fine. Just let me know," he said.

Boris considered shape-shifting and trying to leap out the window, but although he'd heard some remarkable stories of cats surviving leaps from upper floors, he felt he had too much to lose to attempt it himself. He wasn't completely desperate yet. That was about to happen, but so far he had managed to hold himself together. These thugs needed him and Bella for their plans. Of course, they didn't seem to realize that the icon had gone missing. He considered telling them that, but hesitated. He didn't know what Bella had revealed, and he didn't want to say anything to contradict her.

"Do I know the person who's coming?" Boris inquired.

"Maybe."

After two more hours of this, the Hierarch heard footsteps in the hall, and then the sound of a key turning a lock. He looked expectantly toward the door and then rose as he saw three men walk into the room. Actually two large men dragged a third into the room and plopped him down on the floor.

"Take a good look at him. He worked for you."

Boris did that, but with all the bruises and the swelling, it was hard to make out his features.

"Sorry. I don't know him."

The larger of the two thugs snorted. "He's the one who made the arrangements for the icon to go missing. We've been questioning him."

"What have you done to him?"

"Had a conversation. He doesn't like to say much."

Boris looked at the man on the floor and felt a stab of fear in his heart. He had never seen anyone beaten like this before, and he didn't want these maniacs to get started on *him*.

"What did you want him to tell you?" Boris asked.

"How he managed to hide the icon in that damned warehouse without letting us find it."

"How did you know it was there?"

The big guy gave a nasty laugh that had nothing humorous in it. "Because he betrayed you as soon as he could. Only he didn't know that the contact he had was my brother, who naturally told me. Small world."

Boris marveled at the level of evil in the universe. Betrayed and sold out at every turn, he sincerely wished something good might happen right now. Anything, however small, just to restore his faith in the possibility of hope.

"Oh, damn," said the thug from the sofa. "I think he just croaked." And all the others leaped at their victim to try frantically to revive him.

Thank you, gods, Boris thought. *Thank you.* The secret had died with the man. At this point, Boris wanted to put as much distance between himself and the Virgin of Saratov as possible.

He wanted to forget about the whole crazy scheme.

Chapter Thirty-eight

Pavel's wiretaps revealed that Bella was now having problems with her Manhattan helpers. The audiotapes confirmed that she had been guilty of stealing something important enough to interest other felons, even if there was as of yet no hard evidence to connect her with the theft of the icon, since she and the others refused to refer to it by name. Still, it would have been too far-fetched to think it was anything else.

It bothered Pavel that Bella had been at the scene of the Hierarch's assassination and had survived. It just seemed too convenient for her to have eluded death when three men in her company had been shot down just meters from where she stood. True, the video on CNN showed a frantic Bella screaming and demanding to go to her husband's side, but something about the scent rang false.

I'm a cynic, Pavel thought. Perhaps she *had* tried to get out there as soon as the firing started. But still, she had stayed inside the door of the restaurant, a sensible precaution. Yes, her bodyguard had been holding her back. Yes, she had shown extreme emotion on camera when she had flung herself over her husband on the sidewalk, but for an instant, for a split second, Bella had exhibited the kind of attention to detail that Pavel remembered from the war. A fleeting trace of checking the scene flickered in her eyes.

Were they all dead? Any sign of life? And then full-scale operatic grief, shown round the world on the news.

Damn, he thought. *She could have planned this.* And if she had planned it, she had arranged for the assassination with one of the many freelance shooters for hire doing a lucrative business in removing people's enemies these days.

Now, if Bella had orchestrated Dimitri's death, was Boris her coconspirator? Pavel hated to think so. Boris was their Hierarch now, a man to whom the Russian Blues owed their allegiance. He was most likely Bella's partner in the theft of the icon, but could he have actually conspired in the death of his own brother?

Pavel knew that if he had proof of Bella's involvement in the assassination, she would face retribution for it. Even if she escaped punishment for the theft, she wouldn't escape payback for the murder.

With that in mind, he dialed a telephone number in St. Petersburg and smiled when a tired voice said, "Yes?"

"It's Pavel. How are things?"

"The same. How can I help you?"

"Any word on the killing?"

There was no need to specify which killing. For the Russian Blues there was only one that counted at the moment.

"Rumors," he said. "Speculation. Some of the brethren learned that a group of gangsters was celebrating at a nightclub two days after the murder. They got really wasted and bragged to some female talent that they just made a fortune for five minutes' work."

"Did she ask what that entailed?"

Pavel's friend laughed. "They were drunk, but not that drunk. The girl didn't try to find out too much since she already knew their reputations, and she didn't want them coming after her. But she said they were toasting somebody named Bella." He let that sink in.

"None of that is illegal. And Russia is full of women

named Bella. They'd claim Bella is a girlfriend, and who could say she wasn't? We need something stronger."

"That's all I have so far. The girl knows a lot of shady guys who come to that place to celebrate successful jobs. They wear shoulder holsters and ankle holsters, and they throw money around like there's no tomorrow. She's spotted lots of gang-related tattoos and heard the slang they use. They're our own homegrown mafia."

"Well, we need more than a girl's suspicions. If she can provide you with names or a snitch, we might be able to do something. I'd like to see our leader's killer pay for the crime."

"So would we all. And believe me, we're keeping our ears open. Some of the brethren have an idea that there might be a way to connect Bella Danilov to it, but it will take a while. Interviews, talks, negotiations."

Pavel took this to mean the Russian Blues back home were going to track down the suspects, interrogate them in a way that would make the old KGB proud, and force them to rat out their accomplices. No holds barred.

"Dimitri was a good man and a great Hierarch," Pavel said. "He deserves to be avenged."

"He will be," replied his friend. "Just as soon as we can pinpoint the culprits."

"Good hunting," Pavel said. "Meanwhile, I'll be keeping watch in my territory."

"Keep us posted."

"I will," he replied.

Pavel hadn't told his contact about Bella's New York sojourn, because he knew that the only way to keep information secure was to put a lid on it. When the time came, he would alert the brethren. If there were any moles among the Russian Blues, he wasn't going to make it easy for them.

What he needed to do now was to try to destabilize the relationship between Bella and her brother-in-law. From what he knew about Boris, he was the subordinate here.

Dimitri Danilov had been keeping him around because he was his brother, and werecats would never throw out a sibling, no matter how stupid and useless, unless there was a serious reason.

Lack of character and an excessive love of booze weren't enough for Boris to get kicked to the curb, but now that he was the new Hierarch, the Russian Blues needed a leader, not a drunk with a dependency on a power-crazed Siberian Forest cat. From the mood of his brethren back home, Pavel wondered if some of them might be thinking of a coup.

Wishing to drive a wedge between the Siberian and her puppet, Pavel reflected on what he knew about his new Hierarch. Boris was really just a handsome guy who looked good in his designer wardrobe, who was the designated host for visiting dignitaries, who kept visitors entertained while Dimitri made the deals. He was an empty suit.

What else? Oh, he had married Marina, a skinny blonde with surgically enhanced breasts and lips who made a ten second splash in the movie business with a B film called *Vixens of Voronezh.*

Pavel had seen the flick while on R and R during the war when he and guys from his unit had gotten drunk after an especially bad week, gone to a dilapidated cinema in the boonies, brought some liquid refreshment with them, and laughed themselves silly at the film. They probably couldn't have sat through it if they had been sober. Now he cringed at the thought that Marina was the first lady of the Russian Blues.

Boris Danilov appeared to dote on her, Pavel remembered. He'd had two children with her. Perhaps she could become a source of worry for the new Hierarch as he hid out in Manhattan, so far away from home. She wasn't the hausfrau type, and Pavel would bet anything that if she were offered a chance to have a good time, she'd take it.

He'd make it his business to try to arrange it.

Chapter Thirty-nine

When Boris's Siberian captors released him on the condition that they were now partners who wanted a cut of the money from the icon deal, and returned him to his apartment, he was badly shaken, especially after seeing the battered were-cat they had questioned.

"These people are savages," he said. "They have no respect for life. They'll kill us."

"They are thugs," Bella said. "They can be outsmarted. If the one who hid the icon is dead, then the others don't know where it is. Since we don't know where it is, either, they can't hold us responsible for that, so we're safe."

After digesting that, Boris said, "Okay. So what are we going to do when our contact meets us, expecting to receive the icon?"

Bella looked annoyed. "I'll think of something," she said.

"You're not going to create a fake, are you? There's no way we could pull it off. I say we just give up on the whole thing. It's getting too complicated. Let's just stay here until we've missed the deadline for the oil deal, go home with our cover story, and collect the millions."

"There's too much money involved not to keep going with this," she said.

Boris shook his head. "All I want to do is go home to Marina and the kids. You do whatever you want."

Bella reacted with a burst of anger, swishing her long tawny hair around as she faced him. "Don't be a chicken-shit! We're in this together. You can't bail now. We go home when we sell the icon and the FSB holds a news conference with us to announce that they were hiding us from terrorists, the threat was neutralized, and they've saved our lives. You're up to your ass in this."

"We've gambled and lost. We can't get our hands on the icon. The Roussels don't seem to have it either. Maybe the crooks you hired stole it and are selling it on eBay."

"Shit, I hope not!"

"I just want to go home."

"You can't! Right now I would suggest that you don't even contact Marina. We have to be off the radar for now. We need to plan."

Boris shook his head. "I need a drink," he said. "You can plan all you want. Have fun." And with that, Boris retreated to the kitchen, fighting the urge to go werecat.

In his office, Pavel was speaking with Mademoiselle Marais. Catherine had set in motion the mechanism for returning the icon, and Pavel was going to provide security for the site of the transfer. Since he knew her contacts were far-flung and varied, he had a favor to ask, as part of this operation. He wasn't sure if she'd say yes.

"We believe Bella Danilov and her brother-in-law were behind the theft of the icon. And they shouldn't get off unpunished."

"I agree. But since we have the icon and they don't, I think it makes it difficult to pin the blame on them."

Pavel smiled. "I'm not speaking of the law courts. I'm speaking of some other kind of punishment."

Catherine leaned forward. "I'm listening," she said. "What do you have in mind?"

"I want to divide and conquer, and Boris is the weak link

in this duo. Let's make him so fearful and anxious that he can barely think straight."

"You sound like my partner, Paul," she said with a smile. "What's the plan?"

"He has to feel humiliated that this Siberian is calling the shots. She has no real standing in his clan. She's just a sister-in-law. He's the Hierarch. From bugging her apartment we know he wants to go back home to his wife, and now Bella is telling him he shouldn't even contact her. Marina is a bimbo, and Boris probably figures if he's gone long enough, she'll start dating rock musicians and leave him in the lurch. I think we should encourage him in this belief."

"And?"

Pavel looked at Catherine and smiled. "You have many contacts among the jet set. What I'm going to suggest is luring Marina Danilov away to Europe with an invitation to some luxurious getaway where she'll be out of touch with Boris and everyone else for a week or so. Would you be able to arrange this?"

Catherine laughed. "I'm not a travel agent," she said. Then she tilted her head back and appeared to think about it. Pavel hoped she had some ideas.

"What is this woman like?"

"Before she married Boris Danilov, she was an actress in low-budget movies."

"Cultural level?"

Pavel reflected. "She seems to enjoy nightclubs and cosmetic surgery. And she's a woman people notice: pretty face, blond hair, big bosom."

Catherine nodded. "I know an aging director with a villa near Nice. He's going to invite some people to stay with him while his fans hold a retrospective. The local cinema will run some of his old movies, and he's hosting a few parties to celebrate the event. Gilbert hasn't made a movie in ten years, but he's considered an icon of film noir. He owes me a favor. Maybe he'd consider inviting Marina Danilov to his celebration if I asked."

"If we can get her out of St. Petersburg, we'll send her a message allegedly from Boris telling her not to contact him for his safety and hers. She'll have a good time in Nice and probably forget about him for a week or so. That's all we need."

"And meanwhile poor Boris will be unstrung, thinking the love of his life has probably run off with a boyfriend."

"Exactly."

"Psychological warfare," Catherine murmured. "Sometimes it's crueler than a knife."

"We'll save the knives for later," Pavel said with a smile.

Chapter Forty

Pavel paid a visit to one of the cubicles in Metro's communications room and said to Ivan, his best hacker, "I'm going to give you an assignment. I want you to get into Marina Danilov's computer and relay a message from her husband. Only we're going to create it. Understand?"

"Okay. What would you like me to say?"

"First go into her computer and read through her old e-mails to see if there are any from him. Then mimic his style. He's going to tell her to go on vacation to get out of town while things are still unsettled. She'll receive an invitation from a famous European director to attend a film festival. It's all arranged. All she has to do is go there, enjoy herself, and stay put until she hears from him again."

"This is true?"

"Yes. We're working on the invitation right now, so find her e-mail address, find his, and let her know how much her husband worries about her."

"I'll start now."

Pavel smiled at the thought of the effect that Marina's disappearance would have on their Hierarch. From their bugging of Bella's apartment, they already knew that Boris was on edge and Bella's nerves were fraying. This should rachet the tension up a notch and provide fuel for further fights, if not plain hysteria.

With a wife like that, a man had to be watchful. If Boris got sufficiently worried, he might even bolt and head for home despite Bella's warning, and before he reached the airport, Pavel's guys would grab him and grill him. At least that was what they were hoping.

When Pavel took Viv home to his apartment, he noticed she seemed sad or at least very tired. He feared all the recent disruptions had taken a toll.

"Things will be better soon," he said as he watched her prepare dinner.

Viv nodded, but her lovely face never lost its melancholy expression.

Pavel looked at her carefully. "Have I made you unhappy?" he asked.

"No. On the contrary," she said with a smile, "I've enjoyed being with you."

"You don't have to stop," he said quietly.

"Ah, but that's the tricky part."

"Why?"

Viv said ruefully, "Because of the old taboos. Because I'm going to try to organize the impeachment of my Leader, and I may find myself facing a fight with members who don't believe the charges and find it suspicious that I'm relying on the help of someone who isn't even a Maine Coon cat. Old prejudices die hard."

"If you take on this fight, you're going to need someone who has your back. I'll help you dig up enough information to convince your clan that your Leader must go. And I never run from a fight. I have no hidden agenda. I would be faithful to you, and I would fight for you if it came to that."

Viv held out her arms and took Pavel into a warm embrace. "How I want to be with you," she whispered as they clung to each other." She raised her face and let him kiss her tenderly as they stood there in the kitchen, surrounded by so much granite and steel. His kiss deepened and she pulled him closer. Their tongues tangled.

"Would your brother object?" Pavel asked as he gently released her from his arms.

"Actually, I don't think so. You two would get along well, as long as you enjoyed going to baseball games in the summer and skiing in the winter. Marc is pretty easygoing."

"Baseball is a mystery to me," Pavel admitted. "But I'm willing to sit through a few games if it makes me better company. I used to ski when I was younger. I enjoy it. I even had mountain-survival training in my younger days."

Viv smiled at him. "Good," she said. "And, of course, you have talents that make me very happy." A wicked glint in her amber eyes let him know which ones they were.

"Would you like to practice these other skills with me after dinner? I believe you should always keep current," he teased as he stroked the outline of her full mouth and kissed her once or twice again. He held her close and felt her heart beating against his.

From the expression in her eyes, Viv liked the idea. She snuggled up against his chest and murmured that she could keep practicing forever if she had to. It would be delightful.

When they had finished dinner, had a glass of Rémy Martin afterward, and settled into a comfortable sofa to snuggle, Pavel glanced down at Viv and saw something strange. She appeared to be in a trance, staring at the windows into the black night. He gently whispered to her and kissed the top of her head, her cheek, her neck, but nothing seemed to bring her out of it.

Alarmed, Pavel spoke to her quietly, asking her if she was all right.

"Yes."

"What are you doing?"

"Listening to the universe," she said softly.

If he hadn't seen her perform an incantation at the bedside of her wounded clansman, Pavel probably would have made a joke, but he knew this woman had a shaman's gifts, so he simply watched and waited.

After a long silence, Viv seemed to come out of her reverie. She nestled against him and said with a sigh, "We're surrounded by enemies, even ones we don't know about yet. Bella is not the only one who's a danger to us. And she herself is at risk."

"That's true. My clan thinks she killed her husband. And she has to be the reason the icon went missing."

Viv nodded. "In my vision I saw her in the center of a jungle. This often symbolizes a complicated life full of lies, deception, and corruption."

"Any hunters aiming at her?" he inquired.

Viv shook her head. "It was murky. But for some reason I didn't feel she was in danger from the Russian Blues. There are others who have it in for her. I can't really understand it."

Pavel knew from past experience that a shaman sometimes had to spend time trying to interpret what his dreamlike trance meant. They were often allegorical or simply so full of subtle clues that their meaning could be open to several readings.

"But it showed her to be in trouble," he prompted Viv.

"Oh, yes. She's up to her neck, and it won't be easy for her to extricate herself."

"We'll do everything we can to add to her problems," Pavel promised cheerfully. "Now shall we take this discussion to a more intimate level, *dorogaya*?"

"Let's make love like wildcats," Viv said, wrapping her arms around him. "No holds barred."

"Who ever said Maine Coon cats were conservative?" Pavel mused as he watched his lady transform to something the size of a panther.

"Come on, *koshka*," she prompted him. "What are you waiting for?"

Pavel took in that silvery fur and those entrancing amber eyes, and he shape-shifted in record time, leaping like a mountain lion on the attack.

So many taboos went by the wayside that evening, it left them both breathless.

Chapter Forty-one

Boris looked at his Palm Treo and grimaced. He pushed some more buttons and gave up, angrily stuffing it into a pocket.

"What's the matter? What are you doing?" Bella asked.

"Trying to get Marina by e-mail."

Bella rounded on him. "What is the matter with you? Someone could trace you. Let it be. She'll be fine. You've already told her you're all right. Point made."

"I love my wife," Boris said.

"Good. You'll see her in a few more days. You can bring her a gift from New York."

"But you don't understand. Marina gets antsy. She'll start going out with her friends if I'm not there."

Bella glared at him. "And?"

"And a lot of her friends are single women who want to meet rich men at trendy nightclubs. They drink too much, and then hit the sack with any guy who'll buy a jeroboam of champagne and talk about romance."

"If I recall, you used to spend most of your time in trendy clubs chasing girls."

"Exactly. This is why I'm worried. She has two small children at home. She shouldn't be doing this."

Bella looked bored. Russian Blues had a different take on these things, she decided. With her clan, a night's escapades meant maybe a bad hangover and some raunchy memories; there was none of this angst that afflicted Boris. Siberians were too adaptable for that. What they did on the prowl stayed out there. They were born cynics.

"Marina was a movie actress when you met her. She needs more out of life than being stuck at home with the kids. Did you ever consider that?"

"She knew when she married me that she would give up her career if we had children. It wasn't as though she was a serious actress who had trained for years."

"Ummm," Bella murmured. "*Vixens of Vorenezh* wasn't exactly *War and Peace*. She played a supernatural slut."

Boris turned red and appeared ready to go werecat, but then gave up on the idea. He wasn't going to respond to provocation.

"Don't try to get in touch with anyone," Bella ordered. "The e-mail's not secure. Marina loves you and will be happy to see you when you get home. She's smart enough to appreciate the danger you might be in, especially after Dimitri's death. She would want you to be safe."

Bella thought Marina was so self-centered, she wouldn't give a damn if Boris vanished from the face of the earth as long as he left her enough money to have a good time. But she tried to focus on a theme that would appeal to her brother-in-law.

"Did she ever tell you she loved me?" he asked pathetically. He looked absolutely vulnerable, a disgusting thing for a Hierarch.

Bella looked him in the eye and said with total authority, "She once told me you were the love of her life."

That worked. Boris seemed to grow taller, and he lost the dejected "woe is me" look she hated so much. The handsome blond Hierarch had returned.

He was so gullible. She thought once again that the wrong man died that day on the Nevsky. His brother would never have allowed her to have such a hold on him. In fact, she was the one who had always been on edge, always trying hard to please Dimitri, always watchful if he spoke too long to an attractive female at a party. Even though people thought she'd kept Dimitri enthralled with some wicked sexual shenanigans, they didn't know the reality of her marriage. Bella had never wanted to lose him. There was nobody else who could keep her in such style.

Catherine Marais had been in touch with the Russians, and she wanted them to hurry up and decide on final arrangements for the pickup. Dealing with them was like walking through a maze.

"What's taking so long?" Ian asked as he and his partner sat in his living room, looking out onto Manhattan at night. "They're not having second thoughts, are they?"

"No. From what I can tell, Mr. Lubov has to clear this with some higher-up, who probably has to contact *his* boss, who may even have to get in touch with the Kremlin. Since it's such a hush-hush deal, this has to mean their secret service will be involved. The FSB always complicates things."

"You know," he said seriously, "I could just teleport the icon over to St. Petersburg. It would get there faster."

Catherine laughed and wrapped her arm around his neck. "I love your sense of humor," she said as she kissed him.

"I'm not joking."

"Darling, you can't do that. I only wish you could. They would arrest you and hold you for interrogation. You would be dust as soon as the sun came up. I don't want to lose you."

Ian smiled. "I love to hear you say that. It makes me feel so cherished."

"Oh, you are," she murmured as she covered his mouth with kisses and let him caress her with that extraordinarily sensual touch he possessed. "You are the dearest thing in the world to me. *Je t'aime à folie.*"

Ian moved his hand along her thigh, and Catherine gave a cry as he touched her intimately. Her body bucked, and she responded by kissing him passionately as he stroked her, arousing her to such a pitch that she began tearing off her clothing so they could become even closer.

"I need you, darling," he whispered as he helped her out of her clothes. "You're the only one I want. Nourish me, Catherine."

She was lying almost beneath him, listening to the beating of his heart. Ian's mouth moved gently along her body, kissing tender parts and nearly making her go out of her mind with lust. Then she felt his fangs.

"Give me what I live for, darling," he said softly as he nuzzled her with the merest trace of those incisors.

In reply, Catherine reached up and brought his mouth down to her throat.

"Quench your thirst," she breathed.

Chapter Forty-two

At Old Muscovy, Marc glanced up from checking sales figures on the computer and looked through the doorway of the office and across the long expanse of room to where Viv stood chatting with one of their bodyguards. All seemed normal.

Two customers were meandering around the displays of paintings and old silver, talking in quiet tones, speculating about where they could hang one of the canvases in their apartment. Marc hoped they'd buy it, although he read a lot of hesitancy in their body language.

That was a werecat gift, reading humans. It often helped when he was trying to close a deal, being able to gauge just how much a client wanted an item. If Marc sensed there was a strong enough desire for a particular painting or bibelot, he'd gently push to make the sale, but if not, he'd let them think it over. Sometimes that worked, too.

Right now, Marc was wondering about another werecat and his motives. Pavel Federov had certainly helped him and Viv. Since Pavel had posted his operatives in the shop and on bodyguard duty, neither Marc nor his sister had been harassed. This was fine. What worried Marc was the affection that seemed to be growing between Viv and the Russian.

He wanted Viv to find a mate, but so far, her romantic history was a series of dead ends. Well, he had to admit his was

a bit spotty, as well. Cat genes didn't exactly lend themselves to fidelity and happily ever after. Divorce was rife
among their kind. Werecats liked to be on the prowl, literally
and figuratively; they generally didn't make good spouses,
although there were notable exceptions.

But they knew enough to stay within the limits of their
sept. An adventure with a foreign cat was acceptable for a
male, but not an admired female like Viv, and now she
seemed to have fallen in love with this Russian Blue. Not a
good idea, especially since she was a high-ranking member
of the clan with a duty to pass on her heritage. With the news
about the Hierarch about to burst into the open shortly, he
didn't want her to create waves of her own. The Leader was
quite capable of turning that into a bombshell to deflect attention from his own case.

Marc had nothing against Russian Blues; he believed
they were fine cats, with an impressive history of their own.
But he didn't want Viv to get sidetracked by one and become
an object of gossip in the community. And with recent de-
velopments, he worried about the clan's reaction. How many
scandals could they take?

He hated to think that Viv might find this foreign werecat
so attractive that she'd consider anything long-term. He
could close his eyes to an affair. He couldn't hold her to a
higher standard than he followed. But the idea of anything
more enduring than a short-lived love affair made him uneasy, especially in view of the circumstances.

Viv was his only sister and he'd told her he'd support her
in her choice of mate.

But he hadn't counted on this!

"Boss, I hacked into Marina Danilov's e-mail and
blocked all mail to and from the Hierarch. She just received
a message from me telling her to pack her things and find a
nice place to go for a week or so while he's off the radar.
Don't try to communicate with him during this time."

"Good. Now I'll have to get our contact in her house to report back to see if she's going to listen."

"Is Catherine Marais taking care of that invitation?"

"Yes. The French director is sending her a flattering letter, asking her to join him and his friends for the mini film festival."

"You think she'll take the bait?"

"Ivan," Pavel said patiently, "this is the kind of woman who still calls herself an actress even though nobody's asked her to make a film in years. Believe me, she'll be delighted to go. Besides, the south of France is a hell of a lot warmer than St. Petersburg right now. Who wouldn't trade ice and snow for palm trees and flowers?"

"Okay. Hope she goes for it. If I were a woman, I'd be a little nervous about flying hundreds of miles to stay with some old guy I've never met."

Pavel knew he had a point. However, Mrs. Danilov would probably check into one of Nice's luxury hotels for the length of the film festival and experience a lovely vacation on the Riviera, with sunburn the only danger on her horizon.

"Marina will come to no harm in Nice unless it's self-inflicted," he said wryly. "And besides, I think the possibility of connecting with a big shot in the French film industry will outweigh any other considerations."

"Still," Ivan said, "I can't believe she'd be that flighty."

Pavel gave him a thin smile, "She's not exactly a genius. And with the husband telling her to go have fun, do you think she'd turn down something like this?"

Next day, word came in from St. Petersburg that Marina Danilov was heading for Nice with a pile of Louis Vuitton suitcases and lots of suntan lotion. She was also confiding to her friends that this was the opportunity of a lifetime to revive her movie career. She was ready. All the Russian Blues had to do was sit back and let nature take its course.

Chapter Forty-three

The lavishness of Ian Morgan's town house always reminded Pavel of the Winter Palace back home. But he noticed that as Vladimir escorted him upstairs for his appointment with Mademoiselle Marais, his expression was distinctly chilly. Pavel glanced at him in surprise.

"What's the matter?" he inquired. "Is something wrong?"

"Oh, nothing. Except that you wouldn't tell me what you had the night you brought in the *object* for safekeeping. You wounded me deeply, you know."

"I'm sorry. I didn't mean to offend you. I just thought it was too dangerous to involve you at that point."

"We're cousins. We're members of the same clan. I also revere the icon."

"Then you wouldn't want me to do anything to put her at risk," he said.

"Of course not. But you could have told me. I would be glad to defend her, too."

"I'm sorry. The need for secrecy was so great, I felt I couldn't reveal the truth at that time, but I'll keep your offer in mind."

Upstairs in the living room, Pavel joined Catherine. Their relationship was strictly professional.

"I think the Russians have finally gotten their act together," she said after greeting him. "And now they're ready to finalize plans to take her home."

"I would guess that the Federal Security Service is going to take charge," Pavel said. "It's natural for the FSB in matters of national concern."

"A group of recycled KGB thugs," Catherine said with distaste.

"Probably," he acknowledged. "But at least the Saratov Madonna will be back where she belongs."

"Too bad she has to travel with them. But we hope they take better care of her now."

"Definitely. Now," he said as Vladimir appeared with a tea service, placed it on a table in front of Catherine, and left the room, "let's go over the plans."

After careful discussion, Pavel and Catherine fine-tuned their strategy. The Russians would meet with Mademoiselle Marais at a restaurant agreed upon by both parties. She could pick a companion to accompany her to the meeting. The Russians would send two men from the Russian UN mission, who would present their credentials and take delivery of the icon. They would be gone before anyone even noticed them.

"You look as though you have some qualms," Catherine said.

Pavel nodded. "This is quite a different case," he said. "But if you recall, that émigré journalist who met with Russian contacts in London at a restaurant didn't live too long afterward. Don't eat or drink a thing while you're there. I don't trust anybody from the state security services. You shouldn't either."

"Will you be nearby?"

"Of course, mademoiselle. I'll have you under surveillance all the while. And someone I trust will accompany you to the meeting."

"I've handled werewolves, you know. I think I can handle these Russians."

He nodded. "My people respect you very much. And we wish to hear about your exploits for years to come."

"Did you ever encounter any werewolves over there?" she asked curiously.

"Once. An old one was terrorizing a Moscow suburb and several werecats died during its attacks. They asked me to hunt it, and although I felt underqualified, I knew I had to help my own."

"What happened?"

Pavel shrugged. "I prepared silver bullets, put myself in its vicinity late at night, and had to walk through the park a few times to attract its attention. Then I found it. He lunged at me, and I stood my ground and fired. It was one of the scariest moments of my life. I fired away, and he suddenly sank to the ground and went into a spasm."

"Did he play possum?" Catherine asked with professional curiosity.

"Yes. I had been warned about this, so I shot him two more times before I checked the body. By the time I observed him, he was really dead."

"You were lucky. Some inexperienced hunters fall victim to their ruses."

Pavel nodded. "I wasn't taking needless chances. But I'm happy to say I got my werewolf." He gave Catherine a thin smile. "It was also the last time I ever tried. I leave them to the experts now."

She looked at him and nodded. Then she said quietly, "I'll take your advice about the security service too. Just in case."

On his way out, Pavel stopped at the door to speak to Vladimir. He felt bad that his cousin was angry with him for not being let into the loop earlier, and he wanted to make amends.

"Vladimir, I know how loyal you are to Mr. Morgan. If I were to ask you to help me in the transfer of the, ah, object, would you be willing to play a part?" Pavel looked intently at his cousin and tried to gauge his reaction.

Vladimir appeared quite startled. "You want *me* to help?"

"Yes. Mademoiselle Marais will be the one to go to the meeting place, and she will take a companion with her. The Russian secret service is involved, and I would feel better if she had someone at her side who is absolutely loyal—someone she and I trust unreservedly. You would be the best choice on both counts."

"I'd be honored," he replied. "I have the greatest respect for Mademoiselle Marais. And the other lady," he added.

"Good." Pavel gave his cousin a slap on the back and said, "I'll be in touch. It will be soon."

And when Vladimir showed him out, Pavel felt he had atoned for his past slight. Catherine would be in safe hands, and he would have a trusted man on the spot.

The delivery ought to go perfectly.

Chapter Forty-four

The chilly silence in Bella's apartment was broken by the abrupt ringing of the telephone. She gestured for Boris is answer it.

Boris grimaced, but he picked it up and said, "Yes?"

Bella observed him. It had to be those men who had snatched him off the street and phoned her before. She wondered what else they had in mind. Boris appeared to be listening intently. Then she heard him say, "Here she is."

Bella flung her long blond hair over her shoulder and said, "Yes?" as she took the phone.

"It's Bill. I'll be brief. We know you don't have the object and the werecat who hid it is dead. But today I have an update for you."

"Oh, yes?" she said, wondering where this was going. It didn't sound good.

"We just learned that the object is going to be handed over to our countrymen very shortly."

Bella had to stop herself from going werecat. All the trouble she had taken to steal the icon, have it shipped out of Russia, and hidden in the warehouse of some American customers so that she could easily access it by a second theft, and this Neanderthal told her this! He had just flushed all her hopes of financial gain down the toilet.

"Shit!" she exclaimed. "Who managed to find it? The

Roussels never knew about it! They're clueless. Otherwise that woman would have fainted when I showed up."

The voice on the other end seemed to laugh. "It's bizarre. My contacts inside the Russian mission told me one of their highest officials was allowed to see the object by the person who had it. He confirmed it was the real article, and then the person who had it made arrangements with him to send it home. All very mysterious and altruistic. And no names mentioned."

"What is his angle?"

"Oddly enough, he doesn't have one. He just wants to give it back."

Bella paused. "He can't be a rogue Siberian. We'd ask for millions."

The voice seemed to sigh. "I know it's difficult for people like us to imagine," he said, "but all he wants to do is return it. Very strange."

Bella amost snarled. Then she said, "What are we going to do now? It's out of our hands, literally."

"Don't be so sure about that."

Bella listened, almost holding her breath. "Do you have any ideas?" she finally asked.

"One or two," he replied. "Do you still have the customer who wants it?"

"Absolutely."

"You didn't inform him of the little glitch in your plans—as you didn't inform *me*?" he said pointedly.

Bella thought about making some sort of apology and then rejected that idea. "I hoped we could locate it," she said rather lamely. "But at least now we know where it's going."

"Yes, and it will be accompanied by the security service," he said, "but if all goes well, we can intercept it before it reaches them."

Bella thought her caller was crazy. "Somehow I think that will be unlikely. Who has the thing?"

"We don't know."

"What do you plan on doing to snatch it? Conjure it out of the air?"

"No," he said evenly. "I have another idea."

Bella shook her head in disbelief. She saw Boris glumly watching her.

"How do you know all this anyway?" she persisted.

"A mole. A little mole who likes expensive clothing and can't afford it on her meager salary. So she moonlights. She has access to private codes and secure lines, and she's always on the lookout for things that might be of interest to her friends."

Bella gave a disdainful sniff. Some little snoop who would sell out her own country for cash. Good.

"Now," her caller continued, "what about the buyers? Have you set up a meeting yet?"

"No. I couldn't, for obvious reasons."

"You realize I'm only letting you in on this because you've already done the groundwork. We split fifty-fifty, and I'll be there when the deal goes down."

Bella's tone reflected her outrage. "Oh, no! I took all the original risks!"

"Very enterprising," he commented. "It's still fifty-fifty. Or we'll just have to keep it around a bit longer and find somebody ourselves."

"That will take time."

"Exactly. That's why it's in our best interest to take advantage of the present opportunity. Fifty-fifty."

Boris appeared to take notice of the conversation now. He looked alarmed.

"Seventy-thirty," Bella persisted.

"Not possible. I have expenses, too."

"You're ruining me."

"Oh, I doubt that. You're quite the wealthy widow now. You must be worth millions in hard currency."

"Everybody always assumes that, but it's not true. Dimitri kept me on a short leash. I need the money! I have a partner. He needs his cut."

"Tell him the bad news then, *dushka*," he said with a laugh. "It's fifty-fifty or it's nothing. You think it over and make the right choice. See you."

"Wait! Don't hang up!"

But he was gone.

Bella snarled as she practically smashed the phone down into its cradle. She felt her skin prickle, as if she wanted to shift. The sensation roiled her innards.

"What did he say?" Boris asked nervously.

Bella gave him a disgusted glare. "He claims someone has the missing object in his possession and wants to return it to the motherland."

"How did that happen?"

"How should I know? The important thing is, this bastard, the one who calls himself Bill, says he can intercept the object before it reaches the Russians. Once he has it, he wants us to go ahead with our little business deal. But he wants his cut. Half the money," Bella said in disgust.

Boris looked genuinely ill. "We need that money. I was counting on it."

"I kept trying to reduce his demands, but he refused to back down. We left it up in the air."

Bella glanced away. She was so sick of the whole disaster right now; she wished she had never thought of trying to sell the holy Virgin of Saratov. Maybe the miracle working went both ways. The Madonna helped the pure of heart who appealed to her for mercy. And maybe she damned thieves who tried to take her away from her rightful place in that chapel where she stayed to help her admirers.

Either way, Bella was feeling pretty well screwed. She even fleetingly toyed with the idea of invoking the powers of her clan's ancient god, Moroz the Dread. But he was so scary and dangerous that she flinched from it. Besides, the most effective way to get his attention and his help was to sacrifice the offspring of a rival clan, and she didn't know of any local werecats with kittens. Rules were rules. Although . . .

Bella roused herself from her despondency and looked at the Hierarch. "We'll go ahead with the plan," she said. "Half a loaf is better than nothing at all."

Boris didn't look pleased, but he kept his thoughts to himself. Sometimes Bella tried to exchange messages with him telepathically, but gave up when she couldn't connect. It didn't surprise her; sometimes she wondered if he had any thoughts at all.

Chapter Forty-five

"Hello. Any word from your partners?" Vivian asked Pavel as he stopped by the shop to confer with his men. They gave him a muted greeting from across the room. Marc saw him and nodded briefly.

"Everything is falling into place. We expect to have the object back in the proper hands very shortly."

"Ah," Viv said with relief. Then she looked up into his beautiful green eyes and asked, "Will it be dangerous?"

Pavel laughed. "No," he said. "Catherine Marais is handling the transfer at a restaurant. The Russians are sending their representatives. After they present their credentials, it ought to take all of three minutes for them to be out the door and away, and probably off to Kennedy Airport for the trip back home."

"This should be a huge coup for the government," Viv said.

"I'm not sure how they'll handle it, but there will certainly be lots of press coverage, with a fair amount of garbage ladled out to readers about how the government worked against all odds to recover it and restore it to the nation."

"Do you think they'll suspect this Frenchwoman of having anything to do with taking it? I wouldn't want her to have any problems because of this. She's doing us a favor."

Pavel reached over and took Viv's hand. "I wouldn't either. Therefore I'm monitoring the entire transaction by video camera as well as positioning my guys all around the perimeter. And a friend of mine who works with one of the government agencies in this country is keeping an eye on it, too. The fact that the object surfaced here interests his group."

"Does Mademoiselle Marais know about them?" Viv asked.

"Yes. It's added protection for her, too."

"Well, I imagine Bella Danilov will have a fit when she opens up a paper and reads that it's back home, safe and sound."

"When the missing Danilovs hop a plane back to St. Petersburg, we'll try to have a group of government types waiting to speak to them," said Pavel. "Bella can make up any lie she wants, but answering questions from the police is going to shake her up. If I know them, they'll find something to pin on her, starting with an investigation into her husband's murder. Bella could probably be charged with any number of crimes, especially regarding the business laws. So could her brother-in-law. If she's controlling him, he's a fool, and he'll most likely be deposed by his clan in the end."

"This is wonderful news," Viv said with a smile. "Of course, with Bella out of the way and the object safely restored to its people, the case will be closed. Then I'll have to turn my full attention to the problem within my own clan."

"I'm already helping with that," he reminded her with a kiss. Clan infighting could be vicious; that was a given. With so many werecats of varying opinions, it might be difficult to convince them their Leader was a criminal. But Pavel would support Viv, even if she were subjected to threats and verbal attacks. He never wanted to leave her.

"I love you, *dushka,*" he said softly, looking at her very carefully. Having Viv in his apartment was one of the best things that had happened to him in years. He wanted to continue.

She looked up at Pavel and said softly, "I like being with you. I like cooking for you, and going to bed with you, and waking up with you. You make me feel as though I've met the other part of me that was missing for so long. I love you, Pavel."

He looked at her tenderly and lowered his face to hers. "Kiss me," he said softly.

Viv gave him a kiss that nearly rocked him back on his feet. One of the bodyguards saw this and smiled. Marc looked gloomy and turned away.

"I love you, too, Viv," he said. "I want you to stay with me. I don't want to lose you."

"When this is wrapped up, we'll have to have a long talk," she said. "There are so many things we should discuss."

"Yes," he agreed. "And we'll have to speak to Marc, as well."

Viv remained silent. She looked down. She had seen Marc's expression when Pavel kissed her.

"That might not go smoothly," she said. "This morning he reminded me of the old restrictions on interclan relationships."

Pavel nodded. "It's not something to be taken lightly," he agreed. "But we can work things out." The set expression on her face worried him. Maybe he had been too optimistic.

Viv nodded and then gave him a quick kiss, which made him very happy. She caressed his face tenderly as he looked into her eyes and caused her heart to skip a beat.

"I can't wait for the moment Catherine Marais hands the object over," he said with a smile. "That will be the start of our future."

For the first time in years, Pavel began to see the promise of a life with a woman he loved. It was long overdue. All those years of mourning were coming to an end. Not that he would ever forget Natalya—never. But he had finally given himself permission to love again, and the joy of that decision reverberated in his soul.

As Viv clung to Pavel, her body throbbed with desire, but uneasily she recalled the Leader's strange behavior. He had made his wishes plain, and even rebuffed, he was quite capable of ruthlessly coming after her to attack her in an unguarded moment. They had to impeach him and restore the clan's rule of law.

Chapter Forty-six

As Marc watched Viv and Pavel exchange kisses, he had to turn away from the sight. Damn it, even though he'd tried to be open-minded, he couldn't bring himself to accept such a flouting of the rules. Their sept respected and admired Viv. She shouldn't do this, especially right now. He decided he had to speak to Pavel.

And he didn't look forward to it.

As Pavel said goodbye to Viv and stepped toward the door, Marc put on his coat and intercepted him, asking if he could talk with him privately. The Russian nodded and almost seemed to expect it.

"I thought we might go out for a drink," Marc said as Viv watched grimly from the other side of the room. She sent daggers at him as she saw him leave with Pavel, obviously guessing what the topic of conversation would be.

"See you later, Viv," he said quietly.

Marc knew Pavel's own clan had its rules about interclan relationships, and Pavel had to understand Marc's worries, but the idea of having to speak to the other man about this delicate matter left Marc feeling awkward. The Russian was a great guy. But he wasn't of their sept.

"Pavel," he said after they had gone to a bar where Marc knew the owner and was allowed to use a private room for his meeting, "I believe in plain speaking, so I'll come straight to the point. I'm worried about what's been happening between you and Viv."

With an icy glance, Pavel turned and gave Marc his full attention. Out of respect for Viv, he forced himself to be polite, even though he felt the American was overstepping the bounds. Both men then shape-shifted into big-cat size and circled each other, wary and alert. Tails were twitching, whiskers bristling. Two irate males the size of panthers prepared for trouble, their growls low and frightening.

"I have the greatest respect for Vivian. She's an amazing female, and I hope to have a long-term relationship with her," Pavel let Marc know for starters.

"You understand the rules. Your clan observes them, too. The whole disaster with Bella Danilov shows what happens when one of our people forgets them."

"Vivian is not Bella," Pavel said, managing to convey a growl even in telepathy.

"Exactly. But the situation with the Leader of our clan might bring down more trouble than Viv deserves. We're going to try to bring him to justice. I don't want the clan saying she's doing it because of a foreign lover."

"She's doing it for your clan," Pavel replied, giving Marc a harsh look. "He's a thief, a lunatic, and a rapist." The growl got louder. "I love her. I want to be with her."

Marc fluffed out his fur, making himself look huge. "I know that. I've told her I would support her in her choice of a mate. But I never imagined she might choose one outside the clan. This is unheard-of," Marc growled. "I love Viv, too. I don't want her to suffer from the effects of a scandal, which *will* happen if you don't back off."

The dark silver Russian moved closer, invading Marc's space. Hisses came his way and he responded in kind. Both animals vied for dominance. "If your Leader threatens Viv or tries to harm her, we'll deal with it together. I'm not afraid of a fight." His green eyes gleamed with animal ferocity. "Vivian is no child. And you're not her father. If she and I wish to pursue a relationship, it is not for you to put obstacles in our path. My intentions are honorable. I will never harm her."

"Our brethren don't approve of these relationships," Marc hissed. "We are what we are, and we should stay that way. I have no quarrel with you. I'm grateful for the help you've given us. But I have to tell you how I feel about this affair with Viv.'"

"All right," Pavel said with growl, "you've told me."

"And?"

"And I will tell you that I have no intention of disappearing from Viv's life. I love her. I want to be with her. And I don't want to be your enemy."

Marc gave a low growl. "Russian," he said, "I would like to be your friend. I have nothing against you. But I can't allow you to harm my sister with this forbidden love."

The big gray cat flexed his muscles, and they rippled like silk beneath his fur. The shaggy red cat matched him and let out a low warning growl. Tensions heightened. Heads lowered. Lips curled back to reveal powerful teeth.

"I've seen some of my brothers ruined by these unions," Marc said. "I won't allow it to happen to her. I admit, I've indulged, but I've always broken those relationships off."

Pavel looked so determined, Marc thought he might even leap at him, but the Russian stayed put, and they both circled each other, sizing each other up for of a fight.

"My intentions are honorable. I don't want you to think that I'm a mindless predator. I can offer her a fine home. All I want is a chance to try to make a life with a mate I love. Isn't happiness a right for all creatures?"

"Yes. But Viv has always been loved and respected by our clan. This may cause them to expel her. I don't know if she could deal with that. She's a descendant of the greatest werecat that ever lived, a blueblood of our race."

"I think you worry that this might make your clan censure you, as well."

"I'm thinking of Viv, not me. I'm a male and can handle anything they throw at me. She's a female," Marc said grimly. "What if it's only her senses that are in an uproar, and she becomes rational once she realizes how her actions are received? And right now members of our clan are looking to her to lead them in the fight against our Leader. Don't take her away from us right now."

To Marc's surprise, Pavel merely growled a few times and then let his anger dissipate. That broke the tension as he took a step back and looked at the other cat, staring at him without flinching, his eyes as fierce as ever.

"I was truly in love only once before," Pavel said telepathically, "and I lost her when she was murdered. I thought it was a sign I shouldn't look for happiness again because I didn't deserve it. Then I met Viv and I felt restored to life. Do you ever think I would ever allow someone to snatch this gift away from me? If anyone tried, I would fight for her."

Pavel's quiet determination rattled Marc, since the shaggy cat had never felt this emotion for any of his past loves. He almost envied the Russian for his depth of feeling. Now he could feel the scent of a powerful male force pouring out of his body, the scent of his willingness to die protecting his chosen female. This was elemental and fierce, the sign of a male who would give no quarter.

Marc knew Viv had a duty to the clan to pass on Krasivaya's DNA, and her life would be complicated enough by fighting to remove the Leader without this extra drama. Marc would stand by Viv if it came to a clash with the clan in a battle over impeachment. But the thought of a complete rupture with the clan over her choice of mate disturbed him. He couldn't bear to see her lose her rightful place in their world.

"I will fight for her," Pavel said again, as he made no effort to hide the growl in his throat. "You must know this."

"Good," Marc replied with a growl of his own. "You may have to."

Chapter Forty-seven

After Marc shape-shifted and returned from his talk with Pavel, Viv was waiting for him. The first thing she did was ask him to step into the office, and when he did, she let him know the full extent of her fury. She was so enraged, she was fighting an urge to shape-shift and go werecat.

"You tried to talk him out of seeing me, didn't you? You have nerve interfering with us. You've fooled around with every female who took your fancy, and I've never once objected to any of your little playmates. Just because Pavel isn't from our clan, you feel you can set the rules now? Well, think again! I love him and I will be his mate, no matter how many voices are raised against us. If I have to defy the entire clan to be happy, I will."

"Viv, this is a step toward self-destruction."

"No, it's a step toward independence. Never has any member of my own clan made me feel so complete. If we have to, Pavel and I will start our own clan, made up of all the werecats who had to flee their own septs to be happy. And don't worry. I'm sure if you make it known how much you disapprove and how disgusted you are, you'll become a martyr to werecat family values."

"That's unfair, Viv. All I want to do is prevent you from making a terrible mistake. You're my sister. Do you think I would ever want to see you unhappy?"

"Right now, I'm not so sure," she replied. Viv glanced around and said angrily, "I've looked all over, and never found a man I've wanted more. Pavel is the one. He's good, he's smart, and he cares for me. It's not a ploy. It's the truth. We would both like to become part of each other's lives."

"Viv," Marc said, "remember your heritage. You're descended from one of the greatest werecats who ever lived, and right now, you're acting like some silly little alley cat."

For an instant, Viv stood absolutely still. Then the corners of her mouth began to turn up in a smile full of irony, and she simply looked at Marc.

"When did they make *you* the Ultimate Arbiter of the werecat code?" she demanded.

Flicking him a disdainful glance, she turned on her heel and sauntered out of the office, leaving Marc scarlet with embarrassment.

Regardless of his romantic problems, Pavel still had work to do. Back at his office, he picked up his cell phone and punched in the number of his friend back in St. Petersburg to check on the investigation there.

"Any word on the boys who were toasting Bella?" he said as someone answered.

"It's going slowly," Yuri replied.

"How so?"

"We've paid visits to two of them. They were somewhat reluctant to offer any news, but we worked on them. Oh, and by the way, they're human."

"Did you manage to persuade them that it's in their best interest to cooperate?"

"Yes, but it took a lot of effort," Yuri said. There was a pause, then what sounded like a sigh. "I doubt they will ever cooperate with anyone again."

Shit. The brethren must have beaten them to a pulp, Pavel thought. He shook his head.

"Well, what about the rest of them?"

"We're pursuing that. I'll send you a report of what we have so far, via our usual method. I think you'll find it unsettling."

"Don't let the brethern act like hooligans," Pavel warned. "If it gets out of control, the reverberations could be dangerous. Stay focused."

"I hear you. I'll send you the report right now." And Pavel heard the sound of the phone shutting off.

Leaning back in his chair, Pavel shut his eyes for a moment. With all the uproar in the Russian Blue clan at the moment, he didn't want the brethren to go on a rampage. It would be too conspicuous. He wanted to avenge their Hierarch as much as anyone, but he wanted to do it carefully, and make sure he had the right criminals. Sloppiness only created more trouble.

When the fax machine finally stopped whirring and spat out the last piece of paper into the tray, Pavel reached for the report and clicked the mouse on his computer to a special software program that was capable of decoding what his St. Petersburg colleague had just sent. He scanned the report, created a file, and then fed it into the program he had produced last year to handle ultrasensitive information.

Yuri began by saying a few of the brethren had gone to the nightclub where the suspected hit men had been partying. They'd started talking with the hit men, bought them drinks, and then kidnapped them, threw them into a van, and took them to a place where they could question them at leisure.

Pavel allowed himself a grim smile. He knew what that involved.

At first, the two fiercely denied they had ever participated in any kind of assassination. They said they had heard about the murder of Dimitri Danilov, but so had everyone who listened to the news. They were innocent. After some of the more intensive methods of interrogation, one of them finally cracked and confessed to being there. He was a drug addict and feeling the affects of withdrawal, but in the opinion of the brethren, he was telling the truth.

Pavel wondered about that. He read on. The second assassin tried to kill his colleague when he heard him begin to talk. Now that could be a sign the druggie was on the level.

Yuri stated that the criminals were questioned about this Bella they had been toasting, and they looked blank. Turns out she was the wife one of them had just divorced, and they were celebrating the divorce as well as the killing.

Damn, thought Pavel. He knew it had been too good to be true. Bella Danilov was too clever to use a bunch of garrulous lowlifes like that. She would have been smart enough to deal through a few layers of middlemen and have the shooters on a plane out of town an hour later. And he doubted she would have used humans. Too unreliable.

Then he suddenly read something that made him stop and read it again.

Before they died, these scum claimed they had met with a tall blond man who used to party in some of the same clubs they frequented. One night, while they were drinking, he complained about having trouble with somebody from work and wondered what it would take to get rid of him. After a few more drinks, they offered to do it for ten thousand dollars each. Four of them. He put together the plan, the idea that they should all dress alike in order to confuse any witnesses, and he kept in touch with them to track the victim's movements that day. While the Hierarch was dining at the Novaya Avrora, the blond man called in the final orders, and they rushed the Hierarch as he left the restaurant.

Pavel read the last line and flung the paper across the room in disgust.

When we showed them a picture of Dimitri Danilov surrounded by his top exectives at a company function this year, they looked hard at the photo and picked out Boris. The bastard contracted the murder of his own brother.

Chapter Forty-eight

"These werecats who grabbed you after they failed to steal the icon are called the Rasputnikatz?" Bella said. "I don't know any Siberian gangs at home who use this name."

Boris shrugged. "Manhattan branch. They found out about the icon and killed the guy who was supposed to get it back. They questioned him very harshly. They're bastards."

"What do they look like?"

"Like gangsters. Black leather jackets. Gold chains. Prison tattoos. You've seen their kind at home."

Bella had trouble remaining calm. She was starting to twitch the way she often did before she shifted. All her hard work was coming undone, her schemes had been derailed, and Boris had managed to involve them with a bunch of gangster werecats who had viciously insinuated themselves into their plot. She cursed their vile luck.

Then, as Bella paced the living room, she noticed that Boris had resumed his old "woe is me" demeanor, wringing his hands as he sat on the sofa, staring at the pattern in the carpet.

"You've caused us no end of trouble," she said bitterly. "All my plans are falling apart."

"Oh, that," he replied.

"Yes, *that*. What else are you moping about?"

Boris raised his light blue eyes and said, "Marina. I can't reach her."

"Boris! What are you trying to do to us? It's too dangerous to get in touch with her."

Bella was struggling with her fury. Suddenly she lost control and shifted, forcing Boris to do the same, both supersizing, the furious Siberian now larger than Boris. He was the size of an African serval to her puma size.

"I just wanted to hear her voice. I wasn't going to give away any information," he said telepathically as he moved away from Bella and her claws.

"Just making the call would give you away if anyone wanted to track you. You can't do this."

"What if she thinks I'm dead?"

"Look," Bella growled, "you've already spoken to her. You told her you were fine. She knows you'll be gone for a little bit. She won't become unhinged if you don't call her, because you've already prepared her. Don't be so possessive!" she hissed, flicking her tail in anger.

Bella moved toward Boris and fluffed up her fur, looking even bigger. He lowered his head and backed away. He could smell the aggression in her. Suddenly, Bella lunged forward and flew at him, rolling over the carpets in a pent-up rage she could no longer suppress. Both cats crashed into the furniture, then leaped to their feet, snarling, eyeing each other with anger, wild and hissing fiercely. Boris tried to hit her while ducking her angry claws. He actually got in a few good shots, making Bella even angrier. He raked her ear two or three times before she forced him down. She didn't expect that from him. To her intense shock, he had managed to hurt her.

"I'm going out," Bella announced as she startled him by shifting again. "I have to get some air. This place is choking me." She stroked her ear. The bastard had really hurt her!

Boris shifted, too, and then gave her plenty of room. He

could see the anger in her eyes, even though he felt pleased she hadn't been able to best him this time.

"Don't try calling Marina," she warned him as she paused at the door. "I'll know."

By way of reply, Boris turned his back on her and walked into the kitchen as Bella put on her coat and slammed her way out the door.

Once outside the apartment, Bella caught a cab and headed for Central Park on a glorious late-fall afternoon. Comfortable in a cashmere coat and used to colder temperatures, Bella strolled with a purpose, searching for something, undaunted by stories of muggers. She was a Siberian Forest cat on a mission; let one of those lowlifes try anything with her, and he'd find out what trouble looked like.

Walking relentlessly, searching for the right spot, the pretty blonde attracted a few admiring glances, but responded to none.

Finally, after serious consideration, Bella found what she was looking for, a secluded area with several birch trees forming a cozy mini grove.

Now all she needed was one more piece of the plan, but that part, the most essential detail, might be tricky if not impossible to locate. However, Bella took a risk and decided to make do with what she had at hand. It was a departure from the time-honored protocol of her clan, but she hoped the desperate circumstances might make it acceptable.

Scouting the area, Bella had located a colony of feral cats nearby. They lolled in the autumn sun, lazy and uninspired, two females with three kittens underfoot. A big male sprawled next to the females, his eyes little slits of contentment while one of the queens groomed him. She had found her prey.

A few other passersby crossed her path and went on their way again, bits of their conversation trailing off as they disappeared from view as Bella contemplated her choice.

Three kittens, but she needed only one. Which would be the right one?

She knew what she was attempting was wrong. These were ordinary cats, not noble werecats. What she intended required a werecat kitten, but too desperate right now to think straight, Bella convinced herself that she could fool an ancient god by substituting this second-rate life-form. She had bamboozled many a human, so maybe her talents as a deceiver would work here, too. Damn it, she felt frantic enough to try.

Chapter Forty-nine

As the little colony looked up at the woman standing over them, one of the females was the first to suspect something odd. She rose slowly on her haunches and began moving away, glancing nervously at the interloper. The other cats, guided by instinct, followed her lead, until all that remained was one calico tabby kitten, staring up into the stalker's eyes and mewing in panic, as if it knew it was in the presence of sheer evil.

"You're the one," Bella said. She reached down, grabbed the kitten as it tried to run to its mother, and shoved it into the depths of her coat pocket, where it promptly released the contents of its bladder in fright.

"Shit!" Bella yelped as she felt the wet spot. The thing had pissed on her six hundred dollar coat! Then as she saw the other cats watching her in alarm, she made shooing sounds at them, took a fake run at them, and saw them scatter in fear. She had what she needed. She was pleased.

Walking back to the stand of birches, Bella carefully created a makeshift altar, forming a circle of stones beneath the trees. She placed a small pile of leaves in the center, looked around with extreme vigilance, saw nobody in the area, and willed herself to shape-shift as the kitten fell from her coat and ended up stunned on the ground.

Like a tiger seizing its prey, Bella, now a splendid, larger-than-life Siberian Forest cat, leaped at the small ball of fluff, fastening her razor-sharp teeth around its neck and flung it back and forth in her grasp while her powerful jaws chomped down again and again, penetrating its neck and jugular, splattering the birch leaves with a stream of warm blood.

It was done.

Assuming the supine position required for the worship of Moroz the Dread, the Siberian cat extended a paw over her victim and silently offered it to the grim master of the forests and tundra, begging for his help. To the fearsome lord of the Siberian werecats, she said that she wanted to finish the job that had brought her to New York, and get back home without any further trouble from the gang that had forced its way into her business. She hoped Moroz found the sacrifice adequate from his wretched and lowly servant, unworthy as she was to address him.

That completed, Bella looked nervously around, shape-shifted once again, and scattered more leaves on the small corpse she had left behind. It was over.

Vivian knew she would be safe as soon as the icon returned to its homeland, ruining the hopes of any thieves who might want to make off with it. Pavel and his team were setting up the final plans for the handing over of the painting, and very shortly there wouldn't be any reason for her to spend the night in his protective custody. The thought distressed her.

Pavel reached out to her, took her hand in his, and kissed it as they sat in his granite and stainless-steel kitchen, with its wonderful view of the city lights. He stroked her cheek with his hand.

"Why so serious? Did Marc give you a lecture, too?" he asked gently.

"Oh, yes. He thinks that it's not right for us to want to be together, that we're practically causing a cosmic collapse if we think about anything more than a fling."

"Hasn't he ever been in love?"

"All the time," she said. "But he thinks I ought to follow the rules."

Pavel gave a shrug. "I don't think he has any right to criticize you. Or me," he added mildly. "Since the Leader of your clan has gone astray, the members ought to concentrate on *his* flaws and keep their noses out of your affairs. Your transgression is mild in comparison."

Viv looked at him and nodded. Then she said, "Back in the early days of our history, wars were numerous and nobody could trust the members of another clan. I could almost understand why they forbade the clans to mate with outsiders. Now it's not the same. We don't always have to be at one another's throats."

"Really?" He lifted an eyebrow and gave her a smile that went straight to her heart.

Viv glanced at him. "Yes. Why? Don't you believe it?"

Pavel looked into her eyes with his beautiful green orbs, and said, "I don't think the clans are as ready for harmony as you seem to think. I love you, Viv, but other Maine Coon cats might want to kill me for it. And Siberians should always be kept at a distance."

"You almost sound as if you might agree with Marc."

Pavel shook his head. "I'm a realist. I've fought humans, werecats, and werewolves in my time. Our sense of 'us' and 'them' seems to interfere with all our plans for building bridges. We find it hard to accept outsiders as our equals."

"Marc is predicting a dire future for me if we choose to start a life together. He thinks I'll be cast out of my clan. But it's *my* future we're talking about here, not his, and this has to be my choice and mine alone." She wrapped her arms around Pavel and kissed his cheek, his nose, his mouth.

"And mine, too. I want to play a part in your life. And I want to make you happy. Whatever your brother thinks of

Russian Blues, we are a loyal breed and good parents. If we make a commitment, we honor it." He kissed her and pulled her close to his chest.

Viv smiled at him. "Then we're both talking about the same thing here. Long-term and serious."

"Oh, yes, on both counts. But," he said quietly, "I think we might have to straighten out your clan's leadership before moving forward with our plans."

Viv looked pensive. "Not 'we,'" she said. "'I.' No outsiders allowed."

"Well," he said as he pulled her close to him, "if your clan ever needs help, just remember you have allies. All you have to do is give the word, and I'll have your back. And if we have to, we'll write a few new rules of our own."

"Thank you," she whispered as she kissed him. "It may come to that."

Chapter Fifty

"Have the Rasputnikatz called?" Bella inquired when she returned to the apartment, took off her damaged coat, and hung it up. Mentally she made a note to find a dry cleaner tomorrow.

"Yes, they did," Boris said. "Bill sounded very pleased with himself. I think he's delusional, and if they go through with this plan, we'll get ourselves killed by the Federal Security Service."

"We're in the United States. They're not going to cause an international incident on American soil. Besides, we have contacts in the FSB who will help us."

"That's a fantasy," he said. "If they find out what we've done, they'll abandon us for fear of being implicated themselves. They won't mind lying and being paid to say we were hiding out from terrorists, but this crosses the line."

"They have no evidence we had anything to do with the theft. If they manage to grab these Rasputnikatz, we'll deny ever knowing them. You're the respected CEO of a mighty profitable enterprise. Who are they going to believe?"

"They'll sell us out in a heartbeat."

"They can say whatever they want. They're just not credible. We're temporarily staying in New York while the FSB investigates the assassination of your brother. That's quite reasonable. So far, the police haven't caught the shooters, and we're living in fear we'll be next. All very normal. And," she said pointedly, "we're not the ones who have the icon, are we?"

At that, Boris seemed to relax a little. "Still, I can't wait to get back home."

"Yes. And when we do, you will meet with your board of directors and present them with your strategy for moving forward."

"They'll be upset that we lost the Siberian contract," he said.

"We'll explain that we had no choice but to disappear after the assassination, for fear we'd be killed by the ones who killed Dimitri. There are murders all the time. Nobody would hang around if he felt in danger right now. It would be stupid."

"Agreed."

Bella paused. Then she turned to Boris and said, "Well, what did Bill want?"

"Oh, he said the officials at the mission were going to finalize plans for picking up the object at a restaurant. It's going to be tomorrow or the day after. They're still fighting over who's going to have the honor of actually handling it and taking it home."

"And the Rasputnikatz think they can thwart the government's efforts?"

Boris gave a shrug. "They claim they have inside help, and they feel their plans are foolproof."

"Well, in forty-eight hours, we'll either hear from them saying they've got the goods, or we'll see them being arrested on the local TV." Then she said thoughtfully, "But if the Rasputnikatz can actually pull it off, our deal will go forward, and we'll have what we want."

"They're crazy," Boris replied. "And they scare me." He could feel the hair on his arms stand up, the human version of fluffing up his fur.

Bella darted him a scornful glance. Boris had few talents

in life other than knowing how to make himself look attractive in his impressive designer wardrobe and take clients out drinking. Eliminate the fine clothing, and he was merely a fool who needed a handler to keep him out of trouble. And give him his orders.

"They're only second-rate gangsters," she said as she opened a pack of cigarettes and lit up. "We're more than a match for them."

Chapter Fifty-one

That night, something odd filtered through the apartment—
a kind of breeze that ruffled the draperies in Bella's room
even though the windows were closed and locked. While she
slumbered under exquisite sheets, with her head on a lace-
trimmed down pillow, a presence began to make itself
known, quietly at first, then louder until perfume bottles
were falling from the dresser and porcelain statues sailed
across the room. A crash signaled that Bella had a visitor.

Terrified, she woke with a gasp and sat up in bed, staring
wildly into the darkness while the noise continued. Now a
stench filled the room, choking her as she jumped out of
bed, wondering what was happening.

"Boris! Come here!"

"He can't hear you, and he can't help you," said an un-
nerving voice. The strange voice seemed close to her ear,
terrorizing her as she staggered in the dark, frantically
searching for the light switch.

Bella cried out in pain as something with teeth grabbed
her by the ankle and nipped her. She screamed as she
crashed against the wall, running her hands all over it as she
tried to find the lights.

More of the toothy things began ripping at her nightgown, and then Bella tripped on the furniture, disoriented by
the darkness and the pain at her feet. She kicked violently as

the teeth sank into her ankles, and when she finally found the switch and turned on the lights, she shrieked as she beheld the sight in her bedroom.

Before her sat a great silver cat the size of a panther, with blazing fiery eyes and ferocious, jagged teeth. The creature surveyed her with an evil expression. Running around the floor at her feet were the ugliest creatures Bella had ever seen—the minions of Moroz—a cross between badgers and weasels with sharp claws and teeth and weird, deep-set red eyes, dark-furred beings that attacked in packs like piranhas. With fangs bared and eyes alight, they watched her.

At the sight of them, Bella screamed and jumped onto the nearest chair, while the creatures leaped at her, trying to bite.

"You know why I'm here," the huge silver cat stated as he glared at her with those fiery eyes.

"No, I don't," Bella replied as she tried frantically to defend herself against one of his minions.

"You called me this afternoon."

Bella stared at him, petrified with fear.

"No," she stammered.

"Yes. Are you so stupid you really don't remember?"

"Lord Moroz! Is it you?"

Despite her fear of those sharp-toothed beasts on the floor, Bella flung herself on the carpet in full submission as Moroz twitched his tail, and they backed off. She prostrated herself before him, shaking with terror, calling on him to forgive her failure to recognize him.

Moroz the Dread sat there, mesmerizing her with his fiery eyes, his expression filled with contempt. His tail twitched with ill-diguised fury.

"Moroz the Dread, lord and master of the forests and tundra, I beg you to forgive me for the annoyance I may have caused you."

"You are pathetic," he said by way of reply. "You have lived a reckless life, abandoning yourself to a frantic pursuit of money and power, trampling on anybody who got in your way, never sparing a thought for your clan."

"Yes, I have done this," Bella whispered, still afraid to raise her face from the floor.

"But you cannot possibly hope to cheat the lord of the forests and tundra by offering him an insulting sacrifice. That is a sin like no other."

Oh, no! Bella thought. *He knew!*

"Oh, yes, he knew. Do you think Moroz is too far away to see the difference between a werecat kitten and an ordinary alley cat?" He flicked his majestic tail, and blinding light flashed around the room, stunning her.

"No," she managed to whisper. Now Bella was so scared she could barely speak. Her throat closed up, and she felt herself hyperventilating with terror.

"Of course he isn't. Moroz saw all of it. He saw your attempt to cheat him and your brazen disrespect for him."

"Oh, no, my lord. There was never any disrespect," she stammered. "Never!"

"You knew this sacrifice was wrong, even as you offered it."

"Please forgive me," she pleaded. "I was so desperate to present you with an offering, and all I could find was a common kitten."

"Nobody has tried to do that in centuries," he said grimly. "They would have been too fearful of my wrath."

"Tell me what I can do to earn your pardon," she pleaded. "I'll do it."

The enormous silver cat just stared at her with contempt. A few of his minions glared at Bella and chilled her with the sound of their growling, and then they began moving so close that she trembled. They gave off a stench that came from the depths of hell itself.

"Please let me make amends," she begged, looking fearfully over her shoulder.

"You can't do anything," he said coldly. "You are a disappointment to me. You are worthless to your clan. All you think of is yourself, never giving any of your brethren a second thought, not even your own wretched family, who desperately need your help."

"Lord Moroz! I have been undone by nerves. Forgive me for that."

He eyed her frostily.

"What can I do to atone for my deception?" she pleaded. "There must be something. . . ."

Moroz the Dread studied her with contempt as he noted her fearful posture, her alarm. Bella tried hard not to tremble, but her scent conveyed her panic. He sensed the terror it betrayed. It oozed out of her pores, adding another note to the odor in the room.

"You are doomed," he said cruelly. "You have insulted me, and you can never make up for that. Your life will be ruined by being linked to Boris until death claims one or the other. He will be your guarantee, and you will be his, bound in mutual disgust but forced to protect the other against your enemies. Inseparable in your wretchedness. Doomed to live and die like castoffs. This is my curse."

Then the great silver master of the forests and the tundra flicked his magnificent tail, and his minions scampered to him. Together in a blinding flash of light, they leaped at her, and she screamed with such terror that Boris finally came stumbling into the corridor to bang on her door and ask if she was all right.

Her heart raced as she sat up in bed and gasped for breath. She screamed and screamed, begging for help as Boris opened the door, looking as if he expected to find an intruder in with her. Bella kept it up as he switched on the light and stared at her. She clutched at the covers, hysterical with fear, eyes wide with terror.

"What's wrong? Was somebody trying to break in? Why are you screaming like that?"

Bella sobbed as she jumped out of bed and threw herself

into his arms, startling Boris into speechlessness. He squirmed uncomfortably.

"Moroz came to visit me," she sobbed. "He cursed me. I'm doomed."

He relaxed. "You were having a nightmare," he said patiently. "That's all it was. There's nobody here."

"You don't understand. He was here. He had his minions with him. They bit me and chased me around the room."

Boris looked at her and through bleary eyes asked, "Where did they bite you? Where are the marks?"

"On my feet and ankles. Look." And she lifted up the hem of her nightgown to show her feet. Bella saw his eyes widen as he beheld the bites and scratches. He froze.

"Maybe you should see a doctor," he stammered, uncertain of what had really happened.

Bella stared at her ankles. She stared at Boris. Suddenly she glanced around the room, afraid to find the vicious creatures who had attacked her. They were gone.

"Go to bed," he insisted. "You had a nightmare and it frightened you. We're both a little bit on edge right now. Get some sleep."

Bella stared wildly around her room. They had been there, and yet there was no trace of anything out of the ordinary. Lord Moroz had come and gone as stealthily as smoke and had placed a curse on her, all because of one mistake. One small transgression.

She felt the weight of her sin as she looked somberly at Boris, the albatross around her neck. Bound to him until death removed one or the other. What a fate.

"Good night," she said abruptly.

Boris nodded as he turned and walked off. "Sleep well."

Chapter Fifty-two

In the elegant Morgan town house the next day, Catherine Marais put down her phone and felt a weight slide off her shoulders. At last the Russians had worked out whatever kinks had prevented them from making the final arrangements for the handing over of the icon. It was on.

She called Pavel immediately. She couldn't keep the delight out of her voice as she announced the good news. "Tomorrow at one thirty. We meet them at the restaurant you suggested. They had no objections. It will be Vladimir and me, and two Russians from the mission."

"Will you recognize them?"

"I doubt it. The only two I've met won't be the chosen ones."

"They'll probably send two agents of the FSB," Pavel said.

"I don't care who they are. As long as we can hand them the package and be on our way, I'm fine. From that point on, it's their job to get the lady back home."

"I'll start on the preparations for the visit. I know the owner. He'll give us access to the place after closing tonight so we can wire it for video. He'll let us know where he'll seat you so we can get a good look at what goes on during the meeting."

"It should take no time at all. The less people know about

what's actually happening, the better. We're going to make it quick and be out of there before anybody knows we're gone."

"Good. I'll call Vladimir and give him his instructions."

"Which are?"

Pavel grinned and said, "Keep his eye on you at all times, and don't let the Russians near you once you hand over the object."

"You're not very trusting, are you?"

"I'm alive because of that habit," he said with a smile in his voice. "But truthfully, I don't think they'll pose a problem for you. You're giving them the thing that the whole country wants returned, and they'll probably get a service citation for carrying it back."

"I can't wait for it to be over," Catherine said with a sigh. "This has kept me in New York longer than I planned, and my partner is e-mailing me to catch the next plane and hurry up to Canada."

"Ah, you're hunting again."

"Yes. Another one of those creatures is on a rampage, creating problems in Halifax. They're trying to keep it quiet, because, well, you know how people get when they hear the word 'werewolf.' Sheer hysteria."

"Who called you in?"

She laughed. "The local government."

"Really?"

"Yes. It's all very hush-hush. I mean, they can't say they're hiring us, but they realize they need more expertise than they have up there, so we got the call. They contacted the *Institut Scientifique,* and we said we'd come take a look. Paul's been there by himself, but he's getting impatient. I can't wait to join him."

"After tomorrow you'll be on your way north then," Pavel said.

"I've already bought my ticket," Catherine replied.

Chapter Fifty-three

The phone rang, and Boris looked at it with grim loathing. Bella flicked him an impatient look. "What's the matter? Answer it."

Reluctantly he did, and the expression on his face reflected his visceral distaste. It was Bill of the Rasputnikatz.

"What's going on?" Boris asked, worried about the answer.

"We have to have a talk. Not on the phone. It could be bugged."

"Okay. Where?"

"Be outside the apartment in ten minutes and you'll see a black BMW waiting. They'll flash the lights. You get in. Okay?"

"Got it."

"Don't make us wait. We don't like that." And then Boris heard a click.

"I have to meet them," he said nervously. "This might not be a good idea. I don't know where they plan on taking me, and I don't trust them after last time."

"Like it or not, we're partners now," Bella snapped. "So go to the meeting and find out what they want. It may be important. And they need you, so they won't harm you," she said firmly. "At least not yet."

With that happy thought in mind, Boris Danilov stood

outside the apartment building in the late-autumn chill ten minutes later, wearing a black cashmere coat and scarf, and wondering if Bill's gang would be punctual. To prepare for the meeting, he'd had a few shots of vodka, but it hadn't helped. He felt himself shaking slightly and couldn't tell whether it was from the cold or from fear. A late-night chat with these guys wasn't what anybody would welcome. They were unevolved werecats, very low-class, not his normal kinds of associates.

Just when Boris hoped Bill had changed his mind, he saw a black BMW pull up to the curb and flash its lights. They were there to collect him.

Dragging his heels, Boris walked over to the car, opened the door, and got in the passenger seat. Bill was at the wheel with two unknowns in the backseat.

"Put on your seat belt. It's the law here."

Boris almost burst out laughing. This was the gang that was going to heist the Virgin of Saratov under the noses of the Russians, and they were lecturing him on *seat belts.*

"If we get stopped and the cops see you're not buckled up, we get a ticket and we get ID'd. We'd rather not take the chance."

"Okay," Boris said. "I understand. Now where are we going?"

"You'll find out when we get there," Bill replied with his usual disdain. "Relax and enjoy the trip."

Even if Boris had been stone-cold sober, he wouldn't have been able to keep track of their route. There were so many twists, turns, and bridge crossings, that he figured Bill must have spent his youth watching spy movies. Nobody could have figured out where the hell they were going in the dark. Boris fell asleep for a while, and then he awakened to the movement of the car slowing down as it entered a garage. A door rattled closed after them and Bill ordered him to get out. He found himself in a small garage, most likely attached to a private home.

"Follow me," the leader ordered, and he took out a key and unlocked a door to a hallway that led to a staircase.

The group went upstairs and Boris realized they were in an ordinary house. It was nothing fancy, not the kind of place that might belong to a crime lord, so he figured it was the home of an underling.

"Sit down," Bill ordered after Boris had removed his coat and scarf. "We have a lot to talk about."

Boris didn't share that opinion, but he couldn't say so. He sat at the kitchen table and faced Bill, who looked quite serious, not a comforting sight. He was a big guy with scars and a short fuse. It was hard to believe he was a werecat; he looked more like a pit bull.

"Tomorrow's the big day." When Boris didn't react, Bill shot him a look of pure annoyance. "Can't you guess? What the hell do you think you're here for?"

Boris was about to reply he didn't have a clue, but he caught himself. That might sound flippant, and Bill could react viciously. "Something to do with the object we're interested in?" he offered, hoping he was right.

"Bingo! The man has a brain after all." Bill glanced around at his henchmen, and they all laughed at the joke.

"You're really going to try to take it away from the Russians, who will have their secret service officers on the case."

Bill grinned with genuine amusement. "Right again."

Now Boris was glad he had made his will. If these maniacs got him killed, Marina and the kids would have an inheritance to live on, and his children would go on to make successful lives for themselves. He didn't want to dwell on the fun that Marina would have pissing away millions on drugs, booze, and boyfriends.

"You look worried," Bill observed.

"Oh, I was just thinking of how those guys will probably

kill anybody who tries to take the icon from them. They're
trained for that kind of thing."

Boris couldn't understand why the Rasputnikatz were
grinning and chortling as if they were in on the biggest joke
in the world and he was the only one in the room who didn't
know the punch line. His sharp nose was overwhelmed by
the scent of contentment seeping from their pores. He knew
his own scent was reflecting something quite different.

Finally Bill got up and clapped him on the back. "Let's
drink to our success," he said.

"Sure."

One of the gang handed him a bottle of vodka and a couple of glasses. He set them down on the table and poured
Boris a drink. "To success tomorrow."

Boris waited till Bill had a glass in his hand, too, and
joined him in knocking back the vodka. "To tomorrow."

Then Bill sat down again and leaned slightly forward, as
if he were about to share a secret. Boris did the same, wondering if Bill was going to reveal this suicidal and ridiculous
plan. Crazy as it was, it would have one virtue: all the
Rasputnikatz would undoubtedly be mowed down by the
Russians as they attempted to snatch the icon. With any
luck, he and Bella could flee once these insane werecats
were out of the picture and then claim to know nothing
about any icon.

"You know," Bill said as he gave Boris an amused glance,
"I have the feeling you don't quite understand what we have
in mind."

"Well, you didn't actually tell me any of the details, only
that you were going to snatch the icon from the Russians
who were going to pick it up." Boris tried not to look as nervous as he felt.

"You worry too much. For one thing there won't be any
contact with the guys who are assigned to get the icon."

Now Boris was truly startled. "But how will you steal it
then?"

"Brains," Bill said with a grin. "We're going to beat them to the rendezvous, flash our IDs, say, 'Thank you for returning our icon to the motherland,' and be out of there in three minutes. By the time the real diplomats show up, we'll be on our way out of Manhattan. Once we have the icon under wraps, that uppity bitch will set up the meeting with her client and we'll make money."

Boris knew that his expression must have reflected his utter shock because the Rasputnikatz were all laughing and poking one another in the ribs.

"Okay," he said. "But why did you bring me all the way over here to tell me? I don't understand."

Bill grinned and poured him another shot of vodka. "Because I'm saving the best part for last."

Now Boris noticed the gangsters were really knocking themselves out, roaring with laughter as if he was the funniest thing they'd ever seen. He didn't get it. He looked much better than they did.

Bill leaned forward and said cheerfully, "You and my second-in-command are going to go into that restaurant and pick up the goods. Nobody knows you here. We'll even give you a disguise. But you're in on this just as much as we are, and this is our guarantee you won't betray us. Agreed?"

By way of reply, Boris rose to his feet, took one step away from the table, and collapsed. He was doomed.

Chapter Fifty-four

Waiting for a phone call from Boris, or for some indication that he was still alive, Bella paced the living room and kept glancing at the clock. He had left hours ago and still hadn't returned. She hadn't a clue as to what was going on, and that made her anxious, since she needed Boris at her side when she returned to Russia to carry out her plans for Danilov Enterprises.

Bella hated uncertainty. Ever since the day Dimitri had died, she had been fearful of the unknown. She needed to feel in control; she had to dominate the scene. When chance made this impossible, Bella's nervous system went on a kind of panic alert: her imagination ran wild and her breathing became shallow. Right now she stood in front of the mirror, frantically studying her pale face, convinced she was about to faint or have a heart attack. She felt so unstable she nearly shape-shifted against her will. Nerves again.

She poured herself a glass of wine. Rummaging in her handbag, she found her tranquilizers and swallowed one with some cool white wine. She had to calm down. She had been through worse than Boris's disappearance. It was just that she didn't trust him, and she hated to have him out of her sight for long. When he was left to his own devices and surrounded by these rapacious Rasputnikatz, there was no telling what idiocy he might commit. He might try to work out a separate deal with them and kick her aside.

Hierarch of the Russian Blues! Hah! He was merely a front man who needed a puppeteer to pull his strings. Now that Dimitri was gone, Boris would need *her,* even if he didn't realize it. Shit, Moroz was right. They did need each other: Boris to know what to do, and Bella to have a finger in the pie.

Why did Dimitri have to die? And why did fate spare her at that terrible moment if not to propel her even higher? She had a destiny. She was born to rise to the top and to see others pushed aside to make way for her. Perhaps that was the reason for Dimitri's death.

Bella sighed. She missed him. It was such a trial, shepherding his inept brother.

Boris was a classic case of a "dutifully resentful personality," a mentor had once told her. He feared to make overt moves against those above him, but he was treacherous and sneaky. He would bide his time, slithering along like a snake, always keeping his head down until it was time to strike. Was Boris hatching some kind of plot with those Rasputnikatz? If he was, he'd better rethink that alliance because Bella wouldn't become anyone's scapegoat. Not for those creatures.

Pavel and Vivian were curled up on the sofa in his apartment, listening to the music of a jazz ensemble and kissing slowly and languidly, as if they had all the time in the world. She caressed him tenderly as she snuggled against his chest.

"Tomorrow's the big day," Viv murmured as Pavel kissed his way down her neck, nuzzling her like a contented panther. They were in human form, but the urge to shape-shift was strong. Viv's pheromones were on "sex-receptive" right now.

"By this time tomorrow night, the icon will be in the

hands of the Russians and probably on her way back to Moscow."

"Will you accompany her?"

"I haven't been asked to, although I'd say yes if I was. Right now, I'm operating behind the scenes, and perhaps that's where I ought to stay."

"Have you lost your devotion to the Madonna of Saratov?" Viv asked in surprise.

"No. When I see the welcome reception on TV, I'll have the pleasure of knowing I helped make it happen. She belongs to the nation again."

"That's a nice thought. I'm so glad we discovered the icon before the thieves did. Evil creatures should never get their hands on a sacred treasure."

Pavel kissed her softly on the lips. "I agree," he said. "But I'll relax only after Catherine Marais and Vladimir hand her over to the Russians tomorrow afternoon. At that point we'll be able to say we've done our job. Mission accomplished."

Viv sighed and cuddled against him, happy to feel those strong muscles wrapped around her, her own guardian angel. No man she had ever met had made her feel the way she felt with him. Not only was Pavel handsome and very smart, but he had a charm about him that practically made her purr.

Even with the hostility from Marc, he hadn't gone ballistic or made an ugly scene or insulted him. He simply listened and decided to do what he wanted. Viv liked that. He could wipe the floor with just about anybody who came at him, but he preferred to use his brains. In a world that seemed to wallow in violence and provocation, she found it a welcome relief to be lying in the arms of a very strong man who spoke softly and meant what he said. Of all the werecats she knew, only Pavel was that disciplined.

"You're not expecting any glitches, are you?" she asked.

"No. Catherine and Vladimir will be under constant surveillance, and the restaurant will be carefully guarded. All the Russians have to do is show up, produce their IDs, and pick up the icon. All our people have to do is hand it over and leave. Very straightforward and uncomplicated."

Viv nodded. Then she smiled seductively and purred in his ear, "Oh, *koshka*, let's not think about that tonight. Let's concentrate on the two of us."

Pavel had no problem with that idea. He took Viv in his arms and kissed her as she slid beneath him and slipped her hands beneath his shirt.

"Let's make love like savage predators who rule the jungle and challenge their enemies to defy them," she whispered as she nipped his ear.

"Where does this wild streak come from *dushka*? You always seem like such a lady," he said as he slipped off her blouse and her bra. "You take my breath away."

Viv took his face in her hands and smiled as they kissed. "And I'm only just beginning."

She let him kiss her ear, her neck, her throat, and send a delicious trail of warm kisses down her breasts. Viv sighed as he caressed her and slipped his hand under her skirt and into the waist of her silky pants. Her stomach contracted as he explored the region to the south and then gently probed the moist lips.

"Oh," she whispered as she felt a quiver. "Oh, Pavel!" Her head went back as she felt a shock that made her hips buck. "Don't stop. Oh, keep going." Viv wrapped herself tightly against him and kissed him passionately as he kept up his probing, making her breath come in ragged spurts. Then he kissed her again and paused to undress as Viv tried to help him out of his clothing as fast as she could.

"Hurry up," she said, wanting him in her arms right now. "I want to make love all night."

Pavel smiled at her with those fascinating amber eyes. He thought that was the best idea he'd heard in a long time. He wouldn't disappoint.

Chapter Fifty-five

"Is it safe to stay here until it's time to go to the restaurant?" Boris looked at the Rasputnikatz and then at the clock. Ten in the morning. He had the look of a corpse. They had forced him into an incriminating role, and now he felt as if his life was over. They would never pull this off.

"Yeah. Nobody will bother us. We've got everything we need: diplomatic license plates, ID badges, good suits, driver. We're good to go."

"My hair looks fake," Boris complained. "I won't fool anybody with this wig."

Bill flicked him an unsympathetic glance. "Do you want me to call the girl back? She's downstairs having coffee."

"Yes. Maybe she can make it look more natural. It looks all wrong, and it will draw attention. You don't want that, do you?"

Bill called downstairs and a cranky young blonde with a tight T-shirt and big boobs came plodding up to see what he wanted. Bill pointed at Boris's hair. She gave him a bored look and said, "What?"

"It doesn't look right," Boris said. "It looks fake."

She placed hands on hips and glared at him. "I'm a professional makeup artist. I've worked on everybody. You hair looks fine."

"No, it doesn't."

"Who the hell are you to tell me how to do my job?"

"Well I'm your client, and I'm telling you it looks like crap."

Boris found the whole experience surrealistic. Here he was, the Hierarch of the Russian Blue werecats, arguing with one of Bill's girlfriends about the wig she had given him. He shouldn't be here. He should be thousands of miles away, back in his own home, back in his office, surrounded by people who treated him with respect and deference. Dealing with these overseas werecats must be punishment for all his recent sins, he thought. They were so overwhelmingly low-class.

The blonde walked around him and took another look. She made a little pout and went to get her bag of brushes and combs. Boris looked at Bill and nodded as if to say, "See. She finally realizes she made a mess."

When she returned, she pulled off his wig, placed it on a fake head, and got busy with brushes and gel. Then she took out a can of blond spray and applied a couple of streaks. When she plopped the wig back on his head, Boris had to admit it looked better. A little too trendy, but better. He wondered if any diplomat in the world walked around looking like this. He doubted it.

"Oh, we got this for you, too," Bill said, with a nod to the girl. He handed her a small package that appeared to contain some dead hairy thing. When she ripped open the wrapping, Boris wondered what on earth it was and where it was supposed to go.

"He doesn't look the type for a mustache," she said. She eyed the thing as if it might bite her.

"Glue it on him. We want him disguised."

While Boris protested, the makeup artist, a female gang member named Donna, got out some sticky substance, smeared it over his upper lip, and smacked the hairy thing down on top of it.

"It makes him look silly," Donna said with a smirk.

"Then trim it a little," Bill ordered.

Boris could have wept with humiliation. All his life, he had been admired for his sense of style. He had been recently listed in the "best dressed" section of a St. Petersburg men's magazine. These two had just reduced him to clown status.

Bill surveyed the new work and gave a nod of approval. The Hierarch looked like a middle-aged man who was desperately trying to hang on to his youth with fake highlights and a macho mustache.

"Okay," said Bill. "Now run through the routine."

Boris darted him a look.

"Tell me what you do at the restaurant," Bill prompted.

"Valery and I go in, ask the headwaiter for Mademoiselle Marais, get shown to the table, show her our IDs, and ask for the bag. She hands it over. We leave. The car is waiting outside to take us back to you."

"Right."

"And why won't the real diplomats be there?" Boris inquired.

"Because my guys will have a little fender bender with their big car, and while you're taking charge of the icon, they'll be standing in the middle of the street screaming at my men, demanding to see a policeman and making a scene. It'll set them back about ten or fifteen minutes, enough time for us to be in and out before they ever show up."

Boris asked for a shot of vodka. Bill produced a bottle and a glass. "You shouldn't drink so early in the day. You'll rot your liver if you make it a habit."

Boris ignored that remark. "Can I go back to my apartment after we get the icon?" he asked. Boris wasn't at all convinced he'd survive the day, but he felt he had to inquire.

"Sure. But we keep the icon until Bella calls her clients and sets up the appointment. We all go to the meeting, and we split the money on the spot."

"Fine."

Bill grinned and cheerfully slapped him on the back. "Don't look so down in the mouth. It will all work out."

Boris nodded. "Yes," he said. "Of course." And he gulped down a second shot of vodka with a look so grim it startled the makeup girl.

She gave Bill a significant glance. "Nerves," she said with a shrug.

Several hours later, Boris felt oddly calm as he watched the urban landscape whiz by the car windows. A few stiff drinks had helped him achieve this state, but more than that, he had simply accepted his fate as punishment for his sins and was prepared to pay the price. He had reached the end of his rope. In an hour he would most likely be dead and unmourned by everyone except his children. If he was lucky, Marina would shed a few tears for the man who had loved her to distraction. Bella would simply be annoyed that he had managed to cause her more trouble.

The idea of Bella facing a snag in her plans actually gave Boris a shred of comfort. If he died as a result of this moronic scheme, it would mean that Bella would be unable to carry out her intentions of selling the icon and making millions. Instead, she would be grilled by the police in two countries, and she'd have to spend a fortune on legal fees.

Chapter Fifty-six

"We'll give you a signal when they arrive," Pavel said.

Catherine and Vladimir nodded and saw the headwaiter walk to the front of the house. Everybody felt prepared for action. From upstairs at his station, Pavel sent her a message on her microphone, just checking to see if all was well. Carmeras outside monitored the entrance, and his men were positioned front and back.

"You're coming in fine. Can you hear me all right?"

"Perfect," he said. "And I have you on the monitor."

In the crowded restaurant, diners were discussing business deals, many of them executives who worked in the neighboring offices. Out-of-town clients enjoyed the elegant ambience. The owner surveyed the scene, keeping an eye on things, with an occasional glance toward Catherine and Vladimir.

"Are you nervous?" Catherine asked her new partner. She thought he seemed grim.

"A little. Nobody looks forward to an interview with the FSB. They're just the KGB in new packaging."

"Well, they're not going to be here very long. Hang on. You're doing well."

Vladimir smiled, but he didn't look convinced.

As Catherine glanced toward the door, she saw the owner give the prearranged signal.

Two fairly tall men—one with highlighted brown hair and a mustache and one with blond hair—entered, paused to say something to the headwaiter, looked inside the room, and followed him across the crowded dining room straight to Catherine's table.

"Showtime," she murmured to Vladimir and Pavel. "Here they come."

"Mademoiselle," the headwaiter said politely as they arrived, "your guests."

Catherine smiled but didn't extend her hand, a precaution Pavel had suggested. She thought that reeked of paranoia, but since he was Russian and she wasn't, she decided to go along with him. Vladimir extended a cordial greeting in English.

"You have something to show us," Catherine prompted the Russian who appeared to be in charge. She saw him look flustered and then nod as he reached into his breast pocket and took out an ID from the Russian mission to the UN, identifying him as Ruslan Dvorsky. The other Russian nervously responded in kind, reached in and fished out his ID. Roman Vladimirov.

"So," Ruslan said, looking eagerly at Catherine, "do you have what you said you have?"

"Yes." And she reached underneath the table and pulled out a rectangular package neatly done up in bubble wrap and nestled inside a tote bag bearing the logo of a New York boutique. "Part of the wrap is loose so you can look inside to verify the contents," she said.

He did. The second man looked. They nodded almost in unison and then rose to say goodbye.

"On behalf of Orthodox believers everywhere, we thank you," he said. That done, both men turned and made their exit, vanishing out the front door and onto the sidewalk, where a car with diplomatic license plates waited. Mission accomplished.

"We saw it and heard it," said a voice close to her ear. That was Pavel on the microphone. "It's a wrap."

"May we leave?" Vladimir asked.

"Yes. Let's go home."

They had only gone three blocks when Catherine received a frantic call from her contact at the Russian mission. "Our men were involved in an accident en route to the meeting. Stay where you are. They will arrive, but later than planned."

When Catherine heard that, she had all she could do not to scream. "Too late," she replied. "Someone already took delivery at the restaurant. Ruslan Dvorsky and Roman Vladimirov arrived to pick it up." She gritted her teeth as she listened to the sound of a gasp on the other end. She could predict what he was going to say.

"We have nobody by those names at the mission. What did they look like?"

"Tall. One was blond. The other one had brown hair with highlights and a mustache."

A stream of indecipherable Russian curse words poured out like a torrent. "You have given our national treasure away to a couple of confidence men," he screamed.

Then the line went dead, and Catherine felt as if some leaden substance had entered her soul. "We've been had," she said to Vladimir. "I've just handed the Virgin of Saratov over to unknown parties. The Russians have no idea who those men are."

She thought he might crash the car, he seemed so stunned. "I have to call Pavel," she said. "He recorded the whole thing. At least we have the men on video."

"But *they* have the icon."

Catherine cursed herself for the whole sorry mess. She ought to have seen it coming. She felt a bitter taste in her throat when she entered Ian's town house and climbed the stairs to the salon. As soon as she sat down, she took out her cell phone and punched in Pavel's number. She got him on the first ring.

"Federov here."

"Can you get over here as soon as possible and bring your equipment? We have a disaster of biblical proportions on our hands."

"What are you talking about? What's happened?"

"Those two Russians were fakes. I just handed the package over to two con artists. The Russians from the mission called to tell me their men would be delayed."

"Are you at Mr. Morgan's house?"

"Yes."

"Stay there. I'll be over as fast as I can."

Chapter Fifty-seven

Before Pavel headed to the meeting at Ian's town house, he placed a call to a werecat friend in an ultrasecret American government agency dealing with international trafficking. This theft required an immediate and forceful response. If they didn't capture the icon right now, they might never get a second chance. Pavel would never forgive himself if the Virgin of Saratov disappeared with a bunch of crooks.

"You had that painting in your hands and you bungled the repatriation? Pavel, what's the world coming to?" his friend Tony marveled. "I thought you gave master classes on this stuff."

"I can do without the sarcasm. I need your help. I have the whole transaction down on tape. You can see the two Russians at the restaurant. Maybe they're in your system because of an earlier theft."

"Okay. I have to tell you, you'll have the Russians from the UN on your back over this. They'll think you engineered the whole thing and you've got the goods stashed in your bedroom. These people are very paranoid."

"I know that. This why I'm reporting the theft to you, and I want your help. The two people who met the fake officials had no idea they weren't dealing with the men who were supposed to receive the painting. We acted in good faith."

Pavel sensed a pause. Then Tony said, "If those guys

showed up with official ID and diplomatic plates on the car, that has to mean they had help."

"But who could have known about the exchange? It was a top-level secret."

"Secret until they had to go through the mechanics of setting it up. Staff had to know. That's what I'm going to suggest to the Russians when I meet with them. Time for them to put the screws on the staff."

"I'm going to talk to the two people who handed over the painting. I'll try to find out if they noticed anything odd about the two ringers."

"Okay," Tony said. "I'll get in contact with the Russians and suggest a joint effort to locate the goods, starting with an investigation of whoever had anything to do with it. Since it's such a big deal, they may cooperate. Their president won't be happy if they fail."

"Let me know what you find out," said Pavel.

"Okay. Now you take a real good look at that video and tell me what you come up with. I'd like to nail these guys, too. Okay?"

"I'll talk to my people and review the video. We'll start today."

As the big black car with diplomatic plates pulled away from the restaurant, the two "envoys" who had just leaped into the backseat exhaled and sank into the soft comfort of leather seats. They had done it, grabbed the icon without so much as laying a hand on anyone. Nice and easy.

Valery immediately took out his cell phone and punched in his boss's number. "It's with me," he said. "Everybody's fine."

"Good," came the reply. "Now drive to your second stop and get into the car they're holding for you."

"Okay. See you in a few."

Boris failed to share Valery's euphoria. While grateful they hadn't been arrested, he still feared retribution over the theft, and he didn't put any faith in Bill's promise that he could go once the icon was in the hands of the gang.

Pulling into a body shop in Brooklyn, the two thieves and their driver got out and turned the car and its plates over to the owner. The stolen vehicle would be cannibalized for parts, and the plates would be melted down and disposed of by this afternoon.

On the way back to wherever their trip had originated, Valery held on to the packaged icon as if it were his baby. He was nervous to let go of it, because the leader of the pack had scared him before he left by threatening to cut off his balls if the painting arrived damaged.

Boris sank down into the backseat as far as he could and wished he were home with Marina and the children and far from all these lowlifes, including Bella. That greedy, vicious, treacherous bitch cat had ruined all the lives she touched. The worse thing was that he couldn't see a way to get rid of her; they were accomplices in this, stuck with each other. What a partnership from hell.

The thought of seeing Marina again brought the only glimmer of hope. Even though he might be forced to include Bella in his plans for governing as Hierarch—if the Russian Blues didn't impeach or depose him—Marina would be his refuge and his sanctuary. Even Bella couldn't take that away from him.

Who was he kidding? His whole life was crap. All of it. Deep down Boris knew he had the moral sense of an earthworm, the brains of a gnat, and the luck of an albatross. He wondered uneasily if the Virgin of Saratov could forgive a miserable werecat who had kidnapped her and committed even greater sins.

To Boris's great relief, the Rasputnikatz released him a block away from his apartment after a stop at Bill's place, where he had peeled off the mustache and wig, returned the dark suit they had given him for the caper, and resigned himself to a high-pitched grilling from Bella. Boris felt so exhausted, he barely cared. All he wanted to do was sleep. Or get so drunk he put himself in a coma. His werecat nature stirred in him. He wished to escape, but sadly he had no place to go, except back to Bella. He couldn't even manage a growl.

"Where the hell were you?" Bella exclaimed as she ran to the door when she heard a key in the lock. "I thought they might have killed you."

"I'm fine. I just want to sleep."

Bella wasn't about to give up. "What did you do while you were with them?"

"Nothing. Don't bother me. Just let me go to sleep."

Worriedly she looked into his bloodshot eyes. "Did they give you drugs?"

"No. Just vodka. I'm fine. But right now I need some rest. We can talk later."

"What about the thing?" she demanded, afraid to name it even in her apartment, out of fear of detection.

"Our friends have it. They'll call you." And he walked off into his bedroom, wishing he could sleep for a week.

Bella stared after him, amazed. "They have it?" she repeated. "You mean . . ." She could scarcely believe it. "How?"

"I picked it up at a restaurant," he said. "Happy? I did what you wanted. Now get the hell out of my way."

And with that, Boris slammed the door in her face, too exhausted for further discussion.

Chapter Fifty-eight

Before heading for his meeting with Catherine and Vladimir, Pavel made a quick call to his office and spoke with the man on duty the previous night who was responsible for keeping tabs on Bella and Boris. Anything suspicious?

"She was in all night. He left the apartment around nine and got into a car with some unknowns. One of our guys tried to follow him, but the driver took such a crazy route, we lost him. We don't know where he is right now."

"Did you happen to get the tag number on the car?"

"Yeah. We wrote it down."

"And?"

"Belongs to some woman from Queens. No rap sheet on her."

"Maybe Boris has a girlfriend here," Pavel speculated. "All right. Keep watching them. Let me know if anything strange happens."

"Boss? We have a problem."

"Yes?"

"We lost the audio feed into the apartment. Maybe it came loose. We'll need to reconnect it."

"We'll use Margot for that. Bella's let her in to clean the apartment before. She doesn't suspect her."

"Okay."

Shit, Pavel thought. *What was Boris doing last night?*

Given his reputation, he was probably tomcatting around Manhattan. But right now, Pavel wanted all his time accounted for. According to the criminals captured in St. Petersburg by Pavel's associates, Boris had arranged for his brother's murder. He was more dangerous than he appeared.

This corrupt Hierarch already had blood on his hands, so what would prevent him from committing a robbery half the country would consider sacrilegious? He had no shame; neither did Bella. It made for a frightening combination.

Vladimir looked so despondent when he opened the door that Pavel felt sorry he had involved his cousin in the affair. He should have used one of his own men. It would have been smarter. Now poor Vladimir, one of the most loyal men Pavel knew, would never cease to reproach himself for letting down the Saratov Madonna.

Catherine Marais looked as if she wanted to kill someone. Usually so composed, Catherine seethed with fury at being duped.

"Did you bring the video?" she asked as Pavel entered the room.

"Yes. It's all here. We can take a look at them from start to finish."

"The Russians know what happened. Lubov called me to warn me his men had been delayed—about five minutes after those two fakes walked off with the icon. I had to tell him we'd handed it over. I thought he'd have a coronary."

"Did you speak with them after they calmed down?"

"Yes. He called back later and explained what had happened to his emissaries. Somebody hit their car at an intersection, and they spent half an hour in a shouting match before the cops came and took down the information. By the time a squad car showed up, the man who caused the accident had escaped on foot, leaving behind a stolen car and no ID. At that point, they figured it was a setup, and they called Lubov."

"The thieves had it all planned," Pavel said in disgust as he looked at Catherine. "This means somebody at the UN mission had a hand in it. They've got a traitor in their midst."

"They know that, too," said Vladimir. "And right now you can imagine the grilling they're putting their staff through."

Pavel had memories of special police agents interrogating captured guerrillas in the war. Very grim.

"Do you think they'll be able to root out the scorpion in their bosom?" Pavel asked.

"Depends on how much pain he can take," Vladimir replied with a cold smile.

"All right," Catherine said. "Let's look at the video."

First came the shot of the two Russians getting out of the car. Next they entered the restaurant, spoke with the head-waiter, and walked to the table where Catherine and Vladimir awaited them. They introduced themselves, produced their identification, and took possession of the package. In the last shot, they made their way out of the crowded room, exited the restaurant, got into their waiting car, and drove off.

"Vladimir, do you think they were really Russian? Could they have been Chechens, Georgians, Ukrainians, anything?"

"Russians," he replied. "They spoke English, but I can tell a Russian when I see one. And one guy wore a hairpiece."

Catherine nodded. "Oh, yes. Not bad, but still not good enough to fool anyone."

"What about the mustache?" Pavel asked.

"I don't know," Vladimir said. "That may have been real."

"And his partner? Was that his own hair, do you think?"

"Yes," they answered in unison.

"All right, then let's take another look at these two. Try to remember if they had anything odd about them—besides the hair."

They watched the video so many times it made them bleary-eyed. Darkness began to fall.

"Mademoiselle, I have to go downstairs to assist Mr. Morgan," Vladimir said softly as he rose to leave the room.

"Yes, of course." She looked upset at the thought of having to tell her lover that they had just had a major disaster.

"I've been in contact with a friend of mine who works for the government," Pavel said. "He's interested in recovering the icon. We'll work together."

"Russian or American?" she asked.

"American. But of course the Russians want it back just as much, if not more."

"Both countries will be after it. If we're lucky, they'll be able to take it back. Meanwhile, it's out there someplace in the five boroughs, in the company of scum."

"If it's still in New York, that would be the best thing for all of us," Pavel said. "If they manage to ship it out of the area, it's gone for good."

"Do you think your friend will have alerted the border crossings and the airports?"

"Yes. That would be his first move. When I leave, I'm going to e-mail the video to him so he can take a look at it and analyze it to see if he can find a match to somebody already in his file. I'll do the same with the Russians."

Catherine had never looked so disgusted. "We'll get them," she said. "And when we do, I'll make sure I'm available to testify at their trial, no matter where I am or what I'm working on. Now it's personal."

Chapter Fifty-nine

Pavel decided it was time to start preying on Boris's weaknesses: his love for Marina and his hatred for Bella. The moment had come to call in the services of their covert photographer in Nice, who had been charged with filming Marina at play.

"What are you doing at the laptop?" Viv asked as Pavel sat there with a look of intense concentration on his face.

"Sending a message to a friend. I'd like him to send us the videos he took of Boris's wife. The Hierarch is crazy about her and incredibly jealous. And Marina isn't above flirting and more. With her partying in the south of France, I'm hoping he took wonderful footage of Marina in some compromising positions."

"Footage that will, of course, be forwarded to her husband."

"Naturally."

Viv grinned. "That's pretty underhanded," she said with admiration. "I love the way technology lends itself to such a worthy cause." She put her arms around Pavel and leaned against his back as he sat at the computer. She gave his cheek a soft little nuzzle as she glanced down at the screen. Her pheromones sent a seductive message to his senses.

"We believe he killed his brother," Pavel said. He enjoyed

the caress and kissed her hand. "We're planning on making him frantic over his whorish wife."

"Boris killed his brother?" She looked shocked. "No. He's too soft. I'd put my money on Bella."

"Our sources in St. Petersburg have tracked down the shooters. They claim he hired them."

"They could be lying."

"Maybe," said Pavel, "but they picked him out of a photo of Danilov personnel and said he had hired them specifically to assassinate Dimitri. Claimed to be an angry coworker."

"Could they be wrong?"

"Of course. But if they were, why would they all out pick the same man from a group photo?"

"You know how people are. You give them something to look at, and if one of them says, 'This is the one,' then a lot of the others will agree."

"In separate rooms at the same time?" Pavel asked. "There was no chance of discussion here."

"Incredible," said Viv with a shake of her head. "What's the motive? A takeover?"

"Who knows? He was in Dimitri's shadow all his life. Maybe he got a case of ambition late in his career and decided to take a risk."

Viv looked shocked. "Are you going to the police with this?"

"Not until we get the icon back. Nobody's going to grab Boris until we do. Some of our guys back home have the shooters under wraps. When the time comes, they'll notify the police. Or decide to take care of it in-house."

"Aren't you worried they might escape?"

Viv was taken aback when she saw the flicker of a smile on Pavel's face. "Not where we have them," he said as he looked her in the eye.

*   *   *

Bella heard a knock on the door of her condo and looked perplexed. She wasn't expecting company. "Get the door, will you? I don't know who it is. I didn't invite anybody."

Bella gestured toward Boris as if he were her lackey. He gave a disgusted look, but he complied, although her tendency to let her human side take over really irritated him. She was a damn diva.

When he unbolted several locks, he opened it and seemed startled. It was Margot, the cleaning lady, standing there beside a trolley loaded with mops, dusters, polish, sponges, and cleaners.

"Hello," she said with a smile. "It's that time again." Margot gave them both a cheerful look and said apologetically, "One of my other customers is away, so I thought I might move you up. If it's a problem, I'll come back on the regular day."

Bella flicked a glance over the living room with its untidy piles of magazines and a few of Boris's bottles, and said, "Fine. The place is a mess. Men are such pigs. It needs a cleaning."

And Margot closed the door behind her and got to work.

About an hour later, Boris sat at his laptop, engrossed in surfing the Web, scanning for stories about Danilov Enterprises, Dimitri, himself, or any progress in the murder investigation. So far, so good. Nothing but unsuccessful inquiries into the assassination. No suspects, no motive, except for the usual business ones. The group who had been negotiating for oil rights with the Danilovs had ended talks, citing their agreement. Fine.

Their contacts in the FSB were doing their job, claiming the investigation was ongoing and they couldn't comment. They dropped hints of terrorist activity behind the assassination and added enough bureaucratic jargon to make it sound serious. To Russian readers familiar with the pattern, it meant the Danilovs were in so tight with the government that nobody was going to find out the truth until it was convenient.

Boris was grateful he was as yet unknown in New York. He still shook with fright whenever he remembered how his knees had trembled as he and that idiot had walked into the restaurant and taken home the icon. How he had managed not to faint at the table was a miracle.

The woman waiting for him was European, but when he realized her companion was a werecat, he nearly threw up, fearing discovery. His sensitive nose recognized the scent, and he panicked at the thought that he might be Russian. It didn't mean he would recognize Boris, especially under that wig and mustache, but it had been enough to rattle him. For some reason, Boris hadn't expected a werecat. Maybe another European or more likely an American. That would have made him feel better.

He couldn't wait to hand over this bad-luck icon to the client Bella had found, hop on a plane, and go home. Yet every step of the way, he had encountered another roadblock. Bella had brought him nothing but misfortune.

He hated this Siberian bitch cat, who had ruined his life, turned him into a thief, and separated him from his wife. He hated her enough to wish her dead. To his shame, he also knew he would never have the guts to get rid of her, either, because he was in too deep.

As he gloomily checked his e-mail, he suddenly found he had a message from Marina. With a delighted cry, he clicked a few times and brought it up.

Chapter Sixty

Pavel picked up his cell phone and heard Tony's voice, his werecat contact in federal law enforcement. Right now, it seemed harsher than usual.

"This Boris must be a real asshole to get mixed up with this crowd. The leader is a lunatic."

"Who are we talking about?"

"Some gang of raggedy-ass morons from Russia who call themselves the Rasputnikatz. They claim to be descended from an illegitimate son of Rasputin."

Pavel frowned. "I seriously doubt he was a werecat."

"Their usual area of expertise is theft, but on a much smaller scale. They send women out as shoplifters. They boost truckloads of small appliances. They steal whatever isn't nailed down—with a few minor sidelines, like dealing dope and smuggling contraband cigarettes. This recent caper is a whole new enterprise for them."

"How did you manage to dig up so much information in such a sort time?"

"I had my guys trace the license plates of the car they used to pick up Boris the night before they stole the icon. Some girl who sleeps with the leader of the pack owns it. She says he asked to borrow her car, and she let him. She claims he told her he was having car trouble, and she doesn't know anything about any icons."

"Of course."

"So we threatened her with aiding and abetting criminals in an international theft of national treasures, and after we revived her, she said she'd give up anybody we wanted as long as she didn't have to do time."

"She isn't afraid of this guy?"

"She is, but she's much more worried about being in jail for a few decades. Besides, we promised that if she rats out her sweetheart, *he'll* be so old when he gets out of prison, he won't even remember he had a girlfriend."

"Good work. So are you going to round them up and bring them in?"

"Hell, no! We're going to let them make plans with their comrades from St. Petersburg to unload the icon. Bella made the original contacts, and we still don't know who the buyer is, so we have to play along and let them handle it. We'll grab them all the night they make the sale."

"Good." Pavel paused. "Have you been in contact with the authorities in St. Petersburg?"

"Not yet. We want to be able to hand them a rock-solid case so they can prosecute these two. We have an interest in somebody they have. We can do a deal here. Everybody wins."

"Understood."

"I'm keeping tabs on their apartment," Pavel added.

"Under the aegis of this agency with regard to homeland-security issues," Tony informed him. "We operate under the radar. Top secret clearance. We stay out of the news. I'm deputizing you as a special field assistant."

Pavel nodded. "Good," he said.

One way or another, Bella and Boris were going down.

As soon as Boris spotted the e-mail from Marina, he clicked on it, expecting to see pictures of her posing with the children in one of the opulent rooms of their St. Petersburg apartment. Instead, he was stunned to find himself opening a video showing Marina and some unidentified men frolicking in a fountain in some tropical land. His wife wasn't wearing much more than a sopping-wet T-shirt, and she was laughing uproariously at her own inability to get out of the water. To his horror, she was acting like a drunken slut.

There were more videos. In one, Marina stood on the deck of some yacht while a scenic landscape of palm trees and flowers filled the background. Next to her, an elderly degenerate playfully removed the top of her bikini while she laughed and laughed, flashing her cosmetically enhanced boobs at the camera.

Boris tuned red with anger at the memory of the bill from the plastic surgeon. Those things had cost him a fortune. And there she was flaunting them in front of strangers. Who were these fucking morons?

Only a feeling a sheer nausea prevented Boris from viewing the whole collection. What he had just seen filled him with such disgust, he wanted to kill somebody. Here he was, in hiding, abused by thugs, at the beck and call of that bitch cat while his adored wife—who should have been taking care of the children back home—was cavorting at a beach resort. He was so angry, he replayed the videos, searching the background for signs that might give a clue as to her whereabouts.

As Boris scanned the screen, he saw the French tricolor waving in the breeze. The slut was kicking up her heels on the fucking French Riviera while he was languishing in Manhattan, risking his life and liberty for Bella's stupid schemes.

This filled him with such righteous anger, Boris did something unusual. He got up and kicked the nearest object he could find, which happened to be a wastepaper basket. It sailed across the room, crashed into a cabinet, and rolled noisily into the corner, where it lay on its side. He kicked it two or three more times, just to vent his fury and hear the unholy racket it made as it hit the furniture, the walls, the tables. His skin prickled, coaxing him with the desire to go werecat. His scent turned dark and musky.

"What the hell is going on here?" Bella ran into the room, nervously darting her eyes around. "What's all that noise?"

"Nothing," he replied, sitting down once more, feeling pleased he had scared her.

"What do you mean nothing? I heard enough noise to wake the dead. What's wrong with you?"

He looked at Bella as if he barely knew her. "Nothing that a few drinks and a new wife wouldn't cure," he said.

Now she looked really bewildered. Then she glanced at the computer screen and saw the video of Marina in a pool, half naked.

"Shit! Where is she, and who is she with? I don't recognize any of those people."

"Me neither. But then, I'm just the poor, stupid husband who lives to get screwed by devious little whores who waste his money."

Even Bella, as selfish as she was, appeared to hear the bitterness in his voice. She glanced at him, not knowing what to say.

"Don't think too much about it," she said finally. "You need to focus right now."

"No! *You* need to focus. I'm as focused as I'm ever going to be. And when I get home, I'm going to be done with all of you," he shouted. "I'm taking my children and going away. We'll go live in England. Or Switzerland. I'll never let her get her dirty hands on them. I'll save the videos and use them as evidence at the divorce trial."

He was still ranting when Bella shrugged and vanished from the room, saying something about him having to work out his problems by himself.

Chapter Sixty-one

That night, Viv and her lover were entwined on the sofa, looking out over the city at night, its millions of lights spread out beneath the window in a breathtaking panorama. Pavel kissed her and Viv nestled against him in delight.

"I always feel safe with you," she said with a sigh. "You make me feel nothing bad will happen to me as long as I'm near you."

"Glad to hear that. Of course, I'd prefer to hear that you shiver with lust when you see me and that you can't wait to hold me in your arms and make love like a wildcat. But 'safe' is very flattering."

She burst out laughing as she slid under him and put her arms around him, caressing him beneath his shirt, nipping playfully at his ear as he drew her into his embrace.

"I don't care what Marc says," Pavel said. "We're meant to be together. And I'm not going to let you get away."

"Promise."

Pavel kissed her gently on the tip of her nose. "I promise. Come hell or high water, it's going to be you and me. Anybody who has a problem with that doesn't have to stay around and watch."

"Make love to me," she said as she threw her arms around him. "Make love as if tonight was the last night on earth and you and I had to make it last forever."

Pavel smiled. He picked Viv up and carried her into the bedroom, where they quickly undressed and dived under the covers.

As Viv ran her fingers through his hair, Pavel kissed his way down her neck. He took her hands in his as she lay stretched on the bed beneath him and held her possessively while he lowered his mouth to her breast and slowly, gently sucked the hard pink nipple.

The sensation raced from her breast to her groin as Viv gave a little cry and quivered as he did the same to her other breast.

"So sensitive," he murmured. "So delicate."

"Oh, *koshka*," she whispered. "Don't stop."

He smiled and then kissed her again on the mouth, exploring her with his tongue, tangling with hers, pleasing her and exciting her at the same time. "Viv, I want you so much."

"I'm yours. There's nobody else I want," she whispered as she opened her long legs and wrapped them around him.

Without missing a beat, Pavel raised himself over her and then pressed into her, entering her quickly, in a steady cadence of love and lust. They tried to outdo themselves, both of them covered with sweat as they mated again and again, obsessed with giving and getting a climax of such intensity that they could feel their hearts pounding in their ears, threatening to burst from their feverish lovemaking.

When Pavel gave a cry of total release and collapsed completely spent in her arms, sated and incapable of moving a muscle, Viv clung to him in passionate possession.

They belonged to each other; nobody was ever going to separate them in *this* lifetime.

In the monitoring command post at Metro Investigations, the man on duty felt his attention drawn to the screen showing the living room at Bella's condo. This view was courtesy of Margot, the cleaning lady, who had also hooked up the audio feed. Right now things were heating up. It looked as if Bella and Boris were about to kill each other.

"What the hell are you doing?" Bella asked. "Where do you think you're going with those suitcases?"

"To the airport. I'm going back to St. Petersburg tonight."

Bella reacted as if he had hit her. "That's insane! What do you plan on doing there?"

"I'm going to file for divorce and take my children out of the country."

"Stop this. You're upset over those pictures, and you don't know what you're doing. All we need is maybe another day, and we can conclude our business and go home. Don't break down now."

"You can conclude any business you want. I don't give a damn what you do any more."

Bella looked frantically around, as if to summon up some argument that might pacify him.

"Are you drunk?" she demanded.

"No. For once I'm absolutely sober."

"Well, I don't think there's a flight to St. Petersburg until tomorrow," she said.

"You're wrong. I just checked on the Internet."

Bella threw herself in his way, blocking his path to the door. "Stop it!" she shouted, savagely pushing him out of the way. " I'm not going to let you fuck this up and spoil my plans. Millions of dollars are riding on it!"

"Fuck the millions of dollars, and fuck you, too, you bitch! I'm sick of being your stooge. I'm going home to the only people who love me. And I'm taking them so far away from you and from Danilov Enterprises that nobody will ever find me again."

As Boris took hold of her arm and threw Bella against the wall, she grabbed an umbrella from the porcelain stand near the door and whaled away at him, screaming abuse as he tried to defend himself.

With a shout of rage, Boris turned into a werecat the size

of an African serval. He sprung at Bella and knocked her to the ground. She shifted into a cat the size of a puma and responded by grabbing him by the scruff of the neck and flinging him against the marble floor, nearly braining him. She let him have it three or four times until he was out cold. Then she vented her rage by circling him, hissing and spitting with fury as he lay there before her. Incensed, she leaped at him and batted him furiously with her paws, her anger consuming her now.

Staggering a little from her effort, Bella shifted once more, gasping from the effort of the fight. Then, reeling across the living room, she sank down onto a sofa and reached for her cell phone.

Her face contorted with stress, Bella punched in a number and said breathlessly, "Get over here and help me. I've just knocked out the Hierarch and prevented him from leaving the country. But he's going to wake up, and when he does, he'll be hard to control."

Someone on the other end must have said something to pacify her, because the man in the monitoring station saw Bella nod her head emphatically, shut off the phone, and go into the next room to get belts and sashes to use as a makeshift restraint until reinforcements could arrive.

Chapter Sixty-two

"Boss, I'm on the monitor here, and I just saw one hell of a fight between the Danilovs. They went werecat, and now she's shifted back and tying him up with belts. I think one of her helpers is on his way over."

Pavel smiled as he heard the message. Confrontations between suspects were always a good thing. With werecats, they were always so close to the edge, it made fights inevitable.

"Keep watching. Call me if things heat up again."

"Right."

Viv cuddled close to Pavel as she draped an arm around him and nuzzled his ear. "Trouble?"

"No. Good news. The Danilovs were just beating each other up. He lost."

For a moment, she went silent, and then she began to rock with laughter. "*She* beat up your Hierarch? Are you serious?"

"That's what my man said, and he watched it on our monitor. They shifted and went at it."

"She's either a lot tougher than I thought, or your Hierarch is very weak."

"Exactly."

"You Russian Blues need a new one."

"Oh, he won't be holding the title much longer, not after we charge him with murder—and theft of state treasures."

"Any contenders among the Russian Blues back home?"

Pavel smiled at her and pillowed his head on her bosom. "You know how things are in any organization. One falls, another rises. I imagine we'll have many claimants for the job. Even as we speak, I can predict that at least four or five ambitious werecats are scheming to replace Boris."

"Are overseas werecats eligible?"

Pavel glanced at Viv and nestled closer to her.

"I haven't checked the rules lately, but the Hierarch has always been chosen from members who live in Russia."

"Too bad. I think you would be a great Hierarch."

At that, Pavel burst out laughing and then gave Viv a passionate kiss. "You American girls have such odd ideas," he said. "They wouldn't consider me."

"Why not?"

"I've lived overseas for several years, and I'm going to announce my engagement to an American of a different clan. If that's all right with you," he said as he looked tenderly into her eyes.

Viv climbed on top of Pavel, kissing him all over and caressing him with abandon.

"I'm all for it," she said between kisses as she turned her attention to very tender parts.

He yelped. "Do that again. Oh, yes. More."

"I'm not really a traditionalist," Viv said as she slid her fingers around his organ and heard him utter a muffled sound of either pleasure or alarm. "We don't have to make a stop at Tiffany."

"Whatever you like is fine with me," he said in a smothered voice, closing his eyes in anticipation.

"Good."

Viv caressed him sweetly and then bent her head to his chest and left a trail of hot kisses all the way down to his belly. She laughed with delight as she saw his stomach muscles contract and felt a sudden growth somewhere else.

"*Malenkaya*, you're torturing me," he pleaded. "Put me out of my misery."

She smiled and proceeded to do just that.

"What took you so long?" Bella demanded as Bill and his driver showed up and she buzzed them into the apartment.

"Traffic. Where is he?"

Bella jerked her chin in the direction of the next room, and the two thugs in black leather jackets went in to investigate. There on the floor lay the Hierarch of the Russian Blues, in human form, securely tied up.

"What the hell are you trying to do?" Bill demanded by way of greeting. "You know you can't go home right now. Not until our business is done."

"I'm through with everything," Boris said, moving and twisting desperately.

"No, you're not. We still need you."

"I went into the restaurant and got you the icon. That's enough. I did my part."

"You did a good job so far, Hierarch. Now stay strong. Don't break down."

Boris writhed in fury. "I just want to go home!"

"You can't go home until everything is done. You and Bella have to return together and let your FSB contacts hold a press conference to claim you were in a safe location overseas while they pursued terrorists who were attempting to attack Danilov Enterprises and the state. Then there will be a news blackout for state security reasons and the matter gets dropped. We go on with our lives. Danilov Enterprises continues to flourish under your leadership." He glanced at Bella as he said this.

"Fuck the company. I just want to go home and see my children," Boris replied.

"You will. But not right now," Bill said patiently. "Certain things have to happen."

"He's hung up about his wife," Bella explained. "The bitch sent him some provocative videos from where she's vacationing, and they pushed him over the edge. She's flashing her tits at everyone on the Riviera, and he's upset."

"What a great wife," Bill said. "If she were mine, I'd beat her black-and-blue when she got home. Why doesn't he just do that?"

"He loves her," Bella replied dismissively.

Boris continued to twist and struggle with his restraints as his captors looked away, trying to decide how best to handle him. Bill gave a scornful glance at the distressed Hierarch and bragged, "Rasputnikatz kick ass. You should try acting like us for a change. You'd be a better Hierarch for your clan."

Boris had settled down a little. He appeared calmer and his breathing had become normal. The others took that as a sign he was returning to his senses. Bella even bent down and said, "I see you're becoming more rational. Good. Just focus on our goal and you'll get through this."

Boris looked up at her and nodded. Then as Bella relaxed, he shape-shifted, burst out of the restraints, and made a surprise grab for her arm, knocking her off balance and throwing her to the floor. Frantically he headed for the closed door, trying to crash it open with his weight, but the door stayed in place. He butted it furiously, taking out his frustration on the unyielding wood.

Immediately Bella and the Rasputnikatz shifted and went after him. Bill was shocked by the bulk Bella achieved when she supersized; at puma size, she looked like a shaggy mammoth compared to her brother-in-law. Boris was far less impressive at serval size. Even Bill was bigger, with his shaggy Siberian coat. Without it, he and Boris would have been fairly well matched.

"You're not leaving," Bella growled telepathically as she

seized the skin around Boris's neck and flung him toward the Rasputnikatz. They grabbed him with quick paws and sent him sprawling over the polished floor. Boris clawed at his opponents and tried to bite Bella, who responded with a nasty swat, raking his face with her own sharp claws. She gave him a couple of good bites, too, hissing furiously as she did.

Hisses, growls, and the smell of anger filled the air, and Bill's subordinate shifted into human form once again and took a small package from the pocket of his jacket. As Bill and Bella fought to restrain their prey, sinking teeth into haunches and limbs, producing feline screams that reverberated on the walls of the marble foyer, the driver unwrapped a tranquilizing dart, approached the combatants, and at the first opportunity, shoved it into Boris's unprotected flank. Then he did it two more times.

The other two cats kept a grip on their prey as Boris slowly lost his will to fight and relaxed his muscles, even as they held him in their jaws. When his head wobbled to the side and his eyes closed, they released him and backed off, rising to their feet and surveying their quarry.

Shape-shifting, Bella and Bill struggled to catch their breath. For spite, Bella took aim at the drugged Hierarch and kicked him viciously in the side.

"Don't hurt him any more than you have to," Bill said, as he pulled her away. "You don't want him to have to go see a doctor who will ask embarrassing questions. Keep the punishment psychological. "

"Get him out of here," she said. "Do you have a place to keep him until we need him to go to the meeting with the client? He has to be implicated in this, too. It's the best way to keep him under my thumb."

"In my basement," Bill said.

"He has to be restrained. Otherwise he'll try to run."

"Steel cage. Strong enough to hold a five-hundred-pound

tiger. The Hierarch won't be that big in his wildest fantasy. I can't belive the Russian Blues picked such a runt."

"He acquired the position by default. They might unseat him, but he'll still be CEO of Danilov Enterprises—which is why he's still useful. I need him cooperative and living in fear of blackmail."

Bill nodded. "All right," he said. "Semyon and I will wrap him in a rug, take him down on the elevator, and load him into my minivan."

"You drive a minivan?"

"It was the first car in the driveway," Bill said. "But lucky for us it was there. Easier to transport him."

"What if he wakes while you're driving?"

"Then I trank him again. Believe me, Semyon just gave him enough to put him to sleep until tomorrow afternoon. It won't be a problem."

"Take him straight to that cage," Bella ordered.

"Of course. Do you think I want to take chances? Now we need you to call downstairs to the concierge and let him know two men are going to be crossing the lobby with an Oriental rug that needs repairs. Can he open the door for us?"

"Why do you need me to do that?"

Bill looked at her with his heavy-lidded eyes. "Because otherwise he might think we've just stolen it, and he might call the cops."

"All right." Bella made the call. Then she directed Semyon to Boris's room, where a suitable carpet lay, and watched Bill and his driver roll the unconscious werecat inside it.

"Give me something to tie it with," Bill directed.

Bella produced some nylon cord, which did the trick. Then with the Hierarch bundled neatly inside the Persian carpet, she opened the door and watched the two men carry him down the hall and into the elevator.

"Keep him safe," she said. Then she went back inside and

poured herself a good stiff drink. Just as soon as she returned to Russia, she was going to find a trustworthy Siberian hit man, give him the address of these Manhattan thugs, and tell him to eliminate them. She would use blackmail as leverage over Boris, but she wanted nobody to be able to get that kind of hold over *her*.

Chapter Sixty-three

Pavel had his favorite fed on the phone just as soon as his monitor called in the news. "Bella's helper is taking Boris back to his place. Can your men track them? One of my guys put a device on the car while the Rasputnikatz were inside Bella's condo. They're ready to hit the road."

"Okay. We'll trail them and find out where the Siberians are taking him. We had to put the girl we picked up in a safe house until this is over. She's been spilling her guts in hopes of cutting a deal. No loyalty at all."

"Good. We'll keep monitoring the widow Danilov. You can have your guys keep tabs on the others. Bella's the one who will get the call from the person who wants the goods, so we won't let up on her. Audio, video, the works."

"Okay. Hope we can do the takedown soon."

"Then you'll alert the Russians?"

"Yes. And we can make a deal with them."

Viv and Marc had their disagreements over Pavel, but at work all went as smoothly as usual. Neither wanted to air their family problems before the customers, and frankly, neither one wanted to prolong the unpleasantness that arose after bitter words concerning Viv's choice of mate.

She knew Marc wasn't happy; he knew Viv would never change her mind. They left it at that and concentrated on business. With the icon in the hands of the crooks, Pavel had removed the bodyguards, since the Roussels weren't likely to be threatened by anyone now. Life was nearly normal.

The night after Pavel's man had seen the fight between Boris and Bella, Viv said goodbye to her brother and headed for the subway to catch the train to Pavel's apartment. Wrapping her muffler tighter to keep out the November chill, Viv walked briskly to the subway entrance, descended the dirty stairs along with a wave of others, caught a train, and arrived at her stop in good time. With her heightened senses reeling from the odor of fuel, stale air, and the occasional puddle of urine on the floors, Viv never noticed or caught the scent of two men hurrying along behind her. They were about five paces in back of her as she walked quickly up the stairs.

After a stop at a grocery store, Viv continued on her way, and as she reached a construction site, two pairs of hands shot out in the darkness and grabbed her, pulling her behind the tall wooden fence that hid them from view. Before she had a chance to fight back, Viv was overpowered, drugged with a chloroform-soaked handkerchief, and carried into the backseat of an SUV with dark windows waiting just inside the fence. Her attackers settled her in, threw a comforter over her for concealment, then pushed open the gate to the site and drove off as quickly as they could, merging into the early-evening traffic.

"Is she all right?" the passenger asked nervously as the driver headed toward New Jersey. "I mean, this is Viv. She's important to the clan. She's practically royalty."

"And it was the Leader who gave the order to bring her in without a struggle. She'll be fine. She'll just have a headache when she wakes up."

"What's going on with him? I've started hearing rumors. . . ."

The driver nodded grimly. "People like to speculate," he said. "What you have to remember is—he's still the Leader. And we're in the Special Squad, so we take his orders."

"But," the man said as he glanced back at Viv's drugged form, "this just isn't right, and I don't like being part of it."

"I didn't hear that," the driver said as he entered the lane of traffic that would take him out of Manhattan's busy traffic and onto the Henry Hudson Parkway and across the bridge to New Jersey. "You're loyal, I'm loyal, and that's what counts. I can't believe he intends to harm Viv. She's too important."

"Then why have her knocked out?" he persisted.

"Let's just concentrate on getting her to New Jersey safely," the driver said. He didn't sound as though he really had an answer.

As Marc was closing up for the night, he suddenly remembered something he'd wanted to ask Viv about the Fabergé picture frames they'd just gotten in from Moscow. He thought she'd put the pieces on display, but he couldn't locate them. Maybe she could tell him where they were before tomorrow. A customer was coming in to see them first thing in the morning.

He punched in her cell phone number and was surprised when his call went straight to voice mail. Maybe she was in the subway and there was no signal. He snapped the phone shut and put it inside his pocket. He'd try again later.

After Marc closed the shop and went home, he decided Viv had had enough time to reach Pavel's apartment, so he called again. He was directed to leave a message.

As he prepared dinner, he felt vaguely uneasy. Viv normally had her phone on unless she was in a situation where she would be requested to shut it off, but since she was only going to Pavel's, it should be turned on. And there was no response to either of his messages.

Don't jump to conclusions, he told himself. There was probably nothing wrong. Their lives were back on track now, the thieves who wanted the icon had it, and nobody would have any interest in them.

As children, Marc and Viv had shared the ability to communicate telepathically in werecat form. Occasionally it carried over into human form. Right now he was trying as hard as he could to make her call him back, and getting no results.

He didn't want to call Pavel's number. He disliked the whole idea of that relationship, and didn't want to call there as if it was perfectly acceptable that his sister, who ranked high in her own clan, was living with him.

At around eight thirty, Marc heard his phone ring, quickly answered it, and was startled to hear Pavel's voice.

"Marc, I got in late and thought I'd find Viv here. Was she detained at work? I can't reach her on her cell phone."

When Viv woke up, she had a violent headache, a sense of disorientation, and no idea where she was. Opening her eyes, she looked around the area and determined she was lying on an elaborately carved bed in a room decorated in spectacular country house traditional, the kind of decor you would find in the more expensive magazines: lots of lush fabrics, with luxurious window treatments and fancy fringe on everything. It was beautiful. But who owned it and how had she arrived here? The last thing she remembered was exiting the subway and walking past that construction site.

Viv tried to sit up, but couldn't quite manage on the first attempt. She forced herself to try again, and after a struggle, she got herself to a seated position, then perched on the side of the bed, wondering if she had enough strength to put her feet on the floor and walk.

Making an effort, she stood on shaky legs and went to the mirror, studying her reflection, trying to determine if she had been injured. Nothing seemed amiss. No cuts or bruises. She was fully dressed in the skirt and sweater she had worn when she'd left the shop, and her clothing hadn't been torn. The only strange thing was her eyes. The pupils were so dilated they looked huge.

She had been drugged and kidnapped.

Frightened now, Viv staggered to the door and tried to open it, but found it locked. She flung open a closet door and saw her coat and handbag inside, but upon opening the bag, she realized her cell phone was missing. She checked her coat pockets. Nothing.

Quickly, she went to the window and peered out into the darkness, trying to get her bearings, hoping she might recognize something, some landmark, anything to give her an idea where she was. The entire area seemed dark, except for lights that illuminated an elegantly landscaped lawn, with a big semicircular driveway and a fence at a distance from the house. A lone figure stood outside in the cold, keeping watch.

As soon as she saw the driveway and the fence, she felt the bottom drop out of her stomach. This mansion belonged to John Sinclair, Leader of the Maine Coon cat clan, her rejected suitor.

Chapter Sixty-four

As soon as Marc and Pavel realized Viv was missing, they joined forces to try to locate her. She could be anywhere. Pavel called some of his men and had them take Viv's subway route. Marc tried to think what she had said a few hours before she left. Something about going shopping for dinner. One of Pavel's men checked all the grocery stores on the way between the subway exit and Pavel's apartment. One grocer remembered a tall lady who matched Viv's description.

"She got as far as that store, at least," said Marc. "Something happened between there and your place."

"I've got the Hummer outside. Let's go check that area. I've got Ivan monitoring incoming calls and signals from tracking devices. If she still has her pendant, she can call us on that. Meanwhile, keep calling her number."

In John Sinclair's mansion, Viv was beginning to regain her equilibrium. She had already tried to open the windows and found them securely locked. She ransacked the room, hunting for anything she could use as a weapon, and discovered her nail file in her bag in the closet. Small, but made of steel, it might be her only hope right now. She placed it in the pocket of her skirt.

Just as she began to hope she might still discover a way

out of the room, she heard footsteps outside the door and it opened, revealing Sinclair and the two members of his Special Squad who had kidnapped her.

"Viv, how are you recovering? I hope you're all right."

"I've been better," she said with fury in her eyes. "And I'd like to leave."

"I'm sorry. Not possible at the moment. First we have to settle some things. For the good of the clan."

"That would be best served by releasing me."

"I'm sorry," Sinclair replied. "Please come downstairs with me. I'd like to speak to you in my office. I have some papers I'd like you to sign."

That didn't sound good, but it would at least give her a chance to move around, she thought. Besides, after her recent experiences with Sinclair, she didn't want a private conference in this bedroom. Too dangerous, especially in her weakened state.

Viv gave his companions a frosty stare. "How did I get here?" she demanded. "The last thing I recall was walking from the subway. It doesn't go all the way to New Jersey."

"I'm sorry, Viv," one of the men said, looking embarrassed. "The Leader wanted to see you and—"

"They did what I asked," Sinclair interrupted. "Now please come with me."

Viv looked at him with contempt and said, "If you expect me to change my mind about marriage, I'll give you the answer right here. Pavel Federov is my mate. And that won't change—except for the actual wedding ceremony." She looked sternly at his aides, Joseph and Matthew, and said, "I invoked my right to choose my mate and he tried to overrule me. You know the rules of our clan just as I do. What he wants it illegal. He's been on a rampage, raping the females of our clan. Two of them contacted me to tell me. And, Matthew, if you think I'm lying, call up Sarah and ask her what he did to *her*."

The Leader turned red with anger and reached for Viv as

they descended the staircase. As he did, she brought back
her elbow and gave him a vicious jab in the stomach. That
broke his grip on her, and she picked up speed and raced
down the stairs and toward the door, adrenaline flowing in
her veins.

Locked. In desperation, Viv struggled with the lock and
couldn't open it. She looked back at the men. Instead of running after her, Matthew was demanding to know what the
Leader had done to his wife, and his expression was furious.
Joseph attempted to prevent both men from coming to
blows. Rebellion had begun.

Running down the corridor, Viv searched desperately for
a telephone, and locating one, she frantically punched in
Pavel's number. By this time, the Leader had reached the
foyer, still arguing with his subordinates, and shouting for
them to get Viv. She heard Pavel's voice, started to tell him
where she was, and before she could say more than "I've
been kidnapped," John Sinclair broke away from Matthew's
grip and grabbed the phone from her hands. In a rage, he
smashed it down into its cradle, and ripped the cord out of
the wall, his eyes glittering with fury.

"Look at him!" Viv shouted. "He's insane. He wants to
force me into a marriage, and he wants to handpick the females for a harem. Matthew, I know you're a good man. If
you don't believe me, call Sarah and ask her. Don't be afraid
of him."

"Don't listen to her," Sinclair shouted. "Your loyalty is to
me!"

"Never in the history of our clan has any leader attempted
to subvert our rules and harm our members. Think about it."

Caught between their oath to the Leader and their respect
for Viv, the men hesitated.

"You have a choice," she said. "Either you can listen to a
corrupt tyrant, or you can call Sarah and ask for verification
of what I've said. How long will it take for her to get here?"

Matthew looked down at the floor for a moment as if he

were trying to derive some help from the intricate parquet pattern, and he finally said, "Joseph, I think we should listen to Viv. It won't take long. And then we'll know the truth."

"Thank you," said Viv as she looked the men in the eye. Sinclair looked ready to kill.

"Marc, I lost her! Damn it." Pavel pressed a few buttons and Ivan was on the phone. "Viv just got a call through but it was cut off. Here's the number. Find the address. Now!"

Marc and Pavel sat in the vehicle while Metro's best hacker did his magic halfway across town. In minutes Pavel's phone rang again. "Unlisted New Jersey number," Ivan reported. "But we managed to locate it." And he gave them the owner's name and address.

"Shit! I never thought he'd do something like this. We've got to get Viv out of there. I think he's gone crazy," Marc said, badly shaken.

"I have a helicopter. That will get us out there fast. But is there someplace where we can land?"

"John Sinclair has the biggest lawn in New Jersey," Marc replied. "It's a huge estate."

"Does he have guards, guard animals, electrified wires on the perimeter?"

"Probably all three," Marc said. "The Leader is very concerned about safety issues. And, Pavel," he said, "this is a clan matter. I think I ought to call people and let them know what's going on."

"Fine with me. But we're getting there first. We're allies now. Call your brethren and tell them to get over there as fast as they can. We'll meet them."

Chapter Sixty-five

Pavel, Marc, and three of Pavel's best operatives boarded the helicopter and took off from a helipad near the Hudson River. They were prepared for a commando raid.

Marc had called his friends Hank, Pat, and Joey to let them know there was a critical hostage situation at the Leader's home involving Viv, and they offered their support.

"The Leader must have gone mad," Marc said. "He's the one who's preventing her from leaving. This means clan war. There's no going back."

There was a pause. Then Marc heard Hank say, "If it's Viv's word against his, I'd take her side any day. We'll meet you there."

Marc turned to Pavel as the helicopter rose over the river and soared into the starry winter sky. "They're in."

Viv, Sinclair, Joseph, and Matthew sat in an uneasy silence in one of the salons in the front of the mansion while they waited for Sarah. The Leader restlessly smoked one cigarette after the other, his eyes narrowing as he glared at Viv in a chair near the fireplace. She ignored him and looked out the window, hoping to see headlights coming up the driveway.

"As the Leader of this clan, I have a right, a duty," he corrected himself, "to see to the welfare of our clan, now and in the future."

Viv turned to him and said, "You had a duty to protect your clan. Instead you harmed it." The hatred she felt for this corrupt and evil creature roiled in her stomach, spreading through her entire body. She felt the desire to shape-shift and attack with fang and claw. She tamped it down. That would come later.

"This must be my wife." Matthew saw headlights as a car rolled up the long driveway and parked outside the front door.

Viv noticed the sweat already forming on the Leader's brow. He took a long drag on his cigarette as he watched his subordinate go to the door, unlock it, and let Sarah enter. Now his hand was trembling. Viv wondered if he was considering shape-shifting.

Obviously nervous, and suspecting why she had been summoned, Sarah walked into the room, glanced around, and recoiled as she saw John Sinclair about to come torward her.

"Sarah," he said kindly, "what sort of stories are you telling about me? Haven't I always been good to you?"

Turning away in revulsion, Sarah looked at Viv. "Did you tell Matthew what I told you?"

"I told him you would have to tell him yourself. Don't be afraid. Just tell the truth."

Matthew looked fearful as his small wife sank down onto a sofa and said, "I can't. I'm too ashamed."

"Sarah. Please. It's not just you. It's others, too. If he's not stopped, he'll destroy our laws and then our clan."

Sinclair took advantage of the female's hesitation and seemed to grow more confident. "Viv is trying to fabricate something and drag you into it," he said as he crossed the room and stood before Sarah. "Don't let her."

Eyes wide with fear, Sarah looked at Viv, then at Matthew. "Get him away from me," she pleaded.

At that, her husband said to her, "Sarah, if you tell the truth, I will never hold it against you. I love you."

As Matthew's mate opened her mouth to speak, the Leader whirled around and said hastily as if he were trying to concoct a story on the spot, "She forced herself on me and I was flattered. Look at her—young, attractive, always flirting with me when I looked her way. She offered herself like an appetizer and, yes, I took the bait. You should keep an eye on her, Matthew. She's such a—"

Matthew went werecat. Viv and Sarah jumped up and got out of the way as Matthew hurled himself on his Leader and sent him crashing to the floor. Sinclair flung down his cigarette and responded in kind. He shifted quickly, his larger-form panther size to Matthew's smaller lynx size. Both animals snarled, clawed, and bit, trying to kill the other. The floor looked like a mass of rolling fur.

In all the uproar, nobody noticed the lit cigarette roll under the damask sofa, hidden by the heavy fringe that went down to the carpeted floor. Out of sight, it slowly began to smolder.

Sinclair inflicted serious damage on his opponent as they battled, but Matthew was too stubborn to give up. With a snarl, he flipped the other cat and clamped his jaws on his flank, making him screech with pain. Seeing her husband in trouble, Sarah shifted and attacked her former Leader, the two medium-sized cats turning the tables on him and chasing him up the staircase.

While the three werecats took their battle to the upper floor, Viv heard a noise outside that brought her running to the door. A helicopter was landing on the lawn, men were pouring out, and she heard familiar voices calling to her.

Joseph walked out onto the porch with her, and seeing the invasion, he called to other members of the Special Squad to let the visitors pass. They hesitated, but since there were only two of them on the lawn and they were clearly outnumbered, they stood down.

Viv flung herself into Pavel's arms as he ran to her, and then hugged her brother. "I didn't think you'd be able to find me. I'm so glad to see you."

"Where's Sinclair?" Pavel demanded furiously.

Chapter Sixty-six

"Keep everybody out of the house," Pavel ordered. "I'm going upstairs. Viv, Marc, tell your clansmen to stay outside."

"We're going with you," she said. "This is our problem, not yours. I can't let you take charge."

"She's right," Marc said. "Give me a weapon. I know how to use a nine millimeter."

Pavel knew how clan rules were. It would cause an uproar among his own clan if they resorted to outside help in such a serious internal matter. "All right," he agreed. "I'm here as backup. It's your party."

Guided by the screeching coming from the second floor, they made their way up the stairs as the rest left the house, Pavel's men staying close to the helicopter, the Leader's Special Squad watching nervously on the lawn.

Sounds of a furious fight led them to a bedroom, where the Leader was tangling with the female, having already killed the male. Matthew now lay sprawled on the carpet, his neck spurting blood. Desperately the female clawed, bit, and growled, trying to kill the larger cat.

Marc took aim and fired about three inches from the Leader, forcing him to flinch, releasing his grip on Sarah as he did. With a desperate last burst of energy, the smaller cat flung herself on him again. This time, she succeeded in sinking her sharp teeth into his jugular, scoring a direct hit.

As Viv watched, she saw the wounded Leader shape-shift, drag himself to a nightstand, and pull open a drawer. Then, with a determination that shocked her, he took out a Beretta, faced them, and with blood splashing out of his wound, he raised it to his head.

"Fuck you all," he managed, nearly choking on his own blood. "Viv . . . bitch . . . I'm in charge. . . . Going out my way . . . Still the Leader . . ." Then he concentrated his remaining energy, and looking pale but still defiant, he squeezed the trigger. Blood and brains splattered the room in a shower of gore.

Pavel and Marc rushed to help Sarah, but she had gone limp. When they turned her over, they understood how badly she was injured. Blood poured from a wound in her chest, where the Leader had managed to tear open the skin, and now the lynxlike cat was dying.

"Let's get her out of here," Viv said. "Do you have any kind of first-aid supplies in the chopper?"

"Some."

"Then we have to use them. Come on."

As the group carried the wounded female down the hall, their senses were flooded with the odor of smoke rising from the ground floor. When they reached the staircase, they froze. The first floor was engulfed in roaring flames, and flames were licking their way up the stairs. In the distance they could hear shouts from their friends, muffled by the sounds of the fire.

"Do you know another way down?" Pavel asked.

"No. We've been here before, but never upstairs. That was off-limits."

Viv stopped, looked at the devastation below, and suddenly went still. As Marc and Pavel stared at her, she closed her eyes and said in a language from the beginning of time,

"Gods of the forest and the tundra, help us. Krasivaya, my ancestor, help us. Come to our aid and guide us out of here."

Pavel had seen Viv summon the gods at Hank's bedside. He prayed they would listen to this shaman again. He added his own prayer—to the Virgin of Saratov.

"Krasivaya, help us," Viv repeated, more forcefully. "Take us from this house of death! Great Mother who protected her people, help your children now!"

Just as Pavel turned around and made a decision to try to get them out to the roof, where his men could use a ladder or even the chopper to rescue them, Marc let out a shout and grabbed his arm. "Come on! We can make it down the stairs."

Stunned, the Russian turned back to see Viv descending the grand staircase as the flames rolled back in her path like some fiery tide, allowing her free passage.

With a cat's fear of fire, Marc and Pavel flinched for a split second and then followed Viv to freedom, through a corridor of safety and straight out the front door, where Pavel's team was already revving up the chopper, prepared for an aerial rescue. As they laid Sarah's limp form on the lawn, she reached up to stroke Viv's hand and quietly breathed her last.

Hank, Pat, and Joey arrived in separate SUVs and watched in amazement as the mansion burned out of control, flames swirling through it as it turned into an inferno, with flames swirling up into the dark sky like a beacon from hell. They were relieved to see Viv standing on the lawn next to her brother and the strangers. They wondered where the helicopter had come from.

After questioning the remaining members of the Special Squad on the premises, the werecats drove home, shaken by the death of the Leader and the fact that he had raped some of the females and tried to force Viv into an unwanted marriage. From a distance the sound of fire sirens shrilled through the night, and the werecats dispersed before they were forced to deal with any inconvenient questions.

Viv and Marc returned to Manhattan on the company helicopter and went to Pavel's apartment to talk. It was early morning, but they were so keyed up from what they had just lived though that nobody thought of sleep. First they had to come to terms with what had happened.

"Viv," Pavel said grimly, "did he attack you?"

"No. He tried once before, but I fought him off. But tonight, while we were outside on the lawn, Joseph told me that Sinclair was setting up video cameras in his bedroom to film something later." She looked at him and locked eyes.

Marc's head went up. "That sick fuck. I can imagine what *that* was all about."

"Well, he never had the chance. And if he had tried, I would have stabbed him, straight to the heart. I had a steel nail file in my pocket, just in case. Or I would have killed him cat-style."

"What will your clan do now?" Pavel asked. "Do your laws cover this?"

"We'll have to convene a special meeting," Marc said. "Tell everybody what took place last night: Viv's kidnapping, Matthew's death, Sarah's death. The previous attack on Sarah. At least Sinclair is out of the picture, and we can try to elect someone normal to replace him."

"And change his rules," Viv added. "He was absolutely paranoid. And cruel. The Special Squad was subjected to what amounted to torture if they disobeyed him. We have to disband the group and reconstitute it along different lines. No cult of the Leader this time. Back to our roots. We'll need a big overhaul," Viv said, glancing at Pavel as she took his hand and held it. "A restructuring that might even accept a mixed marriage."

"Yes," Marc agreed. "We have to have a better system so that nobody can seize control the way Sinclair did. He was more dangerous than we ever suspected. And we were all guilty for having let him get that far."

Pavel spread his hands in a sympathetic gesture. "We all suffer from the need to rally around the strong man and delude ourselves into thinking he knows more than we do. Just remember the mistake and don't repeat it," he said softly.

An hour later, Pavel called one of his men to give Marc a ride back to his apartment, and he and Viv were alone, so grateful to have each other after what might have happened just a short while ago. They could still smell the trace of smoke on their clothing.

He took her in his arms and drew her very close to him. "*Malenkaya*, I am so grateful I didn't lose you tonight. The gods kept you safe."

Viv pressed her head against his chest and said with a sigh, "I wish we had all survived the night. Sarah, Matthew . . ." Her voice faltered.

"I would have killed Sinclair myself if he had survived," Pavel said flatly. "He was lucky he was able to do it himself. Alpha male till the end."

"You make me feel so cherished," Viv said softly, as she looked up and gently kissed his face. "I never want to lose you."

Pavel's mouth found hers and he kissed her tenderly, pulling her closer and deepening his kiss as she responded passionately, wrapping him in her arms and clinging to him as if she never wanted to let him go. "You never will," he said.

With that, Pavel and Viv staggered into the bedroom. She sprawled on his bed as he sat down and undressed quickly, eager to posses her. Viv practically ripped off her clothing in return, and when they had peeled off anything that would stand in their way, Viv climbed on top of him and let her long, silky tresses fall across his face and chest, arousing him with his need for her. After what she had just been through, all she wanted was Pavel in her arms, his strength surrounding her, his love enveloping her.

Pavel seized her, kissed her passionately, and took hold of her as she slid herself underneath him. With a gasp, he entered her, and Viv cried out as she and Pavel rocked and writhed in total passion as they both tried to give each other as much pleasure as anyone could stand and still survive. After their brush with death, all they wanted to do was hurl themselves into the passion of living. They mated with such force that Pavel feared he may have hurt her.

Viv gasped as she and her lover collapsed in a sweaty pile of arms and legs, wrapping themselves in each other's embrace. "I love you and I know you wouldn't hurt me. You've always been tender with me, even when we lose our minds and mate like wildcats. It's the thing I love most about you. That and your gorgeous body," she teased.

"Darling Vivian," he murmured. "We're going to make each other very happy for years to come." And he kissed her with such sweetness that it brought tears to her eyes.

Chapter Sixty-seven

Boris's fight with his sister-in-law had resulted in his incarceration inside a formidable steel cage in Bill's basement, big enough to accommodate a tiger. Since Boris's big cat form was only as large as a serval, he had plenty of space. But he would have preferred more luxurious quarters.

Boris knew they wanted him to change back so they could use him for the meeting with the client who wanted the icon; therefore he stubbornly maintained his werecat persona, angering his captors.

"Look at him," one of the lower-ranking associates sniffed disdainfully, "the Hierarch of the Russian Blues. No pride at all."

"He'll see reason sooner or later. Or he'll starve." And with that, Bill led his henchmen upstairs while the Hierarch languished in his cell, miserable and lonely.

Once Bill and the Siberians left, Boris surveyed the room and found nothing helpful. The dampness of the room chilled him and the mold-covered cement walls depressed him. He thought of his present accommodations as a sort of werecat gulag.

How had things turned out so badly for a Hierarch of the Russian Blues? he wondered. A Hierarch commanded respect and reverence. None of them had ever sunk as low as himself, a gofer for a status-crazed, corrupt, utterly crooked

Siberian Forest cat. This is where his misdeeds had led him, and truthfully he knew Bella was merely a distorted reflection of himself, just as evil and just as worthless, simply more vicious. Two of a kind when you came right down to it.

Curling into a large but depressed ball of fur, Boris quietly sought out the oblivion of sleep.

Bella reached out with ill grace and yanked the phone off the hook the next morning as the shrill ringing woke her up. "Yes?" she asked, sounding like a bear being rousted out of hibernation.

"This is Lev," the voice said. "I believe you remember me—and our agreement?"

At those magic words, Bella sat up in bed, leaped to her feet, and became all attention. "Yes. Of course. How are you?"

"A little tired of waiting. I heard through the grapevine that a certain something went missing. Is everything all right?"

"Yes. Fine. We have the merchandise," she assured him. "All we have to do is set up a time and a place for delivery."

"Good. And the payment will be in cash as we agreed."

"Ah, excellent."

Bella nearly shimmied with the excitement of gaining those millions. Then she remembered her deal with the damned Rasputnikatz, and she frowned at the idea of sharing.

"I will be able to meet with you on Thursday night. Is that acceptable?" Lev asked.

"Of course. Name the place."

Lev paused as if considering several possibilities. Then he suggested a hotel in the area of a well-known New Jersey outlet center, with a large parking garage. They would rendezvous in a suite there. When they arrived, they were to ask at the desk for Mr. Morris, and someone would come downstairs and escort them up.

"How many will there be?" he asked.

"Myself, possibly my brother-in-law, and another gentleman."

"All right. I'll have my people there as well. You will bring up the item, we will inspect it, and then if all is satisfactory, we will proceed to payment."

"Fine," said Bella. "What time should we arrive?"

"Eight o'clock."

"We'll be there."

"And don't keep me waiting," Lev said. "Time is money."

"Exactly."

When Bella hung up the phone, she raised her arms high above her head in a delighted victory sign and even did a little dance to express the joy she felt. Millions were within her grasp. Life was good—even if her uncooperative brother-in-law had gone werecat and lay caged in a cellar in the outer boroughs. Trust him to pull a stunt like that just when she needed him.

Chapter Sixty-eight

An employee notified Pavel as soon as Bella got the call that they'd all been waiting for. Things were gathering momentum.

"Tony," he said as he phoned his friend in law enforcement, "it looks as though the deal will go down on Thursday night at a hotel in New Jersey. The contact called Bella to make the arrangements."

"Okay. Who's going to be there?"

"Bella, her brother-in-law, and probably Bill of the Rasputnikatz."

"And on the other team?"

"The buyer and some associates."

"Then we should count on at least six to eight of them, with some of them armed and dangerous."

"Definitely. And I'm going with you. I'll take my best crew." Pavel suddenly sensed a hesitation. He asked, "Are you still there?"

"I don't know about outside help. I think we should keep this federal," Tony said.

"How many Russian speakers do you have on your team?"

"None."

"Then you need us. Remember, we're your associates. We go to the party together."

"You and your men all have weapons permits for New Jersey?"

"We've got the paper. We're good to go."

"You take orders from me. None of the Wild West stuff that got those Blackwater guards in trouble."

"My men are disciplined. We'll be under your command."

"Okay. I'll put you in as interpreters. Do you know who Bella is meeting?"

"Sorry. All we know is the client has to be rich. She's expecting a big payout."

Tony paused. Then he said, "What do you think he wants with the goods? Private collection all for himself?"

"Who knows? These people have so much money they think they can buy anything, break any law. They live in their own expensive little worlds."

"Well, after Thursday, he'll be living as a guest of the state."

Pavel laughed. "He may turn out to be just some greedy little tycoon with a yen for priceless art. In that case, he'll be scared to death when you lock him up. By the time the cell door closes on him, he'll offer up anything he can think of to make you happy."

"My favorite kind of prisoner," Tony said with a laugh.

At Old Muscovy, Marc and Viv found themselves back on the same side once more, and still seething over Viv's kidnapping.

"Sinclair was much more disturbed than we ever suspected," Viv said. "We should have seen the signs, but people who knew what was happening were afraid to talk."

"He managed to hide so many things. If it hadn't been for the attacks on you and Sarah, we probably never would have realized how vicious he was. I've sent out a notice to all the brethren to attend a meeting so we can let them know what happened and start choosing a new Leader. Hank,

Joey, and Pat will give their testimony and so will Joseph, who was privy to a lot of Sinclair's actions. He secretly taped him while he was throwing away clan money in the casinos in Atlantic City and Las Vegas and taking his mistress on vacations at our expense. And other things," he said with disgust.

"I'll be at the meeting, too. I'll tell them what Sinclair did to me and Sarah. Charla, another female, will testify, too, if she's needed. And since Pavel and I are mates and have no intention of breaking up, they may decide to expel me."

Marc shook his head. "Then we'd lose the best of our clan," he said quietly. "I don't think anyone would be willing to do that. I'm sorry I acted like the 'defender of werecat family values,' as you put it. You're right. It's none of my business, and I'll support you when you announce your choice of mate. After what we just went through, I can't imagine a better brother-in-law."

"Thank you. It means a lot to me."

He nodded. "It's just the two of us, Viv. You're my family. I can't afford to lose you. And if Pavel can adapt to American sports and split a season baseball ticket, he'll fit right in," Marc said with a wink.

Well, Viv thought gratefully, peace had been negotiated and life was back in sync.

Chapter Sixty-nine

A good takedown meant meticulous planning from start to finish. So with that in mind, Pavel and two of his associates met with Tony and one of his men, drove across the Hudson and down Route 3, and then headed for the hotel where Bella was due to rendezvous with her client.

While Pavel's men entered the hotel and cased the place, on the pretext of looking for a suitable venue for a conference with available rooms for out-of-town visitors, Pavel and Tony checked out the large parking garage located nearby, several floors high and open on the sides. Then they surveyed the entrances and exits of both hotel and garage.

After lunch the group gathered at Tony's office in a large building in downtown Manhattan and plotted strategy. The agency was so far under the radar that, although it had the highest security clearance, its personnel was mostly werecat, its offices were obscure, and its purpose largely unknown. The office door carried the sign NORTH TRADING COMPANY.

Knowing that the mysterious buyer would be staying at the hotel under the name of Morris, federal agents were to enter, present warrants, get the room number, and prevent the desk clerks from making any phone calls upstairs while Tony, Pavel, and another agent would go to the room, burst in, and make the arrests. A backup team would be waiting outside, ready to go in if needed. Agents in the lobby would secure it, while a van containing another contingent would be in front, waiting to herd the thieves in for the ride to jail.

"We'll send an agent in there as a member of the cleaning staff. He'll find out whatever he can about Mr. Morris before we show up. Bug the room if possible," Tony announced.

"Do you think they might put up a fight?" one of his men asked.

"With a few million dollars in play? Sure," Tony said.

"Bella and her brother-in-law went at it the other night in the apartment. He was going to leave and go back to Russia. She managed to knock him out and tie him up before she called her associates and they took him away," Pavel said. "She's pretty frisky."

"What does this woman look like? Brunhilde?" one of the feds asked.

"No. Medium height, slim build. Very attractive," Pavel said with a smile.

Tony shook his head in amusement. "Boris must be a wimp."

"That's his rep, but according to my sources, Boris was the brains behind the assassination," Pavel said.

"No shit?" Tony looked astonished.

"I've been making inquiries back home. My people are planning to take the information to the federal prosecutor after we get Boris in custody. If the brethren don't change their minds and kill him themselves."

"What's the motive behind the assassination? Taking over the Danilov empire?"

"I don't know. Before that, Boris never showed any signs of initiative in anything. Then he goes nuts and orders a hit on Dimitri. Nobody can figure it out."

"He'll be a good bargaining chip with the Russians," Tony said. "I told you we have an interest in a case over there right now."

Pavel nodded. "Now, from my knowledge of Boris's character, if there's going to be any violence during the take-down, I doubt he will provide it. Bella might get hysterical and try to resist arrest, and their buyer will probably have armed bodyguards. Bella's thugs will definitely be packing. Prepare for it."

"Kevlar for everybody," Tony said.

In the basement of Bill's house in Queens, Boris still languished in his cage in feline form, moping and practically inert. One of the Rasputnikatz looked in on him from time to time, trying to figure out how to get him to shape-shift back into human form.

"Hey, you," he said, banging his hand on the cage, "are you going to stay like that forever?"

Boris got up and turned his back on his visitor as he moved away and settled down toward the back of the cage. That pissed off the Rasputnikat, who then opened the cage and shape-shifted himself, surprising Boris.

The shaggy Siberian stalked into the steel enclosure, swaggering a little as he headed straight for Boris, who was actually larger, but sleeker, the size of a well-muscled serval. The stocky Siberian stupidly advanced toward the prisoner, who backed up and snarled at the intruder, hissing with a ferocity he hadn't previously displayed. The visitor seemed unaware of the change.

"What's the matter?" the Siberian asked in the telepathic language of its kind. "Scared to be in the same cage with the big boys?"

"Fuck you. Get out of here."

"Make me."

Quivering with pent-up rage, the big cat sprang at the intruder and knocked him right out of the cage. As the Rasputnikat went flying across the room, Boris leaped after him, attacking him with fangs and claws, setting off an uproar of earsplitting screams and hisses, yowls of pain and fury, while the sounds of falling objects added their own distinct notes as the big cats crashed into furniture and knocked over anything in their path. Bits of fur floated in the air as the cats tried to kill each other, two wild animals bent on murder.

Upstairs Bill heard the racket and came racing down to the cellar. He nearly collided with the large cats, then shape-shifted to try to enforce order, biting and clawing at both until they yielded and stopped fighting.

Limping off to the side, Boris flopped down on the floor and began to shape-shift, ending up in human form and looking as if he'd been beaten up. The Siberian did the same, while Bill watched in disgust.

"Look at you," he said with a sneer. "Brawling like some street cat. My boy nearly tore you up."

Boris glanced over at the winded Siberian. "I think you've got it wrong, pussy. I just kicked the crap out of him."

"Well, you got lucky," Bill said in embarrassment as he glanced at his whipped henchman. The guy was practically wheezing; he also sported a black eye and a few facial abrasions for good measure.

"Whatever you say."

"Look," Bill said, "you're acting like a fool. All you have to do is cooperate with us for the next couple of days, and we all make some money and you go home. Be strong."

"Go get me something to eat," Boris said. He glanced at the Rasputnikat still sitting on the floor, stunned and shaking his head. "And tell fur ball over there to treat the Hierarch of the Russian Blues with more respect. Or the next time, I'll tear out his throat. He knows I can do it. And if he ever again treats me so disrespectfully, I will."

The two Rasputnikatz stared at him as if they were seeing him for the first time as Boris turned his back on them and walked out of that cellar as if he were John Wayne.

Chapter Seventy

Pavel and Viv went out for dinner at a little restaurant in lower Manhattan the night before the takedown, and Pavel just wanted to relax and enjoy Viv's company. Everything had been planned. He and his team had gone over contingency plans. Now all he had to do was wait.

"It's tomorrow, isn't it?" she asked as they nibbled sushi appetizers. "I want to be there."

"Sorry. It's a private party. Top secret."

"You're going to be there."

"*Malenkaya*, I'm the official interpreter."

"Very clever."

"They need Russian speakers for this one. They don't have them."

"How many of your men will be there?"

"A few."

"All official interpreters?" she asked with fine irony.

"Yes."

"The wonderful world of law enforcement. Very interesting."

Pavel took her hand and kissed it. "It's top secret. We're dealing with werecats in the federal system who are in such deep cover that even the highest branches of security don't know about them."

"I still want to be there," she said.

"Sorry."

"Bella Danilov nearly got me killed when her henchmen kidnapped me. They shot up one of my friends. She's broken every law on two continents. I want to see her taken down."

"You'll have to sit this one out."

Viv glared at him with fire in her beautiful amber eyes. "This is important to me," she said. "I want to be part of it."

"You're a civilian. The feds won't allow it."

"So are you, and they want you there."

"I told you why." Pavel gave Viv a smile that sent a little shiver of desire down her spine. "You're too precious to me to want to see you in harm's way. I'd never forgive myself if you got hurt."

"Then let me watch from a distance."

He shook his head as he gave her another high-voltage smile. "Darling," he said quietly, "there are places that are too risky for the woman I love. I went through a terrible loss once. I won't live through a second one."

Viv shook her head. "I'm going to be around for a good long while, *koshka*," she said. "I'm not going away."

Bella felt a rush of relief when Boris called to say he had shape-shifted back into human form and he was ready to play his part.

Surprised at the about-face, she said, "Good. I'm glad you've come to your senses. When this is over, we'll catch a plane for home and be back in St. Petersburg giving a press conference."

"You think so?" he said.

"Sure. This is the last thing we'll do before sending the money to the Caymans."

"I have to keep the Rasputnikatz company until tomorrow evening. I'll see you then."

"How are you getting along?" she asked curiously.

"Couldn't be better. I kicked the shit out of one of them before." And with that, Boris hung up.

What was wrong with him all of a sudden? He didn't seem like himself. Was he joking about beating up one of the Rasputnikatz? They all seemed tougher than he was. Hell, *she* had beaten him up.

He's obsessed with that stupid bitch, Bella thought. That had to be it. The fool was deep in the throes of a meltdown over the extramarital escapades of the vixen he'd married. *Get a grip,* she thought, rather uncharitably. *The world is full of sluts with big boobs. Move on.*

Russian Blues, she thought with contempt. *So idealistic and moronic.*

Chapter Seventy-one

Viv and Pavel finished dinner. Then they took a leisurely route home, enjoying the lights of the city on the early November evening. When they reached his apartment, he drove his SUV into the building's garage, and he and Viv took the elevator upstairs, where they kissed all the way till they reached their floor.

"You're very sexy tonight, *dushka*," he murmured as he pushed aside her long auburn tresses and kissed his way down her throat. "Such an adorable, tough, distracting female."

Viv laughed as he wrapped his arms around her and drew her close to him as he fiddled with the key and finally succeeded in opening his apartment door. They practically fell inside, laughing and caressing.

Suddenly Pavel scooped her up in his arms and carried her into the bedroom, although she was still wearing her overcoat. Viv kissed him fiercely as she struggled to take off her coat with some help from Pavel, and they broke apart only to fling off their clothing before pulling the comforter off the bed and sliding under the covers.

"Ah, I've been waiting for this moment ever since dinner," Viv said. "You're my dessert."

"What a delightful thought," Pavel said. "Nobody's ever called me that."

"You are. And I'm about to sink my teeth into your gorgeous, firm flesh and cover you with kisses."

"Sounds exciting."

Viv climbed on top of him and made Pavel utter a sound that was a cross between a growl and a sigh. "How is that?" she asked as she caressed him. "Does that please you?"

"Oh, yes. Do whatever makes you happy," he teased.

She smiled. "I'm going to do what makes *you* happy, *koshka*."

"Ah, even better."

As Viv slid herself along his magnificent, well-muscled body, Pavel sighed and took her thick hair in his hands as she found the place she wanted to visit. He felt a soft tongue create little circles on his belly as he clenched his muscles involuntarily; then he gasped as she followed that up by blowing on the wet skin. Viv nearly yelped as his hands gripped her hair in a reflex that almost pulled out the roots.

"Sorry," he said. "Keep going."

"Behave yourself. I won't look good if you tear out my hair in the throes of passion."

"I'd love you just as much," he whispered as she lowered her face to his nether regions and began to stroke him with her tongue, making Pavel nearly jump out of his skin as she kept on licking, caressing him, leaving a wet trail down the shaft and working her way up to the tip. He could barely talk as she nearly brought him to a release so fierce, he could hardly breathe or concentrate on anything but the desire to finish.

With the swift movement of a cat, Pavel seized Viv and flipped her over so that she was beneath him. As she wrapped herself around him and brought her knees up, he plunged deep inside her, half incoherent with lust as the two of them joined together in a passionate union that sent covers sliding off the bed and both of them gasping and moaning as they rocked back and forth, Pavel thrusting deeper and deeper inside her as Viv groaned with the force of her response. When they had climaxed, they broke apart and lay next to each other, chests heaving, eyes glazed, so worn out they couldn't even speak.

After their breathing returned to normal, Pavel took Viv in his arms and buried his face in her bosom. "Ah, *malenkayav*," he whispered. "So beautiful, so ferocious. My passionate, elegant mate."

Viv caressed him with one hand as she lay snuggled against him on her side. "Koshka, there's nobody else I've ever wanted the way I want you. No member of my own clan ever appealed to me like this. I used to think I was cursed," she said sadly. "Then after the gods parted the flames for us and allowed us to pass unscathed, I knew we were meant to be together. If it wasn't so, we never would have survived. I believe they blessed us at that moment," she said softly.

They nestled together, tired and feeling a delicious sense of completion. Viv sighed.

"I have to ask you something," she said as last. "And it's important."

"Yes?"

"I know you were in love with a woman who was killed during a botched rescue in that theater. I know it took you a long time to come to terms with it. Will that cast any shadows over us?"

Pavel shook his head. "I love you, Viv. I loved her. I can't change that. Natalya will always be part of my past. But I let go of that when I fell in love with you. No ghost will ever stand in your way, *dushka*. You're the here and now, my future and my life. There is nobody else."

Viv snuggled against him and kissed him tenderly. "I'm glad you said that, Pavel. Otherwise, I would always wonder."

"Darling," he murmured as he nuzzled her cheek, "you will never have to wonder about anything. You're my one and only."

Sinking into a deep sleep later, after making love two or

three more times, Viv felt happier than she had in years. She had a lover she truly desired, a future ahead, and no doubts about his affection.

Life was beautiful. And then she thought of tomorrow night. She was going to be there. And he was going to be furious.

Chapter Seventy-two

Chapter Seventy-two

With several agents in place at the targeted hotel bugging "Mr. Morris's" room, checking guest lists, and setting up for the evening's raid, Pavel and Tony assembled their troops, assigned locations, ordered vehicles, and got the weapons ready. It was going down that evening.

"Will we notify the Russians when we make the bust?" Pavel asked.

"Yeah," Tony said. "But only after these guys are in cuffs and being processed. I'm not letting anybody try to muscle their way in on my collar. And we have to set the time and place for the exchange."

"Good."

"Bella's appointment is for eight o'clock. We'll get there ahead of the pack, monitor the guests, and nab them at the time they're exchanging cash for art."

Pavel nodded. "And we'll have the pleasure of sending the Virgin of Saratov back to her homeland, where she belongs."

"Bella and Boris are going back to the motherland along with her. Let the Russians deal with them. And if it's true Boris engineered Dimitri's murder, they'll put him away for so long, he'll be an old man before he gets out."

"If he survives long enough to get old," Pavel said.

*   *   *

In Bill's home, Boris woke up late and sent one of the Rasputnikatz to look through a selection of designer suits stashed in the basement so he could show up for the meeting in style. He didn't plan on returning to the apartment, and he knew Bill wouldn't approve a little premeeting shopping on his own. Fortunately for him, his larcenous host had hijacked a bunch of Armani suits last week and had a nice variety on hand.

"Try these on." The Siberian he'd beaten up presented him with an offering of four suits and hung them in the closet. "Bill said he had shirts and ties, too."

Boris nodded and waited.

"Do you need anything else, Hierarch?"

"Not at the moment. I'm going to try them on." He gave the Rasputnikat a dismissive glance and watched him leave.

As soon as the door was closed, Boris inspected the Armanis and opted for a sharp-looking dark charcoal pinstripe. After he had dressed, he looked at himself critically in the mirror and tried on the others. Two were an excellent fit; two looked just okay. Boris decided on a navy pinstripe with a blue shirt with French cuffs, gold-striped tie, and gold paisley pocket handkerchief.

The old Boris had returned, stylish, handsome, and ready for the party. All he had to do was get through tonight, and he could be on his way home with millions in the offshore accounts and a new lease on life. This New York detention would be behind him, and he would be free to take the children and find a suitable home somewhere in Europe, far away from Bella, Marina, and business. It was all he longed for.

In her apartment, Bella made a few phone calls to wrap up her stay in Manhattan and then began packing her bags. She and Boris had seats on a private jet flying out of JFK shortly after midnight. She was heading home in style, with millions in her bank accounts. Once home, Bella planned on taking over a few more companies, and under her tutelage, Boris could learn to cast his net wide, turning Danilov Enterprises into the biggest conglomerate in Russia. With her as his closest adviser.

At around six o'clock, Viv said goodbye to Marc at Old Muscovy, and instead of taking the subway to the apartment she now shared with Pavel, she hailed a cab two blocks from the antiques shop and told the driver to take her to her apartment in New Jersey. Once there, she changed into jeans, a turtleneck, and sneakers, put on a down jacket and gloves, and descended to the garage to get her car.

From her home to the point of rendezvous took no time at all, and by seven thirty, Viv had arrived at the hotel's parking garage, entered, and found an empty space on the second level. Switching off the engine, she sat in the dark car and prepared to settle in for a solitary vigil.

With the engine off, the car gradually cooled, and Viv sound herself shivering as the cold night air seeped into the vehicle as she waited. Glancing at her watch from time to time, she could just barely make out the numbers, but she thought it must be close to eight.

Come on, she thought fiercely as she watched in disgust as an occasional BMW or Mercedes pulled into the garage and cruised the levels, searching for a space. One car looked like a possibility, but at second glance it contained three young women, not the one Viv expected.

Damn it. What was with these Russians? They had a business deal to conclude, illegal millions to collect. What made them so slow?

Just as she was about to resign herself to the fact that perhaps Bella and company had arrived earlier and were already inside the hotel, a silver SUV made its way up the incline leading to the second level and slowed down as it looked for a space. With the engine purring, it roamed to the next level and resumed its hunt. In the passenger seat Viv saw Boris Danilov, whom she recognized from pictures.

Viv's heart jumped as she heard them stop the car one level above, heard doors opening, and then heard the sounds of them slamming, followed by the horn as somebody clicked the remote and locked up.

Russian voices filled the air, becoming louder in the chilly night air as three men in overcoats came down the ramp. As Viv slunk down in her seat, she heard the voices and footsteps grow fainter. Daring a glance, she lifted herself up to look out the window, and she could see that one of the men carried a kind of portfolio. She fought a desire to go werecat.

With her heart beating wildly, she saw a second car ascend the ramp and search for a space. Behind the wheel sat Bella Danilov, dressed warmly in mink.

As Bella drove closer, Viv dipped her head until the car passed by. A minute later, she heard the familiar sounds of parking, a door opening and being slammed shut, and then the door being locked with a remote.

She must be running late, Viv decided. Sharp, clicking footsteps made their way down the ramp, as Bella hurried to catch up with her henchmen. The sound of Russian curses floated by as the woman hastened to her appointment, and then the footsteps grew faint and faded away into the night.

Okay, Viv thought. *The players are all lining up. Where are Pavel and the feds?*

In the lobby, one of Pavel's men sat with a drink in his hand, looking like a businessman trying to pick up a female guest with the ID tag from the convention of Realtors going on in the ballroom. As he leaned close to the young woman, they both noted the arrival of Bella and her party coming through the glass entrance doors.

The young brunette bent forward, her long hair hiding both their faces as Bella's group passed by, heading toward the reception desk. "It's on," she said quietly into a mini-microphone hidden in her neckline. "Showtime." And with the flick of a wrist, Pavel's man snapped a photo of the group, sending it up to his boss and Tony on the second floor.

"We give them time to go inside, we listen to them make the exchange, and then we go in." Tony looked around at his team stationed in the room located directly opposite the one "Mr. Morris" had booked and he said, "Any questions?"

"How soon do they seal off the lobby?" Pavel asked.

"Right about now." There was the crackle of a walkie-talkie, and a voice rasped the message that the SWAT team had taken control of the perimeter, and one of the Russians who had accompanied Bella's group was under arrest and being taken out to the van.

The men fell silent as they heard voices from across the hall, the sound of knocking, and then another Russian voice greeting Bella and her companions and inviting them inside.

"What's he saying?" Tony asked softly.

" 'Welcome. Delighted to see you. Is that the merchandise?' "

And then the door closed.

Chapter Seventy-three

"Madame Danilov, delighted to see you again," said the shortest man in the room as he greeted Bella with a kiss on the hand. "Always a pleasure to do business with you."

"The pleasure is all mine," she said with a high-voltage smile as she greeted the bald billionaire. "These are my associates: Boris Danilov, my brother-in-law, and Bill Sirpsky, the head of the Rasputnikatz here in New York. Gentlemen, this is Lev Patritsky. I'm sure you've heard his name many times." She glanced at the two other men in the room, big guys with looks mean enough to melt steel. "And his associates."

The large men gave curt nods in the manner of thugs who didn't put much stock in social niceties. Breaking legs and arms probably came more naturally to them than polite conversation.

Bella turned to her henchmen and cut her eyes to the portfolio Bill carried. "Show him," she said.

Bill was about to reach in and remove the icon when Lev intercepted it and took the bag himself. With nervous hands, he lifted the Virgin of Saratov out of her packaging and held it up so he could get a good luck. In his eyes, Bella saw such relief that she thought he might cry with emotion.

"Stepan," he said to the smaller of the two musclemen, "take a good look."

As Lev Patritsky held it up, Stepan studied it with attention so close, Bella wondered if he was going to whip out a large magnifying glass and go over it inch by inch.

"My art expert," Lev explained as he glanced at Bella and her group. "He grew up in the town it came from. He's looked at it for years."

Stepan gazed at the medieval icon while the rest of the party watched breathlessly. His eyes roved over the details of the painting, studying, examining. Then with a curt nod, he said, "*Da*, it's genuine. Look. This is the mark that the Swedish bullets made in the seventeenth century. It's authentic. And here is a small chip in the gold that I remember, too."

"Okay," Patritsky said as he expelled his breath in a whoosh of relief. "We can do business. Here is the money."

As he spoke, he snapped his fingers and the larger of the two assistants stepped up to Bella and presented her with a metal briefcase. He placed it on a table, flipped it open, and said, "It's all there in bundles of hundreds. Please count it. We don't mind."

Across the hall, Pavel quietly translated the words, " 'It's all there in bundles of hundreds. Please count it,' " and nodded to Tony. "The deal's gone down. The money's on the table. Let's go."

Lining up, weapons in hand, the team exited the hotel room and gathered in the hall on both sides of "Mr. Morris's" room. Tony banged loudly on the door. "Open up. Federal officers."

In the space of a second, they could hear shouts, the sound of things crashing and men screaming at one another. Bella's voice rang out, shrill with fury, cursing everybody and blaming Patritsky for screwing up.

Two of the feds attacked the door with a wooden ram made for such moments and popped it open. Inside the room, everybody was scrambling, the bodyguards with guns drawn, Patritsky screaming at them, Bella frantically trying to scoop up bundles of hundred-dollar bills from the floor. Only Boris seemed oddly still, as if he'd been turned to stone, watching it all with dull, tired eyes, too stunned to move.

"Hands in the air! Get 'em up. Put your weapons on the table. You, don't make any sudden moves, or we drop you," Tony shouted.

Outnumbered by a group of men wearing federal police vests and armed with shotguns, the Russians let themselves be grabbed, frisked, and ordered to stand with their hands against the walls and their feet spread wide apart. Several policemen helped them energetically, and Patritsky shouted his protests at the treatment.

"Shut up and hold that pose. We're not done with you," Tony snapped.

"This is where all your stupid ideas have got us!" Boris flung at his sister-in-law as an officer shoved him up against the wall to frisk him. "You trouble-making bitch. You've ruined my whole family."

"Oh, go fuck yourself! You're such an asshole your own brother wanted to let you go. You don't believe me? Well, he told me shortly before he died that he was going to put you in charge of human resources at one of his holdings in Siberia because you were too incompetent for St. Petersburg!"

At that, Boris became unhinged and he lunged at her. Two of Pavel's men grabbed him and pushed him up against the wall again, kicking his feet apart to keep him off balance.

"You gold-digging slut!" he shouted as little bits of spittle sprayed her in the face. "My brother thought he was so fucking clever. He was always the smart one, the go-getter, the fair-haired boy who could do whatever he wanted while I had to stay in the background and be content with the crumbs that fell off his plate. Well, I want you to know that he's not around anymore because *I* was the one who had him removed. Me! Stupid Boris. Boris the jerk. Boris, whose wife he screwed when he sent him on business overseas!"

All the Russians went dead quiet and just stared at the outraged Hierarch. Patritsky's jaw dropped. Bill appeared stunned. Even the stolid musclemen looked shocked.

Then Bella broke loose and leaped on Boris, hurling him to the floor. She sank her teeth into his neck and held on even while Tony and two of his men tried to pry her off. While they struggled to pull them apart, Boris shrieked and thrashed around on the rug, beating at her with a hatred that he unleashed like a flood. He punched her in the face, the body, the chest. He bit her like an animal, trying to tear her flesh.

"You had my husband killed because he screwed your wife?" Bella screamed as she fought back. She grabbed his hair and banged his head on the floor as federal agents tried to pull her off him. "Everybody screwed that slut! You stupid, motherfucking bastard!"

Suddenly as they rolled around the floor and landed behind a couch, Bella stopped screaming curses at Boris. He went stone silent as well. Suddenly animal sounds filled the air, making everybody's blood freeze. Before the feds or Pavel's men could get a look at what happened, a large, shaggy cat emerged, a beast the size of a panther with blood dripping from its fangs.

"Damn it!" Tony said. "She shifted."

"Take a look." Pavel stepped around behind the sofa. "She got him good."

Boris lay inert on the rug in big-cat form, his face and throat savaged by the larger one, his eyes staring at the ceiling but seeing nothing. Blood gushed from his jugular, pouring bright red stains onto his dark fur and the beige carpet.

As the humans in the room stood around, unnerved, wondering how the hell a woman could have done that, and where had those two beasts had come from, Pavel watched the large cat walk away from the living room and into the next room, where the door to the balcony was cracked open just a bit. He was right behind her.

Earlier, Patritsky had left the door to the balcony slightly ajar in order to bring in some cool air. Now the large tawny beast walked to that door, and as Pavel followed it, the animal pushed open the door, creating an exit for itself to the balcony.

Tony and the other werecats in the room froze as the animal jumped up onto the outside railing and leaped two stories to the grass below. In an instant Pavel shape-shifted and followed her, leaping into a tall fir tree to break his fall and then jumping down to the ground and racing after her, hitting speeds that would have qualified him for the Olympics. The feds ignored questions from their prisoners and started herding them down to the vans. Later, the agents would erase their prisoners' memories of those beasts.

Chapter Seventy-four

Winded by her leap from the second-floor balcony, the shaggy Siberian got up from the ground and began running toward the parking garage with Pavel right behind her in the form of a sleek and speedy cat the size of a panther. Men guarding the approaches to the hotel never spotted the animals because the big cats took a roundabout route that hugged the shadows of the bushes. Thick landscaping provided cover in the night, and the cops got the call to be on the lookout for two big cats only after Bella and Pavel had already bypassed them while they waited for the team to arrive with the perps.

Realizing she was being followed, Bella hunkered down just outside the parking garage and leaped in from the side, putting herself in there before the other cat could do the same. Its fur standing up from sheer nerves, the large Siberian stalked the aisles, searching for the car. In the harsh fluorescent lighting, it looked even bigger than it was, its fur making it huge. Blood stained its coat and whiskers, even its paws. Low growls rose from its throat as it sought escape.

Jolted to full alert, Viv caught sight of the cat, and suddenly she felt her heart race. That had to be Bella. She must have escaped from the hotel and then come here to find her car. Where were Pavel and his men? Did they realize she had shape-shifted? At the sight of the blood, she wondered if

Bella had attacked Pavel. Was he still alive? Frightening thoughts poured into Viv's mind as she watched the blood-stained creature pace the aisles.

If nobody stopped her, Bella Danilov would flee the country and live out her life in luxury, enjoying the profits from her crimes. Viv was outraged at the thought. She was glad she had disobeyed Pavel; right now she might be the only one able to take her down.

As silently as she could, Viv got out of her car and shape-shifted. Bella had already started up the ramp to the next level, but Viv was right after her, a large, very angry cat the size of a mountain lion.

With muscles twitching from concentration, Viv stalked her prey like a stealthy beast of the jungle, and then as the Siberian paused and turned around, alerted by some sixth sense, Viv crouched and leaped, her adrenaline in overdrive.

Feline screams pierced the air. Bella went sprawling on the hard floor of the garage as Viv crashed down on her, biting with all the force she could command. The Siberian screamed with pain and tried to bite back but only succeeded in getting a mouthful of Viv's thick fur as both big cats spun around like dervishes, raising a cloud of dust from the dirty cement floor. Roaring with fury, they leaped to their feet and attacked each other, ready to kill.

Viv chomped down on Bella's sensitive tail as the other cat tried to tear her face, causing such agony to her spine that they could hear the noise even outside the garage.

"You're going to jail," Viv told her by means of the telepathy their kind used. She bit Bella's ear and tore off a chunk as the other werecat shrieked and tried to use her claws.

"I'll kill you!" Bella screeched as Viv sank sharp teeth into her cheek, ripping off a few whiskers. But she was the one who was bleeding. She whipped around, trying to bite her attacker in the neck and sever her spine. Viv made a lunge for her and flipped her over before she could do any damage.

Pavel's roar echoed from a distance, and both cats jumped in surprise. Bella then seized the opportunity to claw at Viv's face and sink teeth into her shoulder.

Enraged, Viv let out a roar that terrified her opponent, and suddenly she morphed into a cat the size of a tiger, furry and furious as she took hold of Bella and grabbed her by the neck. Violently, she swung her from side to side as easily as if she were a toy.

The wounded Siberian moaned in pain as her much larger enemy took a few steps back and flung her headfirst into a concrete wall, bouncing her off the side of a car and picking her up again to throw her against the grille of another one before she was done.

Utterly spent, the Siberian lay on the ground, panting from pain and exhaustion, looking at Viv as if she expected the coup de grâce. "Kill me and get it over with," she said telepathically. "I'd rather die here than face prison in Russia."

"Too late," Viv replied. "You're out of options."

By the time Pavel, still in werecat form, reached the scene of the fight, Viv was standing with one paw on Bella's head, holding her down. To her lover's amazement, she was the size of a tiger.

As Pavel approached and shape-shifted, Viv turned to him and began to morph into human form. "She's yours. I caught her trying to escape," she said as she sensibly kept her foot on the Siberian's neck.

"Thanks for listening to me," he said. "It's nice to think that you're safe and sound at home."

"If I were, I wouldn't be able to present you with this damaged trophy, darling. It's all yours."

She felt her foot pushed aside as Bella shape-shifted and rolled over on the cement floor, sobbing in distress. She had lost everything she worked for: husband, money, reputation. She was ruined and battered, utterly destroyed.

Viv stepped aside and flicked her a disgusted glance.

"You're lucky Viv didn't do to you what you did to Boris," Pavel said. "He's dead. You'll be as good as new in a few hours."

"The bastard murdered his own brother. If it hadn't been for him, I'd never be in this mess."

Bella groaned as Pavel helped her to her feet while several of his men and the feds entered the garage with weapons drawn. They stopped as they heard voices and shouted, "Federal officers! Come down and show yourselves."

"It's Pavel. Vivian Roussel is here with me. We captured Bella Danilov."

"Pavel, it's Ivan. You're all right?"

"We're fine. Stay there. We're bringing in the prisoner."

Chapter Seventy-five

Several months later

"Pavel! Come in here. It's CNN. You have to see this!"

Walking into the bedroom, Pavel glanced at Viv, who was pointing to the large TV screen on the wall. "Oh."

"Sit down," she said as she reached for him and pulled him down on the bed beside her. There on the TV was a clip from the inauguration of the new chapel of the Virgin of Saratov.

Gorgeously robed priests led a procession around the newly refurbished church, swinging censers of incense as they moved. A choir chanted hymns in the background. At the head of the procession was one of the highest-ranking churchmen in the country and behind him walked representatives of the government, all coming together to give thanks for the recovery and reinstallation of the icon, back home in a renovated church—with a million dollars' worth of security equipment installed.

"I can't believe how beautiful it is," Viv said as she stared at the TV screen. "Those colors are magnificent. Are those the original paintings on the columns?"

"Yes, restored and looking like new. The artists did a fantastic job. They were still working on it when we finished our part."

"Now nobody can get in there and steal the icon."

"Not even a cat can get near it without setting off alarms," he said with a smile. "Once they place it in its niche in the iconostasis, it activates a signal that will send an alarm if it's ever moved, even a fraction of an inch. Once that signal goes out, metal doors slide into place and isolate whoever is in the chapel. The police will receive the alarm, as well as the new security station, and with all that racket, half the town will know something's up, as well as the head of the FSB via a private hookup. I think we've covered all the angles."

"I missed you while you and your crew were over there. I was proud that they asked you to do the job, and I knew that you felt it was your duty, but I am so glad that you're home."

"So am I, darling. This is where I live now, and you're part of my life." Pavel kissed Viv tenderly on the mouth and sank down onto the bed with her. "I missed you so much I declined the offer to attend the official ceremonies. I couldn't wait to get back to you."

She smiled into his green eyes. "Tell me what happened to Bella."

"There's something of a mystery about her fate, but from what Tony said, Madame Danilov arrived in St. Petersburg escorted by him and a subordinate, and sometime during the transfer by helicopter to a prison on the outskirts of the city, she suddenly threw herself out of an open door at a thousand feet, and fell to her death in the Gulf of Finland. The Russians searched. They never found the body."

Viv's eyes met his. "Did Madame Danilov happen to have an all-werecat escort by any chance?"

"Yes," he said mildly.

"And now nobody will ever know what she really was. The secret is safe. Tell me, do you think your werecat secret agent friend ever actually planned to turn her over to the Russians?"

"I think he planned to go through the motions to facilitate

the deal he wanted. The man he traded Bella for was human."

Viv shook her head in wry appreciation of the werecat capacity for treachery. "Well, Bella got just what she deserved. No tears for her. But what about Boris? How did they repatriate the body? You told me he died as a big cat."

"They got in touch with his wife, who was vacationing in France, and gave her the sad news. Her reaction was 'Cremate the remains and ship them home.' She contacted the funeral parlor and put it all on her credit card. He's headed home in a small urn, and she's still tanning in Nice and spending his money."

Viv shook her head. She couldn't even bring herself to comment.

"Umm," Pavel said as he kissed the hollow of Viv's throat while she wrapped her arms around him and languidly caressed him. "There's one thing I have to ask."

"Yes?" Viv said as she kissed him along his jaw and finished up with his mouth.

He pulled apart from her kiss and said, "How did you manage to turn into something the size of a tiger? When I saw you and Bella going at it, I thought something else had joined the hunt. You never became that large before."

"Ah," she said with a smile, "you noticed."

"Noticed? It's difficult to miss a gorgeous creature the size of a tiger!"

Viv laughed. "I have many secrets, *koshka*, and I may reveal them someday. These talents go back a long way, back to the time of my ancestor Krasivaya, when our survival depended on our skill in battle and in the magic we could use against our enemies."

"My clan can supersize, but we can't reach those proportions. It's never been documented."

"Aeons ago, in the time of the ancestors, Krasivaya fought a battle against the evil Siberian Forest cats. At that time, she had rescued one of the lesser gods of the forests whom the Siberians had displaced from his sanctuary. To show his gratitude, this ancient forest god gave her the gift of supertransformation. Instead of becoming the larger size allowed to members of her clan, she and all her descendants could call on their shaman powers to increase their size in cases where the battle required it."

"And that night in the parking garage, you needed it."

"Definitely. It was the only means I had to prevent Bella from getting away. I was so afraid something had happened to you during the takedown that I called on all my strength to deal with her and stop her at that moment."

Pavel smiled. "I was glad you did. If you had listened to me and stayed home, we would still be looking for Bella."

"Ah, so you like it when I show some initiative," she said as she wrapped her arms around him.

"In some cases," he said with a grin.

"What about now?" Viv teased as she caressed Pavel with a hand that wandered all over his superb form, stroking, gliding, demonstrating various ways to arouse him.

"Oh, yes. Keep going."

"*Koshka*, you are the most wonderful cat I've ever known," Viv murmured as she started undressing him. She pushed back the coverlet and slid it down the bed. "Let me demonstrate just how far my affection goes."

He wrapped an arm around her as she kissed him, slipping her tongue in and out of his mouth, swirling it around, kissing his neck, his chest, his lips.

Viv tore off her remaining clothes and nestled down under the covers with him. She wrapped her arms and legs around him and kissed him tenderly, playfully nipping at his ear. Pavel had a sharp intake of breath and responded with a kiss that made the little rosebuds on her breasts harden.

"Darling," Viv whispered. Then she shape-shifted and turned into a striking feline beauty the size of a mountain lion. She prodded Pavel with her paw, and he shape-shifted in turn, changing into a sleek gray cat the size of a panther.

With low, throaty sounds, they seized each other and let their instincts take over, ready to celebrate their bond.

There was hardly an object standing in the apartment when they were through.

Also Available
from
Melina Morel

DEVOUR

A werewolf...
A vampire...
And the woman who wants them both.

The dashing Pierre du Montfort is a werewolf who's
never had trouble hiding his cursed heritage. But now
with his dark secret about to be unleashed, he's willing
to do anything—and savage anyone—in order to
stay alive.

Beautiful and intrepid werewolf hunter Catherine Marais
has no qualms about her destiny. Nothing will stop her
from destroying the last Montfort werewolf. Not even Ian
Morgan—the 200-year-old vampire whose electrifying
touch could tempt Catherine to indulge in a forbidden
darkness from which she may never return...